To Jessica
all the lo
own Happi
Tessa
To Todd
XOXO Todd

PRAIRIE HEAT

A COWBOYS OF THE FLINT HILLS NOVEL

TESSA LAYNE

T♥L

Shady Layne Media
www.tessalayne.com

Paperback Edition ISBN-13: 978-0-9983275-0-1
Print Edition
Cover Art by Razzle Dazzle Design
Published by Shady Layne Media

Welcome to Prairie!

Where the cowboys are sexy as sin, the women are smart and sassy, and where everyone gets their Happily Ever After!

Prairie is a fictional small town in the heart of the Flint Hills, Kansas – the original Wild West. Here, you'll meet the Sinclaire family, descended from French fur-trappers and residents of the area since the 1850s. You'll also meet the Hansens and the Graces, who've been ranching in the Flint Hills since right before the Civil War.

Prairie embodies the best of western small town life. It's a community where family, kindness, and respect are treasured. Where people pull together in times of trial, and yes… where the Cowboy Code of Honor is alive and well.

Every novel is a stand-alone book where the characters get their HEA, but you'll get to know a cast of secondary characters along the way. Additional books in the series:

PRAIRIE PASSION – Brodie Sinclaire & Jamey O'Neill (on sale Feb 10 2017)

Receive Notifications for Upcoming Releases
http://tessalayne.com/newsletter

PRAIRIE RAPTURE –
Ben Sinclaire & Hope Hansen (coming in 2017)
PRAIRIE STORM –
Axel Hansen & Haley Cooper (coming in 2017)
PRAIRIE OBSESSION –
Travis Kincaid & Elaine Ryder (coming in 2017)
PRAIRIE FIRE –
Parker Hansen & Cassidy Grace (coming in 2018)
PRAIRIE FEVER –
Gunnar Hansen & Suzannah Winslow (coming in 2018)
PRAIRIE ECSTACY –
Colton Kincaid & Lydia Grace (coming in 2018)
PRAIRIE LUST –
Jarrod O'Neill & Lexi Grace (coming in 2018)
PRAIRIE REDEMPTION –
Cody Hansen & Carolina Grace (coming in 2018)

Visit www.tessalayne.com for more titles & release info
Sign up for my Newsletter here
http://tessalayne.com/newsletter
Hang out with me! Join my Facebook Reader Group –
Prairie Posse
facebook.com/groups/1390521967655100

CHAPTER 1

BLAKE SINCLAIRE GRUNTED as he maneuvered his Ford F150 into a tiny parking space in front of Frenchie O'Neill's. The big truck stuck out like a sore thumb in the suburban Chicago neighborhood that was a mix of hipsters, young families, and scientists from Fermilab. He'd be on the road home again soon. But not soon enough for his taste.

He'd give anything for a cold beer and a sit-down on the porch with his brothers. After spending the week dealing with scientists and wranglers at Fermilab, and enduring endless rounds of networking, he was more than ready for the solitude of their ranch in the Flint Hills. He dug out his phone and hit speed dial.

His brother Ben picked up on the second ring. "How'd the transfer go?"

"Off without a hitch. The bull is temporarily isolated in a far corner of the grounds, the cow seems to be integrating well. I'll check on the herd again early tomorrow, and then start the drive home. I'll be damned glad when this is all over."

Ben chuckled into the phone. "Gotta put that fancy MBA to use, big brother."

Blake snorted. "As long as they purchase our livestock and meat, I'll be happy. The director at Fermilab recommended I host a meet and greet here at Frenchie O'Neill's. The chef is outstanding, and the scientists like to hang out here."

"What's the plan?"

"Get in, get out. Shake a few hands. Chef O'Neill's well connected and invited a number of her colleagues. I instructed her to fill 'em up with food and booze."

Demand for their bison was growing. Over the last few years he'd learned the easiest way to bring new clients on board was to let them taste the product first. Nine times out of ten they were hooked after the first bite. "I'll leave them with my card and follow up when I get home. I'm confident our Chicago clients will double."

Ben let out a low whistle. "That would be a big help."

"It'll tide us over until we can set up the hunting lodge and diversify our income. Did the plans arrive?"

"Yes." Ben's voice held a note of hesitation.

Blake was instantly on alert. "What is it? Old man Hansen hasn't been mouthing off about us again, has he?"

"Man, you gotta let it go." A note of exasperation crept into Ben's voice. "I think you need to come up with an alternative building site.

"Like hell I will," he growled. "You know I swore on mom's grave we'd get our land back."

"But we don't need it."

"Yes we do. It's ours. It belongs to us. To our family." Why couldn't his brothers understand this?

"It's only a few hundred acres. Is it worth tying yourself up in knots and continuing a family feud?"

Words caught in his throat. Ben was right. No one liked the longstanding feud with the Hansens, but it was all they knew. And he couldn't let it go until he'd righted the wrongs done to his family.

"Hell, Ben. We've been over this before. It's about the

Sinclaire legacy."

"All I'm saying is that the Sinclaire legacy can remain intact without that bit of land."

"Not without the homestead."

Ben made a disbelieving noise. "Just think about it on the drive home? Maybe we can come up with a different solution."

Blake clenched his hand and softly beat it against the steering wheel. A sense of defeat settled over him. Hell and damnation. Discussing Warren Hansen always made him grouchy. Not the best frame of mind to be in before a final few hours of schmoozing.

After a moment he let out a frustrated sigh. "Fine. I'll think about it." He hated it when Ben was reasonable. "Gotta go. I'll see you tomorrow night." He clicked off, jammed on his Stetson, and stepped out of the truck into the cold Chicago wind.

This day couldn't end fast enough. He was a rancher, not Joe Schmoozer. As far as he was concerned, events like the one he was hosting were only slightly less awful than walking across broken glass in a pool of lemonade. But until his family's operation could grow a little bigger, he'd have to continue wearing both hats. There was too much riding on the ranch's future if things went sideways.

He wasn't in a mood for small talk, but he'd endure it. Suck it up for the family, just like he always did. And if the end result was a hunting lodge and the diversified income necessary to secure his family's legacy… well, he'd do that and a whole lot more. He'd do anything for his brothers and little sister.

The cocktail party was in full swing as he stepped through the door into the posh restaurant. An atmosphere of warmth and delicious smelling food immediately enveloped him. Handing his Stetson to the hostess, he surveyed the room. From the looks of it, the guests were enjoying themselves. Several servers circulated trays of food, and drinks were flowing.

Good.

Hope brimmed up, temporarily chasing away his foul mood. Load 'em up on great food and good booze and they should open their wallets.

He circulated through the room, shaking hands with the men he'd met over the week. If the happy smiles on their faces were any indication, the food was a hit. The ranch would be in good shape after tonight if they came on board.

Chef O'Neill caught his eye and bustled over.

"You're late, cowboy."

"He who walks in last wins the deal."

"I see. More wheeling and dealing tonight?"

"Never waste an opportunity."

She raised her eyebrow archly. "Well then. You'll be pleased to know the scientists love the tenderloin marinated in the Buffalo Sweat. Although it did raise a few eyebrows until I clarified it was a porter from Manhattan, Kansas." She leaned in close. "And the chefs you invited are dying over the pâté and the bison bourguignon en croute."

Impressive. She didn't miss a thing.

She tugged on his elbow. "Come on. I've saved you a few bites." She led him over to the buffet table and grabbed a plate covered in plastic. She removed the wrap and handed it to him.

He picked up a round of toast spread with pâté and popped it into his mouth. She'd outdone herself. He tasted the bite of cognac, but it didn't overpower the flavor of the bison. The result was rich and earthy. Next, he bit into the bison bourguignon. Again he was surprised. He was used to bison fajitas, steaks and chili. This elevated the meat to a whole new level.

"Chef, if you ever want a ranch job…"

She shook her wild red curls and rolled her eyes. "It's Jamey. Didn't we agree to dispense with this cheffy business? And I have everything I want right here, thanks. But put a good word in for me with the other chefs. The kitchen is still a man's world."

"Of course. Anything else I can do for you?"

She brightened, her eyes sparking devilishly. "Well there is one thing. I have a friend I'd like you to meet. She doesn't get out much."

"Oh?"

He worked to keep his smile from slipping. He didn't want to come across as an ingrate, but the last thing he wanted this evening was a set-up.

"You know how these scientists are. She's a bit shy."

Before he could stop her, she spun on her heel and ducked through the heavy velvet curtain separating the restaurant from the bar.

Great. Now he was on the hook for entertaining a socially awkward scientist. Hopefully she'd know a few people in the room and he could leave her with them and make his excuses.

Shaking off his irritation, he stepped over to the beverage station. "Scotch. Neat."

Jamey had tried to sell him on Irish whiskey, but he was a scotch man through and through. He savored the smoke as the liquor slid over his tongue.

She popped back through the curtain and tugged at his elbow. "Come with me."

Downing the scotch faster than he liked, he placed the empty glass on a tray and followed her through the curtain to the bar. The atmosphere was much more relaxed – a nice contrast to the upscale velvet and leather in the front. Here, he could exhale and loosen his tie.

The bar was filled to capacity. Patrons spilled out onto the tables next to the dance floor. A small band was setting up onstage. Jamey bobbed through the crowd and stopped halfway down the bar.

No. No fucking way.

Maddie Hansen.

Of all the gin joints.

It had been fifteen years, but he'd recognize her anywhere. Large sapphire eyes rimmed with square black glasses frames. Eyes that were the spitting image of her father, Warren Hansen. The din of the bar faded as his focus narrowed to only her.

Something passed between them that was at once both deeply familiar and disconcertingly erotic.

His mind went blank and his cock surged in awareness. It didn't matter that he was in Chicago for the sole purpose of peddling his bison, or that his family hated hers. All he wanted to do was devour the full, sweet mouth tilted up at him. He fought the urge and groaned inwardly as her tongue darted out to wet her slightly parted lips. God, he wanted to taste her.

He glimpsed surprise and curiosity in her blue depths. And was that a hint of something else? An invitation for him to forget everything but the two of them? He hoped so. But whatever he'd observed quickly faded as startled recognition clouded her eyes.

Jamey flipped her head and smiled broadly. "Blake Sinclaire, this is my best friend and roommate–"

"Madison Hansen," he finished for her. Roommates, huh? Best friends?

"Wait." Jamey slid a sly glance at Maddie. "You know each other?"

Maddie smiled tightly, her eyes snapping. "Ah… Yes. Yes, we do."

It could have been worse. She could have denied ever knowing him. He'd take a small victory.

He leaned in close to her, kissing her cheek. "Try not to look so shocked, sweetheart," he murmured low into her ear. "I promise I won't bite."

"I'm not your sweetheart," she hissed back.

Jamey clapped her hands. "Excellent. I'll let you two reconnect." She winked at him. "Don't worry. I'll take care of your guests until you're ready to rejoin the shindig." She scooted past him and disappeared through the curtain that separated the bar from the restaurant.

Holy. Hell.

He'd never forget the first time he'd met Maddie. The event floated in front of him, crystal clear.

He'd been driving home from the Feed 'n Seed in Prairie, the small town near their ranch, when he caught sight of a group of kids in the vacant lot down the street from Dottie's Diner. Something about the scene up ahead hadn't felt right. He'd driven by slowly and seen Kylee Ross with her usual entourage—including his brother, Brodie, who was always trying to impress her. The gang had surrounded a girl and dumped the contents of her backpack on the sidewalk. They seemed to be chanting something.

Maddie had been scrawny back then, all elbows and knees, her hair bleached nearly white from the sun. Her face had been pinched in anger and defiance. He'd slammed on the brakes and pulled a u-turn, rolling down the window and shouting for her to get in.

Stalking around the truck, he'd blasted everyone, but especially his brother for picking on a girl. Then he'd picked up her school things, shoved them in the backpack, and tossed it in the back of the truck. He remembered being surprised that she hadn't cried. She'd been tough as nails.

"You're one of the Hansen kids, aren't you?"

She nodded, refusing to look at him. "Maddie." She looked out the window.

"You want me to take you home?"

She shrugged.

"Hey." He reached over and ruffled her hair. "You okay?"

She nodded, still refusing to meet his gaze.

"Wanna talk about it?" His little sister wanted to talk about everything all the time.

She pursed her lips and shrugged again.

He noticed her bloody knees. "Who did that?" His voice sharpened in anger. "It wasn't my brother was it? I'll beat him good if he laid a finger on you."

"Kylee Ross." She practically spat the name.

He should have realized that day Kylee Ross was always bad news. Too bad he'd learned the hard way where she was concerned.

But the young girl he drove home back then hadn't said anything more about Kylee.

"Drop me off here," she'd insisted. He'd stopped the truck at the edge of Hansen property. "My cousins will tan your hide if they catch you on Hansen land." She opened the truck door and hopped out, but she couldn't reach into the bed to grab her pack.

He jammed the truck into park and retrieved it for her. She took the pack and put it on, hunching her narrow shoulders against its weight. Gratitude flashed in her eyes. "Thanks," she mumbled, and scrambled down the ditch, climbing over the fence to her family's property.

And now here she was. All grown up and no longer scrawny. Definitely not scrawny. Mother Nature had blessed her with curves to die for. Curves to sink his fingers into and caress until her skin pebbled in delight. But according to gossip he'd overheard at Dottie's Diner she was also very off limits.

"Dottie mentioned you're a doctor living with some old man. What are you doing in Chicago, living with a chef??" Now that he'd met her, the rumor disappointed him. Even if she was a Hansen.

"PhD, not MD." She rolled her eyes. "When are you people going to realize the news from the diner isn't reliable? I'm a scientist," she snapped. "Particle Physics. And my roommate is obviously not some old man."

She brushed a stray lock that had broken itself free from her tightly wound bun behind her ear, then pushed her glasses up her nose. He imagined winding the silky looking tress around his finger. He shifted his weight uncomfortably. He needed to stop this line of thinking and get a grip.

She pushed her glasses up her nose again.

Ah-ha.

Her tell.

So she was nervous.

Well that made two of them. Not that wild horses could ever drag that admission from him. He was overcome with the urge to … impress her. That was ten kinds of bad. The kind of bad that wrangled you a date with an aisle and an altar, and there was no place for that scenario in his life. Not with the responsibilities he shouldered.

He cleared his throat, suddenly wishing he hadn't downed his scotch so quickly.

"So… what are you doing in Chicago?" Quite possibly the lamest opener since… ever. He'd done better asking cheerleaders to the prom.

She shot him a look of challenge and exasperation. "I'm an Associate Scientist here at Fermilab. What are *you* doing in Chicago? You're the cowboy."

Dang she was sassy. She'd obviously inherited the Hansen trait of not backing down from a fight.

"I'm sure you know about Fermilab's bison herd. I delivered a pregnant cow and a two year-old bull. We ranchers are committed to preserving genetic diversity. Something you scientists are familiar with?" He didn't keep the sarcasm from this voice.

Her pretty mouth tilted downward. "Look. Nice to see you again and all, but don't let me keep you from your party."

Hansens were bad news. Always had been. If he was smart, he'd turn and walk away.

Right now.

Too bad that was the last thing he wanted to do.

She piqued his curiosity.

He wanted more of this… banter.

And whatever else that was zinging back and forth between them.

Throwing caution to the wind, he extended his hand. "Why don't you join me?" He knocked his chin back toward the front room.

Her eyes narrowed suspiciously. "What's in it for you?"

"The company of a lovely lady to help pass the time at a somewhat boring but very necessary event?"

She snorted. "That's a nice line, but it won't work with me."

He spread his palms. "Consider this a favor then. I helped you out of a pinch once. Now you can help me." He gave her his most charming smile. The one that his housekeeper, Mrs. Sanchez, said crinkled his eyes, and made her pinch his cheeks and call him niño.

She pushed her glasses up her nose, staring at him in disbelief.

"You're calling in a fifteen year-old mark?"

He shrugged nonchalantly. "I know you Hansens hate to owe anyone. Just giving you the opportunity to wipe the slate clean."

"You're kidding." She scowled at him, eyes flashing. "I've always heard you Sinclaires are the most arrogant bunch of–"

He leaned forward, interrupting her. "Surely you're made of stronger stuff, Dr. Hansen?" He'd push his advantage while he had the chance.

She crossed her arms. "Surely you know you can't manipulate me."

"Wouldn't dream of trying." He lowered his voice. "But I'd like you to join me."

The look in her eye softened a fraction.

"Please?" Hell, when was the last time he'd begged? For anything? Let alone someone's company?

Her breath came out in a whoosh and she nodded. A tightness in his chest released, surprising him. She reached for her glass, squared her shoulders, and slid off the stool. "Fine," she said, raising her chin in challenge. "Though I'm certain I'll regret this."

He winked at her. "I'm certain you'll never forget this." As long as she thought he was arrogant, he might as well play the part.

He settled his arm at her hip. As they moved through the crowd, his hand skimmed over the soft material of her skirt.

Jesus.

Was she not wearing panties?

Awareness surged through him.

He splayed his fingers, testing. Sure didn't feel like it.

Damn. He'd give his left nut to find out.

He held the curtain open nodding for her to step through into the gathering. He dipped his head, steeling himself against the tantalizing scent of her hair. "You can tell me which scientists wear high-heels in their office."

"That's the problem with you cowboy types. You think all scientists are poofs."

He raised an eyebrow. "Aren't they?"

She studied him over the rim of her glass. "We're pioneers. Same as our ancestors. Only we think before we speak."

Zing.

Well wasn't she a surprising bit of sass? He should have expected that, given her father. "Boldly going where no man–"

"Or woman," she corrected. "And I don't see cowboys pushing to be the front of the line for space travel." She took a sip of her wine, regarding him intently.

Was it possible to be jealous of a glass? His balls tightened as she licked the remains of the liquid from her lips. There were so many things he could imagine that pink tongue doing.

"As long as we're discussing gross generalities, why don't we discuss how cowboys are an oversexed bunch of Neanderthals who can't accept the possibility women have more than fluff between their ears?"

He stiffened. "I'm not a Neanderthal."

She raised her eyebrows skeptically.

So what if he'd been checking her out nonstop since Jamey had connected them? So what if the first thought that entered his mind was what she'd look like naked beneath him? That didn't make him a Neanderthal. That made him a flesh and blood man.

"I'm not," he repeated defensively. "But I am human. And there's nothing wrong about appreciating a pretty woman." He allowed his eyes to slowly rake over her curves. Her tongue darted out nervously to wet her lips as a slight pink flush crept up her neck. The vein there fluttered wildly.

Huh.

So she wasn't as cool and collected as she projected. As if in answer to his thought, she pushed her glasses up her nose again.

Her tell.

Huh.

Damn if that movement didn't go straight to his cock.

It would not do to sport a raging hard-on in a room full of observant scientists. He needed to shut that shit down fast. Ripping his gaze away, his eyes landed on a painting.

Of a nude. A voluptuous reclining nude. With long blonde waves cascading over her shoulder.

Not helping.

So not helping.

This wouldn't do at all. Steeling himself, he went to the place he hated. His worst nightmare come to life. He hated thinking about that afternoon twelve years ago and the disastrous results, but it always did the trick. The vision was permanently branded in his mind and nothing sucked the sex out of him faster. He shook his head, clearing the cobwebs and forcing himself back to the present.

She tilted her head, analyzing him over the rims of her

glasses, like he was some kind of specimen. "You okay?"

Great. Nothing got past her.

He swallowed, nodding. "Yep. Have you tasted the food yet?"

Her eyes narrowed skeptically, but she didn't press the matter. "No. But if it's Jamey's it will be incredible."

He ushered her to the table. "Everything on the table is made from bison from Sinclaire and Sons."

"When did you move to bison? Weren't you always cattle?"

He nodded, grateful to be on safer turf.

"Ben. He convinced us to switch five years ago. Said it made financial as well as environmental sense." Pride welled in his chest. He loved what he and his brothers had built together.

"And did it?"

"So far, so good. But we're a small operation and need to continue to diversify. We've built the herd to seven-fifty, and we're developing a nice A-list of clients across the country, thanks to creativity like Jamey's." He handed Maddie a cracker smeared with pâté, enjoying the ecstatic expression on her face as she savored the taste.

Shit. Food was off limits too. All he could think about was doing things to her to elicit that same reaction. He couldn't resist offering her another bite, this time of the bison bourguignon, just to see it again.

Her eyes rolled back and she let out a satisfied sigh. His cock stood at attention, loving the sounds she made. He bit back a groan as she slowly licked her fingers. "Oh my God. That's so good. That's bison?" She grinned, her eyes lighting. "Jamey's the best."

No. Your reactions are the best.

When was the last time he'd talked business with anyone but a client or his brothers? Or allowed himself to enjoy a purely sensual moment like this? This was dangerous territory. He needed to shift focus quick.

He grabbed a glass of wine for her from a passing tray. "Refill?" She shrugged and accepted the glass. Lightly touching her elbow, he led her to the makeshift bar. "Scotch please."

She smirked. "So I see Jamey hasn't convinced you of the finer points of Irish whiskey."

"Old habits die hard."

"What other habits do you have, Blake Sinclaire?"

He stilled. The way she said his name. It rippled over him like a breeze dancing through prairie grass.

Holy. Hell.

"If you spoke to Dottie at the diner, she'd tell you I'm an old grumpus. If you spoke to Anders at the Feed 'n Seed, he'd tell you I pay my bill promptly on the fifth of the month." His eyes narrowed. "And if you asked most mothers in town, they'd tell you to run, not walk away as fast as you could. Everyone knows that Sinclaires and Hansens mix like oil and water."

Her eyes widened at that. A half smile lifted the corners of her sweet lips.

"I'm a Hansen, cowboy. We run toward challenges."

He snorted, shaking his head.

"Don't tell me you avoid them?"

"Challenges?"

She nodded, raising her eyebrows in cool assessment.

He shrugged. "Let's just say I calculate the odds before making a move."

Her eyes flared.

Where in the hell was this conversation going? His chest felt like a balloon about to burst. Except for the occasional flick of her tongue, which drove him to distraction, she seemed cool as a cucumber. What would it take for her to drop the cool facade? He'd love to find out.

"How very scientific of you." She drained the rest of her wine and signaled the server for another.

"You don't have a corner on the intelligence market."

She cocked an eyebrow. "Considering I had a doctorate by the time most people discover college nightlife, I feel pretty confident."

He took a sip of his scotch. "I see the apple doesn't fall far from the tree."

Her face remained impassive. "Say more."

"Warren Hansen is the cockiest bastard I've ever had the misfortune to wrangle with."

Her lips twitched like she was trying not to smile. "There's your problem. If you want to come out on top, the last thing you do is 'wrangle' with my father." She took a sip of her wine, amusement flickering in her eyes. "I'm surprised you haven't figured that out. You've tried to buy back the disputed land, how many times now? Three?"

Zing.

He stifled the anger that flamed to life every time he thought about the fact that Warren Hansen had stolen the Sinclaire family homestead from his father. Land he desperately wanted to use for a hunting lodge. Not that he'd ever let on to a Hansen he already had plans in the works.

No. They'd only use it against him.

Bitterness rose in the back of his throat. "Warren Hansen swindled that property from our family and it's an insult to our honor to beg for it back."

She tutted, shaking her head. "Swindled? Those emotions

will get the best of you every time, Blake."

He clenched his jaw. He did not need to *wrangle* with another Hansen over *his* property.

She spoke to him as if she was talking to a child.

That rankled.

He was a fucking grown man with an MBA.

He made deals.

Big deals.

With important people.

He wasn't some greenhorn basking in the glow of her intelligence.

She smirked. "You seem to be as bad a poker player as your father."

He opened his mouth to make a smart reply, then snapped it shut again, glaring at her.

She sighed, the look in her eyes too close to pity for his like. "I don't know why I'm going to tell you this, but in spite of what you said about the mothers in town telling me to run, you seem like a nice man… for a Sinclaire," she added.

For a Sinclaire. That was a small victory.

"First off. Practice your poker face. Warren can read you like a book."

He scowled. "I have a great poker face."

She arched an eyebrow in question.

Fine. Maybe he didn't. But he'd sure as hell start practicing. "Go on."

"You can't go at him head on. You'll lose every time. Figure out his pinch point and use it. And whatever you do, don't challenge his pride."

He could kiss her for that. Right here. In front of everyone.

The temptation was overwhelming, her mouth so perfect. He stepped closer.

CHAPTER 2

OH GOD, OH GOD, oh God. He's going to kiss me.

He looked like he wanted to devour her. Right here. In front of her colleagues. She never should have had that third glass of wine. Or the fourth. She was asking for trouble where Blake was concerned. His scent buzzed around her like mosquitoes, making it impossible to string logical thoughts together.

Logic told her he was interested. Logic also told her Blake Sinclaire was the last person she should mess with. Even though she had no intention of ever moving back to Prairie, if her family discovered she'd gotten cozy with a Sinclaire, they'd accuse her of being stark raving mad. Nope. Sinclaires should be avoided at all costs. She was already in the family crosshairs over her profession, and their criticism for that provided more than enough heat.

So what on earth was she doing giving Blake Sinclaire counsel on how to deal with her dad? For a split second she'd felt sorry for him. Her father could be an ass. Heck, *was* an ass. She knew that better than anyone. Especially after her most recent conversation with him. There was no way he'd ever sell to a Sinclaire. Not now. Not ever. Even with his health concerns.

Did anyone even know how the feud had started? Did they even care? Each family took offense at the hint of a slight.

As it was, she'd probably said too much to Blake. No doubt she'd hear about it if word got back to her cousins or her dad that she'd said anything. But that look in his eyes when he talked about the property tugged at her.

His head tilted in.

She backed up a step.

Not because she wanted to escape. Quite the contrary. If she kept smelling him she'd lose rational thought and do something stupid like throw herself at him. Blake was sexy as sin. And her pussy throbbed insistently when she focused on his mouth. A mouth she suddenly wanted to taste more than her wine. But she simply couldn't let that happen. And not only because he was a Sinclaire.

Disappointment flickered in his eyes. And something deeper. More… sinful. Her pulse thrummed in her ears.

A throat cleared to her side.

"Ah, Ms. Hansen?"

She turned, surprised someone here recognized her. She'd scanned the room as she'd entered and hadn't seen any of her close colleagues.

"I'm Gary Armstrong, Research Associate at the James R. Macdonald Laboratory in Manhattan, Kansas."

"Oh, yes. At K-State. I'm aware of it."

The man was a few inches taller than she was, but next to Blake he looked insignificant.

"I found your presentation this afternoon to be very thoughtful. I'm passing it along to our lab director. I think he'll find it intriguing."

"I'm flattered. But it was a team effort."

He nodded. "Of course. But the application of your research in experimental AMO physics could be quite interesting. If you're ever in Kansas, please visit us."

"I'm sure Maddie would be happy to stop by the next time she passes through Manhattan," Blake interjected smoothly, placing his hand at her waist.

She shot him a warning look. What the hell was he playing at?

"Oh?" Gary's eyes darted back and forth between the two of them.

Great. She could see the gossip wheels already turning in his mind. No doubt the combination of a cowboy and a physicist would feed the mill for weeks. "I have family an hour south of Manhattan. I get down when my schedule allows," she clarified. Leave it to an arrogant Sinclaire to horn in on her conversation. Well two could play this game. Sending Blake a syrupy smile, she changed the subject.

"Gary, are you aware that the food you're enjoying tonight was raised right down the road from your lab? This is Blake Sinclaire, a Kansas rancher whose spread is not far from you." She patted Blake's arm. "I'm sure he'd love to tell you all about his bison. Now, if you gentlemen will excuse me, I need to visit with the chef."

Anything to put distance between them. She spun on her heel and wove through the gathering searching for Jamey. She should have known better than to let Jamey talk her into coming out tonight. It only ever ended in disaster. And this time it was drawing up old memories and new, tetchy sensations. She should have stayed home in her fuzzy pajamas to binge watch Dr. Who reruns.

Jamey bustled up holding an empty chafing tray as if she knew Maddie would want to talk.

Maddie confronted her, hands on hips. "What on earth were you thinking, Jamey? Have you lost your marbles?"

"I told you he was testosterone on a stick, didn't I? And

all this time, I thought the men in your hometown were a bunch of yokels."

Maddie rolled her eyes. "They are." Well, one of them wasn't. At least not now. Not that she'd ever admit it outloud. Especially to Jamey.

"That." Jamey tossed her curls back toward where Blake was still standing deep in conversation. "Is no yokel. And from the way he was undressing you with his eyes, I'd say you've more than captured his fancy."

She pursed her lips, shaking her head. "What are you trying to pull here? You know our family's history with them. It's best we stay far apart from each other." Even as she said it, her heart sank a bit. Blake addled her. Made her insides all twisty and her skin burn. A sure sign that she should stay far away from him.

"Sinclaire, schminclaire. Did you happen to notice how hot he is?" Jamey dropped one side of the tray to fan herself. "Lordy. The only battling you should be doing with him is under the covers. Climb down out of your ivory tower and bury the hatchet, Mads. Before you shrivel up into a dried out old cat lady."

"I am far from that." Indignation roiled in her chest.

Jamey speared her with stern eyes. "Don't make me get my Irish whup-ass out."

Oh no. She'd been on the receiving end of that look more than once over the last twelve years of their friendship. "Don't go there. Not tonight, Jamey." She shook her head vehemently.

"Can't talk more, Mr. Hottie is on his way over. But listen to me." Jamey's eyes turned serious. "It's time for you to drop this whole 'romance is an impediment to my career' act."

"Well played, Maddie, well played." Blake's voice in her

ear sent shivers rippling down her neck, settling right at her apex. Her thighs clenched automatically in response. Of all the times to be without panties. She could shoot Jamey for forgetting the laundry today.

She turned on him. "What was that all about back there? Since when do you get to speak about my schedule?"

His lips quirked, and humor danced in his eyes.

God, he should not do that.

Look at her like that.

Turned her insides to jelly.

He tsked. "Touchy, are we? I expected more control from a Hansen. Especially one as… tightly wound as you seem."

"What's that supposed to mean?" she snapped, irritated at how unsettled she was around him.

He smiled laconically, and she watched in fascination as he undid his tie with one hand, stashing it in his jacket pocket. He arched his brow. "Oh I think you know." He unbuttoned his top button.

She licked her lips, trying to not to ogle the skin he'd just exposed. "Enlighten me." Damn. Her voice came out all breathy. Excited even. And her heart was suddenly pounding.

He dipped his head close and his breath warmed the spot under her ear, sending shivers dancing down her spine. "Care to dance?" His voice scraped over her nerve endings like a five o'clock shadow. Her nipples liked the sound.

A lot.

She shook her head. "Oh no. I don't dance." *Especially with hot cowboys.*

His eyes gleamed.

Damn him, he was toying with her.

"Why not, Dr. Hansen?" He leaned in closer. So close his lips brushed her ear. So close, she could see a hint of dark curly hair at the top of his unbuttoned shirt. Her pulse le... at the jolt of electricity that buzzed through her.

"You're not... scared, are you?"

She didn't miss the note of challenge in his voice. Pressing her lips together more in an effort not to tilt her head and meet his lips with her own, she inhaled deeply.

Mistake. Big mistake.

Her brain cells swirled in delight. Smelling him was like breathing damned fizzy water.

"I'm not afraid of anything," she answered loftily, adjusting her glasses.

He threw his head back in laughter. Rich, dark toffee laughter that warmed her belly as much as any Irish whiskey.

His hand pressed at the small of her back, propelling her toward the crowded dance floor. "Even I know a whopper when I hear it." He turned, pulling her into his arms.

Hard thighs pressed against hers as he expertly maneuvered her around the dance floor. His hand engulfed hers in warmth and strength. It took all her self-discipline not to rake her other hand down his shoulder, relishing the corded muscles that heated her palm. This was a body perfectly chiseled from long days of labor. A Rodin statue come to life.

His hand splayed across her hip keeping her pressed tight against him. Awareness surged where their bodies touched. Could he tell she had no panties?

He angled his head closer, his breath sending warm shivers to her achy nipples. "I've figured out what makes you tick."

She tilted her head back to study him. The light in his eyes scorched her, launching her pulse like rocket fuel. "Highly improbable, but shoot."

"You're afraid of losing control."

er face impassive. "Not." It was a non-issue. control. Ever.

hy is your pulse hammering like a stampede of

...es of heat flamed through her. "Because my… ah… pheromones are confused."

He made a noise of disbelief in the back of his throat. "Your pheromones?"

"Yes." She nodded emphatically.

A growl rumbled in his chest, and he pinned her with a look that made her squirm.

"I'm calling bullshit, Madison."

"What?" She blinked her eyes at him.

His lips quirked, but the challenge was unmistakable in his eyes. "You're a physicist. You don't know shit about biology."

"How do you know?"

His eyes narrowed as he dipped his head closer. Invading her space. His breath tickled deliciously at her temple. "I think you're so terrified of losing it, you tell yourself whatever lies necessary to believe you're in control." His hand drifted casually down and cupped her ass. He leaned his head back to catch her eyes, and squeezed.

The jolt went straight to her clit, proving his point. Her heart pounded loudly in her ears. Refusing to look away just made it worse. Her skin heated and prickled. She was overcome with the urge to grind her hips into his.

No, no, no, no. She couldn't give into these sensations. Not in public, not ever…not with *him.* She'd walk barefoot on hot coals before admitting he did things to her no one else ever had. Not even Marcus all those years ago. Before she'd wised up and put herself on a romance-free diet.

"Are you challenging me?" Her voice came out too breathy. Like she anticipated whatever was coming next. She really should have slowed down on the wine. This was all it was.

The wine.

Not chemistry.

Yeah. Keep telling yourself that.

His hand pulled her closer. Close enough there was no question of his arousal. Close enough that she was pressed into him from knee to shoulder and she was eye level with the hollow in his neck. A hollow that smelled like pine, and salt, and delicious pheromones.

"Oh, no. I'm absolutely confident." His chest rumbled as he talked, the vibrations setting off sympathetic vibrations where they touched. "I bet you're glorious when you lose control, Madison." The way her name rolled off his tongue started a fire in her belly.

"Wouldn't you love to find out."

"I aim to."

The certainty laced with the laughter in his voice triggered something bold inside of her. She couldn't let him win. He'd leave here and laugh all the way back to Prairie. That was *so* not happening.

She inhaled deeply, letting his proximity set her body buzzing. Her nipples puckered to hard points at the thought of what she was about to do.

Slowly, she lifted her head. Then inching just slightly forward, brought her lips to the hollow of his neck and tasted. Shivers cascaded down her body, and her clit throbbed with wanting.

He tasted just like he smelled. Of musk, salt, leather and pine. Of a masculinity that egged her on. She flicked her tongue over the hollow before she drew the cord of his muscle between her lips and gently sucked it in.

His breath rushed out in a hiss as his arms tightened into a vice-like grip. They had practically stopped dancing, not that anyone had noticed.

Ignoring the tremors in her own body, she risked a glance up. Raw lust glared down at her. A small smile tugged at the corner of her mouth. "Now who's afraid of losing control?"

Spinning on his heel, he wheeled them both around, and quickly threaded them toward the glass doors leading to the courtyard.

The quiet of the courtyard echoed in stark contrast to the noise of the band and patrons. Her ragged breathing sounded loud to her own ears.

His grip not releasing, he navigated randomly placed chairs and tables until they reached a darkened corner, half in shadow from the glow of a lantern. The scent of lilacs dripped in the air. Propping his hand against the wall, he let go, glaring at her.

The night air did nothing to cool her feverish skin. Lifting her hand, she traced a finger from his delicious hollow, still damp from the ministrations of her tongue, slowly down his shirt.

He grabbed her hand and held it away from him.

Hmm.

So. Turnabout wasn't fair play. Interesting.

"What do you want?" he rasped, the edges of his voice grating over her like hot coals.

What did she want? Him obviously, but that was out of the question. Too dangerous, for starters. She bit her lip, unsure how to answer.

"Your eyes tell me you want this."

Before she could process what was happening, his mouth had claimed hers.

Fiercely.

Possessively.

The tinder they had been dancing through ignited in a rush, instantly blazing to an inferno.

His tongue did not politely seek entrance. It demanded she open, which she did willingly. How could she not, held in thrall by his sheer magnetism? As soon as his tongue slid against hers, burning coals melted at her apex. Swirls of desire raced up through her, pulling her toward him like he was some kind of black hole and his gravity was stripping her bare.

She melted into him, letting his weight support her, and pressed her hands up his shirt, tantalized by the hard muscles beneath her palms. Her tongue curled against his, meeting his thrusts with an enthusiasm that surprised her.

His body radiated heat.

And strength.

And raw animal power.

Her hips rocked against his in an effort to slake the building pressure at her core.

Quick as a whip, he pivoted and had her pressed up against the wall, his knee between her legs. He released her lips, breathing heavy. His eyes narrowed in suspicion. "Are you playing me?"

She couldn't hide the smile that quirked the corner of her mouth. "Just staying in control." Barely, but he didn't have to know that.

He stilled, then gently removed her glasses, tucking them safely in his pocket. That simple movement sent a little thrill of anticipation through her. Who was playing who?

He placed his hands on either side of her head, fingers

massaging and searching for the pins that held her thick waves securely in place. Her breath hitched as he lowered his head. He stopped, his lips so close that if she tipped forward she could touch them.

"Never challenge a Sinclaire where control is concerned. We'll win every time."

He brushed her mouth in the barest of kisses. Her pulse launched like a rocket booster and her breath lodged in the back of her throat. Still moving his lips barely against her, he swept his hand up her side to rest just under her breast, his thumb sweeping her already taut nipple.

His mouth smiled against hers.

Realization dawned. He was totally playing with her. No doubt about it. If she was smart, she'd walk away right now. Right back home to her fuzzy pajamas, bunny slippers and geometric equations.

But she wasn't.

She was hungry.

And tense.

And prickly, and hot. White hot chemical reaction hot. And dammit if she wasn't going to meet his challenge head-on. He might be a Sinclaire, but she was a Hansen, and Hansens didn't back down and cower in corners.

A slow grin spread across her face. "Bring it on, cowboy."

He growled pulling her flush against him, his hands cupping her ass.

She'd just unleashed the Kraken.

And she loved it.

"The first one to make the other moan wins." His breath was hot in her ear. His tongue ran over the sensitive cartilage, sending pulsing shivers through her nipples to her clit.

"Wins what? A cookie?" She panted, her hands tracing the

hard as rock muscles in his arms.

He raked his teeth down her neck to her collarbone, biting gently, then soothing it over with his tongue. Every place he touched made her clit throb harder.

He was good. Really good. Like he had a road map of her personal buttons.

"The chance to call the shots next time." He ground his hips into hers, pinning her to the wall.

She shook her head. "No next time." She wouldn't survive a next time. She was barely in control as it was. A next time would reduce her to a puddle of goo. She needed to carry this out to whatever ending they were determined to write, and escape with her dignity.

His response was another low growl before his lips claimed hers. Something unlocked deep inside as his tongue slid with hers, swirling her to dizzying heights. Was it possible to shatter from a kiss?

Hands tugged her blouse from her skirt, and calloused fingers caressed the flesh below her breasts in lazy circles, leaving goose pimples in their wake. If he was going for the slow burn, it was working.

Her arousal overflowed and slicked her thighs, heightening the ache that threatened to overwhelm her. She clenched, in a half-hearted attempt to stave off the building ache. He just made her feel too damned good.

But she refused to go down without a solid attempt to break him first. Reaching inside his denims, she yanked his shirt loose, feathering her fingers over the ripples that could only be his abs.

Sweet baby Jesus.

She had to feel them again.

Moving her fingers back toward his belly, she pressed

harder this time, letting her fingernails get in on the action.

The quick intake of air through his nose was the only indication that she was having an effect on him. That, and the rock solid erection pressed dangerously close to her pussy.

She should end this quickly and just ride him right there in the shadows. But truth be told, she wanted this to go on just a bit longer. The curiosity was too tempting. She'd never been with a man that made her… feel.

Feel what? Wanton? Desired? Like she couldn't think about anything except stripping her clothes off?

"Stop thinking, Maddie," he muttered into her mouth.

She pulled back. Had she spoken aloud?

"Your thoughts are racing a mile a minute."

Sparks raced up her neck. How could he tell? She hadn't meant to think. It was just something she did. All the time. She shook her head, squinting slightly to study him. His face was inscrutable.

"You think I'm the kind of man you can kiss while you work quadratic equations in your head?" He shook his head at her slowly, the corner of his mouth pulling down. "Don't play me for a fool, Madison."

He kissed her again. Hard. Then pulled away, his breathing as ragged as hers. He scrubbed his hand over his face.

"I should have known better than to tangle with a Hansen."

The ache between her legs protested as he spun on his heel and stalked off toward the door. With her glasses.

She leaned her head back against the brick, fighting waves of humiliation. What in the hell had just happened? Blake Sinclaire had beaten her at her own game. But she hadn't lost control… had she? Doubt assailed her and an ache twisted in her ribs. She'd lost this evening. She'd definitely lost something.

CHAPTER 3

BLAKE'S MOOD MIRRORED the storm clouds building several miles to the west. From the ranch's vantage point in the heart of the Flint Hills, he and his brothers could see storms long before they arrived. They'd have rain before nightfall. He stalked from the barn to the large front porch and grabbed a beer from the mini fridge plugged underneath the window.

His mother would roll in her grave to see the front porch looking like a bachelor pad, but the ability to grab a beer without removing one's boots trumped propriety.

Another downpour would flood the south acreage completely, making it impossible for the bison to stay close. Not that calving couldn't happen on the far acreage. It was just inconvenient. And costly.

It also made any controlled burn out of the question. Not that wildfires would be a concern immediately, but the longer the cedars grew, the more costly they were to remove. They were already beginning to take over down by the homestead thanks to years of neglect from Warren.

The cool liquid slid down his throat, slaking his thirst, but did nothing to slake his temper.

His thoughts drifted back to Maddie. Damn if she hadn't crawled right under his skin like a chigger in May. He couldn't get the blazing hot encounter they'd shared out of his mind. Three weeks of sleepless nights had made him grumpy and restless. His balls tightened again just thinking of her.

Of the way her tongue glided with his. The way her scent filled him as he breathed her in. He had the hard-on of a lifetime, and no amount of showering and hand time seemed to relieve it.

He groaned and began to pace, shaking his hands and hoping movement would take the edge off the raw, itchy sensations fraying his nerves like a sheet in a windstorm.

A shower was the wrong thing to think of. Not when all he wanted to do was soap Maddie's body, graze his hands over the flare of her hips, slip his fingers into her wetness. Stroke her until she clung to him, her breasts dripping with slippery soap bubbles pressing against his chest.

He was certain she'd been more than wet the night they kissed. He'd bet a year of beers at the Trading Post that if he'd slipped his fingers up her skirt, he'd have found her naked as the day she was born, and wet.

So wet.

"Gah." He threw the beer bottle into the recycle bin with extra vigor. Damn her for captivating him then holding him at bay. Was he not scientific enough to hold her interest?

He was the one who held people at arms' length. Not the other way around. He knew she'd wanted him. *Knew* it. And she'd drifted somewhere while he was seducing her. Trying to bring her to her knees. He'd be damned if he ever begged for kisses.

Especially hers.

He was in serious trouble.

He was supposed to be thinking about prepping the south pasture for calving, and all he could do was fantasize about getting naked with her. In multiple naughty ways.

Damn Maddie Hansen and her perfect little mouth for haunting him like this. If he ever saw her again, he'd sure as hell make sure the only thing she was thinking about was him. And when she melted under him, he'd fuck her six ways to Sunday and wouldn't let up until she'd screamed herself hoarse saying his name, begging for more. Too bad the one thing that haunted him more than her kisses was the look in her eye when he'd thrown the family feud in her face and stomped off.

"Take a breather and go into town. Nothin' you can do about the weather."

His brother, Ben, joined him on the porch. Blake clenched his jaw, nodding once.

"Yeah. Piss or get off the pot. Are we going into town or not?" His youngest brother hopped up the steps and gently cuffed him. Blake shook him off.

"Shut up, Brodie. We'll go."

Sometimes. No. Most times, Brodie was a pain in the ass. Ben got him. Knew when to give him space. Right now, he needed space. Brodie was a damned bull in a china shop who didn't know when to shut up. One day, it was going to get him into a mess of trouble.

"I heard Warren Hansen's pretty sick."

He swore Ben had inherited their great-great and so on grandmother's sixth sense. He always knew what to say, and when.

"Yeah? Where'd you hear that?" And why hadn't Maddie mentioned her father was sick? The answer floated right in front of him.

Why would she tell a Sinclaire?

She wouldn't. He clenched his jaw, beating back his frustration.

"Didn't have to hear it. Saw it at Dottie's." Ben pinned him with a stare.

Blake raised his eyebrows in question. Dottie had her finger on the pulse of everything that took place in Prairie. If Dottie knew it, everyone knew it. But if it happened at Dottie's, the news traveled faster than a prairie fire in a stiff wind.

"Cut to it, Ben," he snapped. "I don't have time to be led to the light. What happened?"

Ben rolled his eyes and took a swig of beer. Clearly enjoying taking his time with his response.

Blake clenched his beer, tamping down the anger that threatened to bubble over. He needed to burn this off, and since sex wasn't an option, that only left sweat.

Or booze.

But he wasn't about to lose control that way. Maybe he should stay home and shovel out the stalls. He was shitty company right now.

"Warren had an episode this morning. Turned grey and nearly passed out. Martha had to come pick him up and take him back to the Stables. Said something about his heart giving him trouble. But my guess is that kind of help doesn't sit too well with him. Best strike while the iron is hot."

"Don't be a fucking poet, Ben. What in the hell do you mean?"

"Go talk to him. I bet you could persuade him to give us our land back. For a price, of course."

"For a price," he stated flatly. "He fucking stole it, Ben. I'm not giving Warren Hansen a Goddamned cent." His brothers didn't know what Maddie already knew – that he'd tried repeatedly.

The sting of humiliation had been too great.

Was still too great.

Anger, hot and raw, spilled over. Goddamn Warren Hansen. The man had known Blake's father had a gambling problem, and instead of sending him home that night twelve years ago, he'd played a few rounds of Texas Hold'em and sent Jake Sinclaire home five hundred acres lighter. Five hundred acres of prime river bottom, and now the Hansens held both sides of Steele Creek, including the Sinclaire family homestead.

Maddie's voice tut-tutted in his ear. *Those emotions will get the best of you every time...*

Ben eyed him curiously. "All I'm saying is that you should go talk to him. If you wait too long, his nephews will buy him out, or his daughter will sell it."

"How do you know?" Warren Hansen was the last man on earth he wanted to talk to. Especially right now.

"Oh, you mean Britannica?" Brodie laughed scornfully. "Yeah, she'll sell in a heartbeat."

"Don't call her that," Blake gritted out, glaring at his brother.

"What?" Brodie cocked his head back, eyes narrowed. "Why not?"

"Why don't you stop being an ass for once and grow up?"

"Whoa. Where's your head, Blake? Why do you care?"

"Shut up, Brodie."

Ben put up a hand, waving off their younger brother. "Think about it, Blake. You know it's good pastureland. It's also good hunting and good water. Gunnar and Axel would be stupid not to buy out their uncle. Problem is, if he dies, it rightfully goes to his daughter, what's her name?"

"Maddie," he supplied.

"Right. And she'll sell to the highest bidder. Do you want

that to be you or her cousins? Or worse?"

Ben was right. Hell, he was right most of the time. This wasn't the first time Ben had talked him down and into a place of reason. It was Ben that had suggested they make the switch to bison five years ago. They were still building the herd, but it had been a profitable move. One that kept the ranch in the black. But not by much.

If he could get his family's property back from Warren, he'd break ground and build a state of the art hunting lodge. Seasonal hunting would not only be good for the land, it would be very lucrative for the Sinclaire coffers. He'd been reading about fancy eco lodges that had gourmet chefs and comfortable beds. Just the kind of thing that would appeal to the same high end chefs and clients he sold his bison to all over the country.

Question was, could he swallow his pride enough to convince Warren to sell? And if not sell, lease?

Aww, hell. For the millionth time in the last three weeks, he wished he could ask Maddie to elaborate on her advice about Warren.

Stupidest thing he'd ever done was not ask how he could contact her.

No.

Stupidest thing he'd ever done was kiss her.

And then he'd let her push his buttons and before he'd realized what was happening, he'd gone and behaved like an ass. That was sure to ingratiate him to her father.

"Fine. I'll do it."

"You want us to come with you?"

He shook his head. "No. You two go on to The Trading Post, I'll ride over and speak to Warren."

CHAPTER 4

BLAKE SWALLOWED HARD and double-checked the roll of plans he carried as he stepped across worn slats comprising the front porch. He'd ridden over across Steele Creek instead of driving. It was faster, and somehow felt friendlier. Family feuding had taken precedent over neighborliness, and maybe it was time that stopped.

He rapped twice on the front door and waited. Looking out across the porch, he was surprised to see the edge of the Sinclaire homestead through the trees, just on the other side of the river. After all the generations of misunderstandings, his heart twisted a little at how close the families must have been at the beginning.

He rapped again, this time hearing a muffled voice and accompanying footsteps. The door opened and a gaunt figure with vivid blue eyes stared out suspiciously. For a moment his breath caught. God, it was like staring straight into Maddie's eyes. Her father had aged even in the short time since Blake had seen him last, though. Ben was right. Warren was ill.

When Blake didn't speak, Warren cleared his throat.

"Cat got your tongue, son?"

"Sir? Warren?"

The man nodded once, his face not giving anything away. God, he looked worse than whatever the cat drug in. "You're back. Did Maddie Jane put you up to this?"

He may look like crap but his tongue still had the sting of a viper.

Warren scowled. "Well she didn't waste any time, did she? Circling like sharks. I'm not dead yet for chrissakes."

"Sir?"

"Well don't just stand there like a ninny. May as well have a cup of coffee." Warren turned and left Blake standing.

He guessed he was making progress. Last time Warren had kicked him off the front porch and told him that he'd shoot him if he ever stepped foot on the property again.

He followed Warren into the house. Except for several pictures of Maddie at various ages, nothing adorned the walls and the furniture had seen better days. Clearly the home had missed a woman's touch for many years. His heart twisted. Surely this wasn't where Maddie had spent her childhood?

Warren grabbed a metal pot of coffee off the stove and poured. But his hand shook when it hovered over Blake's mug. Ben wasn't kidding about Warren's condition. Blake had never seen the man look so frail.

"Sit." Warren motioned to the Formica table in the corner with his head. "You think showing me your plans is going to convince me? The only thing those plans are good for is kindling."

Shit. He'd gone about this all wrong. Maddie had told him not to meet Warren head-on. And what had he done?

He'd come over here with the idea of treating Warren like a potential investor bringing the plans for the hunting lodge he'd had drawn up. He should have known better. He did know better, but he hadn't listened. Instead, he'd rushed over, letting his emotions rule his head.

He nodded, pushing down the flames of shame that licked up at him. He would not let this man shame him. Hell,

Warren had stolen the property from his father. Shame sparked to anger, and he forced himself to let it dissipate by taking a long sip of his coffee. He hid a grimace. It wasn't as good as his. Not by a longshot.

He slowly set the mug down and looked Warren square in the eye. Sweat beaded across his upper lip. Was that a tell? Was Warren nervous? The kitchen didn't feel very hot.

"With all due respect, sir. We're talking about property you stole from my father."

"Jake tell you that?" he growled. "Jake owed me a lot more than that property, son. I accepted it as payment fair and square."

"You knew he had a problem."

"Everyone knew he had a problem. The only person who refused to see it was Jake."

Anger blazed in Blake's gut, and pressed his hands into the cool Formica in an effort to remain calm. Warren raised his hand and cut him off before he could speak.

"Why are you here?"

Blake swallowed. Hell, he might as well cut to the chase. This conversation was going to the shitter like the previous ones.

"I heard you haven't been well." He paused, studying Warren's face for any type of reaction. There was none, but those blue eyes pierced him. Longing for Maddie stabbed through him. He pushed his feelings aside, willing himself back to the conversation. "Rumor has it you might be…" He stopped suddenly, unsure of how to continue. Warren looked like shit, and having this discussion felt predatory.

"Spit it out, son." Warren's voice fell heavy between them.

"Aw, hell." He scraped his fingers over his day old stubble. "We heard you might be selling… I wanted to make an offer."

Warren's mouth pressed into a thin line and his eyes flashed. Anger, resignation, something else. Pain? Something about this whole encounter felt off.

"Why in tarnation would I sell to you? You're a Sinclaire."

Blake refused to take the bait. "You know that land was ours before you stole–"

"Won it."

"Fine." Blake straightened in his chair. "You're not going to make this easy, are you?"

"Why should I?" Warren glared. "Nothing worth fighting for is easy, son. Especially matters of the heart."

"You think that's what this is? A matter of the heart?"

"If it wasn't, you wouldn't care two hoots."

Well damn if he didn't have a point. This land had been in his family since the 1850s. At some point along the way, the Hansens and the Sinclaires had a falling out. Repeatedly, as the wounds got passed down the generations. But he'd be damned if he'd let a developer come in and take what was rightfully theirs. As much as it galled him, he'd rather the Hansens have the land than a stranger. At least they had an understanding.

Speculation flashed across Warren's eyes. Instantly, his guard came up. Years of negotiating experience indicated Warren was ready to pounce.

"Tell me about yourself, son."

Why was he abruptly changing the subject? Shit. He should have listened to Maddie instead of riding over here, plans in hand, like this would be a done deal. He'd been foolish and headstrong. Fine. He could play this game too. *Answer the question with a question.*

"You have an MBA, sir?"

Warren sat back and laughed. "Ha. Don't need no business degree, when I've got the smarts up here." He tapped his temple.

Blake nodded. "Remind me not to get on your bad side."

Warren's eyes narrowed. "Who says you aren't?"

He was going to be a tough nut to crack.

Blake took another sip of his coffee, his mind racing. What was Warren after?

"I see you're not married."

"Haven't met the right person." Not that it would matter if he had. He wasn't marriage material. Not with his burdens.

"You should be."

"Huh?" He cocked his head, not following.

"Married. You should be married. You're hell bent on getting back Sinclaire property but who you gonna give it to?" Warren pinned him with eyes that he seriously needed to stop looking at. This was not the time to be thinking about Maddie.

He shrugged. "My brothers' children. They'll get married someday."

"How old are you, son?"

"Thirty-two."

"Just how much longer are you gonna wait until someday?"

Warren's uncanny ability to push his buttons reminded him too strongly of another Hansen. The urge to fidget in his chair rushed through him. But Warren was a Texas Hold 'em player. If he so much as twitched, he'd give something away. *Just like she told you.*

"What exactly does this have to do with the property, sir?"

"You're the first born, aren't you?"

Blake nodded curtly, tired of the questions.

Warren chuckled to himself, then caught his breath, wincing. "Know how I know? You're jus' like your father."

He stiffened, fisting his hand. Like hell he was like his father. Jacob Sinclaire was an SOB who'd drunk himself to death and had given away five hundred acres of family history and God knew what else to hide it.

He opened his mouth to object, but Warren raised his hand. "Jake knew when he'd been beat. He might not like it, but when you're a gambler, you learn when to take your winnings away from the table." He leaned forward, a wild, hungry light in his eyes. "You want the property, don't you? You can taste it." He paused, a bead of sweat glistening above his lip. "You've wanted it back your whole life. And you're not so proud you refuse to come in person and ask. Repeatedly. I like that about you."

Blake's mouth went dry. His senses were on high alert zinging danger signals at him left and right.

"You even came here with a plan." Warren's eyes glittered shrewdly. "Now, if I was a betting man, and sometimes I am, I'd bet you put the cart before the horse and have plans to build because you're convinced someday you'll wear me down and you'll get your land back.

Jesus. How in the hell had Warren Hansen just gotten inside his head?

"I'd also bet you'd site it down by your old homestead. That's where I'd build something." Warren's hard stare sliced right through him. "See, you're too much of a gentleman to build on this side of the creek. You'd stay on the old family dividing line in case I changed my mind, because there's no way in hell you'd let a house fall into Hansen hands."

The guy was half-cracked. Whatever meds they were

pumping into him had knocked a screw loose. Blake could feel a noose tightening around his neck and he was powerless to stop it. All of his negotiation training had gone out the window. It was like he was seventeen again, arguing with his father. He stood.

When losing a deal, change the dynamic in the room. Warren stood too, and grabbed the pot from the stove, refilling Blake's mug without asking. And even though his hand shook like an old woman, he reasserted his control of the conversation. Damn, Warren was good. Although clearly not well. Whatever ill feelings he harbored toward the man, Blake couldn't deny he was tough as nails.

"Love costs, son."

"Sir?"

Warren leaned his hip back on the counter, looking grayer by the second, sizing Blake up.

"Build your house." Warren waved at the roll of plans still sitting on the table. "We can work out the payment details another day, but before you break ground, before I sign anything…"

The silence stretched between them.

Warren smiled slyly. Like a cat about to wolf down its prey.

Damn.

He'd done it. Whatever his tell was, Warren had figured it out and used it against him. He was going to go to the devil. He'd been set up and played for a fool. The trap door opened and the noose snapped around his neck.

"Marry my daughter."

"Sir?"

"You heard me. My daughter is in need of a husband."

He stared at the old man, slack jawed. Was Warren treating his daughter, his precious daughter, if the number of pictures were any indication, like a piece of livestock?

A lightbulb went off in his head. *Find his pinch point and use it.*

Well hell and damnation. Was Warren's pinch point Maddie? That was a fine turn of events. He'd always said he'd do whatever it took to reclaim his property. But would he make a deal with the Devil to get his property back?

He had to get his land back, no matter what the cost. For the future Sinclaires. Ben and Brodie were bound to settle down soon. He'd give the land to the first one of them to marry and have a family. Then it would stay Sinclaire land forever.

Maddie Hansen was the hottest thing he'd ever met. No doubt about it. She drove him crazy with need. But what would she have to say about this? He couldn't see any possible scenario where she'd believe marrying him was a good idea. In fact, if their previous encounter had been any indicator, she'd kick his ass into next week if she learned about this conversation.

"Uh… Have you spoken to Maddie about this?"

Warren paused, grimacing. "Pah. That girl wouldn't know the right thing for her if it was a rattlesnake on a pile of laundry."

"I doubt that very–"

Warren gasped audibly, his eyes bulging out, mouth open.

"Shit. You okay, Sir?"

Warren gasped again, eyes rolling back, clutching the counter as his knees gave out. *OhGodOhGodOhGodOhGod.* Blake stepped forward to catch him as he pitched forward. Christ almighty. Warren Hansen was going to die in his arms. What would Maddie say then?

CHAPTER 5

MADDIE SLOWED HER horse to a walk as she approached the stables. One of the Fermilab perks she enjoyed most was the stable they kept on site. When she'd been a student at MIT, she'd desperately missed her horses. Even though there'd been no time for regular rides. But shortly after she started at Fermilab, she'd convinced her cousins Gunnar and Axel to drive up her Palomino, Daisy, and another mare for Jamey. Her uncle was the best horse trainer in the region, and she was secretly thrilled her cousins had opted to stay in the family business. At the very least, they helped keep an eye on her dad.

She dismounted and led Daisy to her stall near the barn door to begin the routine of unsaddling and grooming her. The ride, an extra long one today, hadn't given Maddie the relief she sought. Maybe the slow steady rhythm of grooming would help. She needed to purge Blake Sinclaire from her mind.

Permanently.

The man had turned her into a heap of irrational…feelings. A shiver twisted down her spine as she attempted to relieve the itchy, tight sensation that was a constant reminder he'd completely unnerved her. She didn't have the time or inclination for this. It was affecting her work. To make matters worse, her heart galloped every time she replayed their last encounter in her head.

Don't play me for a fool, Madison.

As if.

The sting of his accusation still reverberated.

She wasn't one of those manipulative, shallow people. If anything, the moment someone showed interest was usually the moment she ran for the hills. She'd learned the hard way back at MIT what happened when you let feelings cloud judgment. It had nearly ruined her academic career, and she'd freeze in hell before she ever let herself make that mistake again.

Daisy nickered and turned her head.

"What?" Maddie reached for a treat from the pail hanging on the post. "Sorry, girl. Be glad you're a horse."

Her phone buzzed from inside the bag she'd hung on the hook outside the stall. In many ways, Fermilab shared the qualities of a small town like Prairie. Both in its relative safety, and in the way it functioned like a gossip mill. She'd fielded no less than a dozen questions in the past weeks about who she'd been seen dancing cheek to cheek with at Frenchie O'Neill's. She should have expected the gossip.

Especially about a man like Blake.

His yum factor was higher than ten rocket scientists combined.

Or more.

And that made him bad news.

At least for her.

And being the subject of the gossip mill was yet another reminder that she needed to avoid entanglements of any kind. Even with a hot cowboy from her hometown.

The phone buzzed again.

"What do you think, Daisy? You think that's Jamey?

Think she's got another prospect for me?" She shook her head vehemently. "No. Thanks."

She was done with Jamey's setups.

Done.

Daisy twitched as she reached a sweet spot on her withers.

"That's right, Daisy. It's better to be alone than in bad company. I've got a date with fuzzy jammies, wine, and Jeopardy reruns tonight."

At least the TV wouldn't screw you over with someone prettier or easier.

Her phone buzzed a third time.

Huh.

Either her work had just won a Nobel, or she was suddenly popular.

"They can leave a message, huh Daisy? We'll finish you up, and then I'll see who's burning the phone lines."

She finished brushing Daisy then checked her hay and feed. Giving her one final pat, she stepped out of the stall and grabbed her bag, fishing for her phone.

It buzzed again as she reached for it. At least it wasn't Jamey this time.

"Aunt Martha. Just promise me you don't have a date lined up for me."

"Oh thank God, honey. We've been trying to reach you for hours."

The smile froze on her face as ice cold fear swept into the pit of her stomach. "What is it, Martha? Is everything okay?"

Martha's voice hitched. "Oh, honey. Your father had a massive heart attack."

Her hands went cold. "What happened? Where is he?"

Tears thickened Martha's voice. "Thank God Blake Sinclaire was there when it happened or he'd be dead. I'm sure of it."

"What was Blake doing there?"

"I don't know, honey, but thank God he was. Rode in the ambulance the whole way. Kept us posted the whole time. Eddie is beside himself. Thinks it's his fault for–"

"What do you mean? Where is he?"

"Oh sweetie. He's in surgery right now–"

"*Where*, Martha?"

"Manhattan. Via Christi. You know we don't have any facilities here. They took him by ambulance. They're not sure..." Her voice rose into a sob. "They're just not sure."

Maddie forced a wave of panic down. "Facts, Martha. Stay with me."

Martha hiccupped and sniffed. "Oh God, honey. You need to get here as quick as possible."

Dread crashed over her in waves. She'd gone through this with one parent. She wasn't ready for a repeat. Not after the way she'd left things with her father. She blew out a steadying breath, pushing at her glasses, holding the panic at bay.

"Okay, Martha. I can get to the airport in about an hour, I'll come as fast as I can. I'll text you my flight information. Have one of the boys come and get me."

Her clearance allowed her to bypass security, provided there was a flight leaving soon. As a last resort she could call the lab director and request emergency use of the plane.

She offered a silent thought up to the stars that were popping out as she hurried to her office to grab her laptop. *I'm not ready to be an orphan.*

★

"FLIGHT ATTENDANTS TAKE your seats."

Maddie clutched the armrests and leaned her head back,

shutting her eyes. For the last ninety minutes, the plane had been tossed around in the air like one of Dottie's donuts in a bag of cinnamon. Finally, they were landing.

She chanted under her breath. "The plane wants to fly, the plane wants to fly."

Her terror for her father only slightly trumped her terror of flying. One of the many reasons she'd made repeated excuses not to come home. Guilt washed over her for the millionth time in the last four hours. She pushed her glasses up her nose.

She should have been the bigger person…

She should have let the bullying go…

Should have, could have, would have.

It wouldn't change the past, and it wouldn't change what was. Which was her father, clinging to life. Nope. Guilt wouldn't change anything.

And what was Blake doing wrapped up in the middle of this? His voice echoed in her mind. *I should have known better than to tangle with a Hansen…*

Had he tried to purchase the property again? Chances were he'd heard from someone that her father wasn't doing so well. Blake hadn't come across as the predatory type, but maybe she was wrong. He'd made her head spin that night, so maybe her judgment had been off.

She exhaled a huge sigh of relief as the back wheels touched down at the tiny airport outside Manhattan.

She reached under the seat for her bag and fished out her phone. A text was waiting from Martha.

He's out of surgery and in recovery. They'll move him to ICU next.

She texted back.

Just landed. I'll be at the hospital soon.

At least he was still alive.

She steeled herself as she stepped into the center aisle. Time to put her game face on. Martha was beside herself, and Eddie would have his hands full caring for her. Someone had to stay on top of things and ask the tough questions.

A blast of wet, spring air smacked her as she stepped from the plane. The kind of air that felt like more storms would move in. She inhaled deeply, searching for strength as she crossed the starkly lit tarmac to the small baggage area. If Gunnar or Axel weren't already there, she'd grab a taxi. She quickly scanned the handful of people waiting, looking for height and blond hair.

She found height. But it wasn't blond hair waiting for her. A pair of piercing hazel eyes underneath a signature black Stetson locked with hers. Blake. Her stomach flipped at the sight of him. He looked more delicious than she remembered. Suspicion immediately replaced anticipation. Where was her family? Why was he here?

She stopped in front of him, her eyes glued to his. Even with the crisis at hand, being this close to him set her body vibrating like a neutrino.

She wet her lips nervously, her mouth suddenly parched.

His eyes flared, but he made no move to speak.

Should she speak first? Given the way he'd left her hanging, she should make him squirm. As quick as it rose up, the fight left her. She adjusted her glasses. Now was not the time. She just wanted to get to the hospital and check on her dad.

"Nice glasses."

She narrowed her eyes. "Somebody stole my favorite pair."

The corners of his mouth curved up as he reached for her bag. She never carried anything at home. Not when the men were around.

"I like the blue frames."

Huh. Was he toying with her?

He turned, allowing her to step past him, and placed his hand in the small of her back, guiding her through the tiny crowd. It was like having a hot coal at her back. She shivered.

"You cold?"

She shook her head. She was, but she'd never admit it. Especially to him. She'd come straight from the stables, grabbed her laptop and called a taxi. She hadn't even bothered to put her work clothes back on, let alone grab a coat.

He stopped in front of an oversized F150 she recognized as Gunnar's. Interesting. He tossed her bag in the bed and opened the door for her, offering his hand to assist with the height. His eyes met hers in challenge.

Was he daring her to take his hand?

Or to refuse?

She paused briefly, her eyes raking down over the white shirt peeking out from beneath his black leather jacket. Down over the worn denims hugging legs of iron to his shiny black boots. Back to his face that held the barest trace of a smile, up to his eyes still daring her to make a move.

Clearly, he'd been practicing his poker face.

She held herself perfectly still. If she disclosed her indecision she'd lose this little battle of wills. Keeping her gaze steady, she arched her eyebrows and took his outstretched hand, doing her best to ignore the electricity zinging up her arm.

It would have been rude not to take his hand. And given the fact he'd helped her family today…

At least, that's what she told herself.

She remained silent as he settled himself in the cab and pulled out of the parking space.

"How far is it?"

"Fifteen, twenty minutes, tops."

She pressed her lips together and nodded, her father's words playing on endless repeat in her head. *I ain't got nothing to slow down for…*

Blake let out a sigh.

"Is this how it's going to be?"

She slid a glance at him, pushing her glasses back up her nose. She couldn't read him in the darkened cab.

He briefly took his eyes off the road. "Madison… Maddie." His voice softened. "Look. I'm sorr–"

She held up her hand, shaking her head, refusing to let him finish.

"No. Not now. Right now I want to focus on getting to the hospital and seeing my dad." A lump swelled in her throat, threatening to choke her.

He huffed out a breath, but didn't argue.

The silence stretched between them.

He shook his head and huffed again. "Maddie. Don't be absurd–"

She waved her hand more forcefully this time, glaring at him. "Please. I don't want to talk about it. Ask me how my flight was."

"Your flight?" He glared back at her the next time he glanced over. "Fine. How was your flight, *Doctor* Hansen?"

His irritation was not lost on her. Not in the least. But if she was going to get through this ordeal in one piece, she had to compartmentalize.

"Bumpy."

He laughed, shaking his head. A bitter edge crept into his voice. "Anyone tell you you're a piece of work?"

She refused to take the bait. Instead, she shrugged, adjusted her glasses, and looked out the window, focusing on the lights moving by. Warren's voice continued to haunt her. *I'm damned sure not gonna wither away to a wisp the way your ma did…*

They pulled into the parking lot, and Maddie hopped out of the car before he'd barely cut the engine. She turned to reach for her bag, but couldn't reach over the wall of the truck bed. Suddenly, she was thirteen and in need of rescue.

Again.

She waited while he locked the truck and took his time coming around the back. His eyes were inscrutable in the shadow of his Stetson. He stopped only when he was toe to toe with her.

He was so close she could see the whisper of dark curls peeking out from the vee of his shirt. If she inhaled, she'd not only smell his aftershave, she'd smell *him.*

Her pulse thrummed in her ears, and she willed herself to not look away.

He pushed his hat back and bent his head toward her, amusement and something harder flickering in his eyes. Surely he wasn't going to kiss her? Not here. Not now. Her mind shouted no, but every cell in her body screamed yes.

Not taking his eyes off her, he reached into the truck bed and lifted her bag. Disappointment briefly squeezed her chest. She didn't want to kiss him anyway. Not really.

Pushing her glasses back up her face, she turned and made for the main entrance, as fast as her feet could take her.

His long strides easily kept pace with her while his hand returned to the small of her back, sending delicious waves up her spine. She slowed once they reached the lobby, unsure of where to go next.

"This way."

He steered her over to the elevator banks and pressed the button. The doors immediately opened. She stepped in and turned, leaning against the back wall, absently watching him push the number six.

Suddenly the fear that she'd been holding at bay pulled at her like a black hole. There was no escape. Her breath hitched and she concentrated on a scuff on her boots.

"Maddie."

She glanced up sharply. The tenderness in the way he said her name surprised her. It caressed her. Slid into hidden crevices. Left her nerves frayed. She could deal with anger, with sparring. She couldn't deal with…with this.

Concern shone through his eyes, but he made no move to stand close to her. As if he knew it would be too much.

"When was the last time you saw your father?"

She swallowed the ache in her throat. "A few days at Christmas." *Well that doesn't count.* Her father was right, it didn't really count as a visit. She'd been home a day and a half at best. Guilt twisted hard in her chest.

Blake nodded, scrubbing a hand over his face.

"You need to prepare yourself. He looks pretty bad."

The elevator came to a stop and the doors opened to an empty hall. He held the door and motioned her through, catching her hand and giving it a reassuring squeeze as he stepped out with her.

Momentarily overcome with dread, she squeezed back, holding on as if he were a lifeline. They turned the corner to the waiting room. Martha immediately cried out, rushing over. She let go of Blake's hand, but not before she saw Gunnar's eyebrows shoot up.

Arms encircled her. "Oh dearie. I'm so glad you're here." Martha's voice caught, and she sniffled, shaking her head. "You poor, poor girl. First your mama, and now this."

Maddie patted Martha's back, consoling the woman. "It's okay Auntie M," she said, using the nickname from childhood. The last thing she needed now was her aunt in hysterics. If she was going to learn anything from the doctors, she'd have to stay calm and rational.

"Where is he?"

"Around the corner," Blake answered.

Judging from the looks on her family's faces, he'd clearly taken charge of the situation. Uncle Eddie sat in the corner, hunched over a paper cup of coffee. Axel and Gunnar stretched out awkwardly on either side of him.

She gave her aunt a final squeeze, then extracted herself the embrace. This was all too familiar. The awkward glances, the hyper emotion from her aunt. It was as if her father was already dead.

Locking her own feelings away for the moment, she took a deep steadying breath, suddenly grateful for Blake's solid unemotional presence behind her. "I think I'll go to the nurses' station and check on him."

"You do that, sweetie." Martha patted her cheek. "It's been a bit of a blur to us."

She strode toward the double doors leading to the ICU, dimly aware of footsteps behind her. She pushed through and stepped into a world that was at once foreign and disturbingly reminiscent of her mother's last days. The hushed voices of the nurses at the center station, the dim light, the muted whirs and beeps from multiple rooms of machines. Death lurked at every threshold.

Putting that behind her, she approached the nurses' station. "Hi. I'm Maddie Hansen. I'm here to see my father."

The matronly nurse looked at her kindly. "Oh yes. They brought him in a few minutes ago."

She nodded.

Her heart slammed into her ribs as her eyes flitted around the bays. Blinking rapidly, she tensed her body to hide the shaking. Her hands were like ice.

"What's the twenty-four hour prognosis?" The words tasted like cardboard in her mouth.

The nurse's lips curved up. "He came through surgery with flying colors. He's a fighter." The nurse stepped back, coming around the station to lead her to the room where her father lay. "What saved him was the CPR."

Maddie glanced sharply at Blake, but his face remained impassive.

"Can I see him?" She stilled, hardly daring to breathe.

Pity flashed in the nurse's eyes, before the professional mask slipped back into place. "Of course, sweetheart, but you have to understand, he's just come through major surgery. And while he did fine, he's very frail."

Frail? No one ever used that word to describe her father. She blinked furiously. She would not let Blake see her in a moment of weakness. Yet his hand was immediately at the small of her back, offering nothing but steady support. She blinked again, pushing back the piercing rush of fear that clawed at her insides. "Let me see him, please."

The nurse ushered her toward a room on the other side of the station.

A solitary light in the corner cast a golden glow over the

room. While she'd braced herself, nothing prepared her for what she encountered. Her father was asleep and hooked up by tubes and wires to various machines. The worst, though, was the ventilator breathing for him. His skin looked the color of oatmeal.

She slid a glance at Blake. "I thought you said he looked pretty bad."

He gave her a partial smile. "He looks like shit." His smile grew a fraction.

She stepped up to the head of the bed, and caressed his forehead with the back of her finger. His skin was cool.

"Dad," her voice thickened with emotion. "I'm here, Dad. I want you to get well, okay?" Grief stabbed through her, lodging in her throat. "I'll come home more. I'll stay longer, just…just.." She heaved a sigh, pushing her frames up her nose. "Just get well… please?" She leaned forward and pressed her lips to his brow. "I love you, Dad," she murmured against his cool skin. "Don't give up."

She had to get out of here. Now. She refused to break down in this room. In front of the nurses. In front of her family. In front of Blake, who was quietly waiting just outside the threshold.

Brushing her cheeks with the back of her hand, she turned and pushed past him. She pushed through the double doors, blindly moving down the hall, turning at random intervals until she reached a dead end.

She leaned forward into the wall, bracing herself. She would not cry. She would not cry.

She. Would. *Not.* Cry.

She never cried. Ever.

Fear settled like metal into Maddie's mouth, and hot tears welled behind her eyelids. She pushed her glasses forward and pinched the bridge of her nose.

Strong hands turned her. Encased her in solid warmth. Life. A tear squeezed out. Then another. And another.

Dammit.

She shook her head against his chest, clutching his jacket like a lifeline.

"Let it out, sweetheart," he murmured above her ear.

A sob ripped through her throat as tears slid unchecked down her cheeks. She hadn't cried this much since Marcus. At least those tears had been shed in private.

"That's it, Maddie. It will tear you up if you hold onto it." He held her tightly. Caressing her head as he continued to murmur softly. "Warren's a cuss. He's not gonna give anyone the satisfaction of dying anytime soon."

After a few moments, awareness seeped back into her body, along with the overwhelming urge to flee. Bracing her hands against the soft leather of his coat, she pushed away, stepping back.

She steadied herself, taking off her glasses and brushing her hand across her eyes, before meeting his. What she found there mirrored her own turmoil.

Pain.

Sorrow.

Compassion.

She swallowed, looking away. "Thank you," she uttered softly. "Thank you for… everything."

She had to get away. The way he was looking at her was entirely too…feely. She had to get back to her family. Put on her capable hat. Pushing out a sharp breath, she replaced her glasses and turned to find her way back.

CHAPTER 6

BLAKE SNAKED AN arm out, capturing her elbow.

Maddie turned, eyes filled with turmoil.

"You're not the only one who's lost parents." He couldn't hide the rough edge in his voice. "I know what it's like."

"But I refused to come home." She shifted away, pinching the bridge of her nose again, obviously working to stave off more tears. He leaned back against the wall, giving her space and wrestling with what to say next.

"My last conversation with Jake was..." he searched for words that would convey the ugliness of their last encounter without going into the lurid details. "Less than pleasant."

Did she notice he referred to him as Jake? Never 'Dad'? Jake had never been a father. Not the kind he'd ever wished for, at least. She studied him intently, but continued to listen.

"Jake had a way of treating people like they were disposable," he elaborated after a moment. "I hated it. I called him out on it the last time we talked." He sighed, lost in a memory so painful he'd pushed it to the recesses of his brain. "I regret... some... No." He shook his head. "Much of what I said."

Maddie narrowed her eyes, pinching out two more tears in the process. His heart squeezed tighter at the sight. He opened his hand, but forced himself to not reach out and wipe them away.

"Why are you telling me this?" She brushed the back of her hand across her cheeks.

Why was he?

Because he had the overwhelming urge to confide his darkest secrets to her? Right here, right now? What in the hell was wrong with him? She was a Hansen. He'd already dipped his toe in this stream with less than stellar results.

"Why are you… why are you being so nice?" she finally blurted out.

Because you wriggled your way under my skin. And you're in pain.

"Will you accept my apology if I offer it now?" Why did it matter so much that she accept his apology? She'd been just as difficult that night.

After a long moment, she nodded.

He reached out and pulled her into a loose embrace. "Maddie. I'm sorry I behaved badly in Chicago. I'd like to do what I can to be… neighborly… Something I think both our fathers had difficulty with."

Unable to resist her tears a second longer, he captured her face between his hands, wiping the wetness from under her glasses with his thumbs. Her eyes darted over his face, before finally meeting his.

"Maybe we can change that?" he asked, afraid he might lose himself in the distraught depths of her sapphire eyes. Give in to the urge to kiss away her pain. "No one is an island."

The hypocrisy of his words hit him as they left his mouth. But he had burdens no one else should be forced to carry. And they didn't matter in this situation. There was no way she'd ever discover them, so it was a moot point.

All that mattered was offering Maddie a few words of comfort. A shoulder to lean on. Even in the face of her unwillingness to accept support. How different would his life be if someone, *anyone*, had been there for him in his hour of need?

He dropped his hands. "You need rest."

She shook her head and stepped back, adjusting her glasses. The moment between them vanished. "I'm fine. I just need some coffee."

"You need sleep. You know as well as I do, you can't make complicated decisions running on empty."

Her mouth set grimly. "Fine. I'll nap in the waiting room."

"Let me drive you home." He turned on the charm and flashed her a grin. "Please?"

"Really. You've done enough. I mean if Dad… if Dad…" She blinked rapidly.

He couldn't help himself. He reached out and grabbed her hand, threading his fingers through hers. "He's as stubborn as they come. He'll pull through."

"Thanks to you." She exhaled a shuddering breath.

His gut twinged at the anguished look on her face. "Let me take you home," he repeated. "I promise I'll bring you back first thing."

She quirked a half smile as she narrowed her eyes suspiciously. "What's in it for you?"

He grinned. "The satisfaction of seeing the look on your father's face when he realizes I probably saved his sorry ass."

That earned him a laugh. And a rueful smile.

A throat cleared at the end of the hall. "Now that you two love-birds have had your moment, can I ask a question?" Gunnar stood leaning against the corner, holding Maddie's bag, barely concealing a knowing smirk.

Awesome.

How long had he been standing there? Maddie's eyes rounded and she quickly untangled their fingers, dropping his hand like it was a red hot branding iron. Damn Gunnar's timing.

Blake jammed his hands in his pockets and nodded. "Ask away."

Gunnar tilted his head at Maddie. "Maddie Jane, doc says to go home and come back tomorrow. They expect him to be fine overnight. No use watching the pot boil. Sinclaire, you follow in my truck?"

He nodded, relieved Gunnar hadn't challenged him.

"Now wait just a minute–" Maddie began, her voice laced with indignation.

"Don't be heroic, cuz. Your presence won't change the outcome."

She opened her mouth to disagree, then snapped it shut, the fight visibly leaving her body.

"Now gimme some sug, and I'll catch up with you tomorrow." Gunnar reached them in two steps, dropping her bag, and leaned down to give her a peck on her upturned cheek.

"Blake?" He extended his hand.

That was a first. But when he took it, Gunnar leaned in and whispered. "Take advantage of her, and your ass is mine." He stepped back, smiling. The smile didn't come close to reaching his eyes.

Not that he'd take advantage of a woman, ever. That wasn't how he rolled. But he knew how the town gossip mill worked and respected the sentiment. Loud and clear. He pushed off the wall and grabbed her bag, resisting the urge to turn around and offer her his hand. With anybody else, he would have.

A harsh laugh practically burst from his throat. Like there

had been anybody else for a long time. Not in nearly twelve years thanks to Kylee Ross. Pushing those thoughts aside, he waited at the corner for her to catch up, and ushered her back through the series of turns to the bank of elevators.

As they stepped through the main doors into the cool night air, she shivered. She'd tried to hide it, but he didn't miss it.

"Wait." He stopped under the lamp post, dropping her bag to remove his jacket.

She shook her head. "Oh no. Really. I'm fine. I'll just grab something from the attic when I get home."

"What did Gunnar say? Don't be a hero? You should listen to him," he challenged gently. "Do me the courtesy of letting me be a gentleman."

Her spine stiffened, but she didn't object. Flattening her lips, she nodded, and accepted his proffered coat. "Thank you," she murmured.

He opened the door of the truck and extended his hand. This time there was no showdown. She took his hand and allowed him to help her up.

Something white hot and possessive flared and puffed inside him. If he was anywhere else but a hospital parking lot, he'd have her pressed up against the seat with his hands running over her.

Wrong place, wrong time.

He shook himself, and gently shut the door, walking slowly around to the driver's side in the hopes his sudden flagpole would calm down. It was a big enough deal he'd convinced her to let him drive her back to town. He turned the ignition and pulled out of the lot.

"Do you want the radio?"

She shook her head. "No, thank you. I'm fine with the

quiet."

She looked frail and vulnerable, hunched in the corner of the cab, wrapped in his coat. More like the scrawny teenager he remembered than the strong, sassy woman he'd met recently. His gut twisted at the difference.

"Gunnar's right, you know. Worry won't change the outcome."

She turned her face toward him, the light from the street lamps casting her features in stark relief. Anguish etched across the plains of her face. But she nodded her agreement.

"Why don't you tell me about your work at Fermilab?" Anything to keep her talking.

She stifled a laugh. "Are you sure? I wouldn't want you to fall asleep while you're driving."

"I'm not the village idiot."

"How long has Fermilab been a client?"

Just like Warren, answering a question with a question.

"Three years."

"And have you asked about any scientist's research in that time?"

Damn she was good. She'd turned the tables instantly.

"Nope." He grinned. "But none of them was a beautiful scientist from my hometown."

Out of the corner of his eye he could see her jaw drop, then snap shut. Ha. "Why do you operate under the assumption that no one but you is interested in your work?"

She remained silent a minute, as if wrestling with what she really wanted to say. In the end she shrugged, adjusting her glasses. She had no idea it was her tell.

"My research is in a very specialized area of particle physics. There are less than fifty people in the country who do what I do. It's highly complicated."

"And?" He refused to let her off the hook.

She huffed, and stared out the window for a moment. "Why do you care?" Bitterness laced her words.

"I don't." He shrugged, entertained at the offense she took. "Get off your high horse before you get your panties in a twist, Maddie."

She scowled and pulled his jacket tighter. God, he loved yanking her chain. He'd pull over the truck and kiss her silly if Warren wasn't hanging over them like a specter.

"You're nothing special. No more than anyone else. You're smart. So am I. You have an interesting career. So do I. Get over this idea that you're so special no one gets you."

She stiffened. "Well it's true."

"What's true?"

"No one gets me."

"Get over yourself."

She pushed her glasses up her nose. He'd gotten to her, all right. A small flash of guilt fluttered through him. He shouldn't push her this way. Not tonight. Not with Warren lying in the hospital.

He reached his arm across the back of the seat, resting it on her shoulders. She shrugged it away. "Come on, Maddie, lighten up."

She turned, glaring at him.

"Lighten up? You want me to lighten up?" Her voice held an edge of hysteria. "My father's life is hanging in the balance and you want me to get over myself and *lighten up?* F-f-f-fuck. You."

His breath caught in his throat, and for a moment the only sound in the cab was the rumble of the engine. Then he threw back his head and laughed. Full bellied.

He slammed on the brakes and pulled the car to the side

of the road. "Warren is going to be fine. Did you not hear what the nurse said?"

Unbuckling his seatbelt, he turned and leaned over. In the dim light of the dashboard, her eyes were huge orbs behind her glasses. He reached out the back of a finger and caressed her cheek. Silky smooth and warm. Just like he imagined the rest of her was. Her lips parted slightly as her breath hissed in at his touch.

"You better practice those cuss words more often if you're going to use them, Maddie Jane."

Her tongue flicked out and her teeth came down on her lower lip, her eyes never leaving his face. His cock sprung to life in his jeans.

"You do that again, and I'm going to have to kiss you." He couldn't keep the rough edge from his voice.

Her eyes widened, and the pulse at her throat thrummed wildly. She half-smiled. "Do what again?"

Shit.

His cock twitched at her tone of voice.

She would never back down. She was a Hansen for chrissakes. Did he really want to go there? He couldn't seem to help it when he was near her. Like she'd cast some magic spell over his cock.

And his brain.

"I've been where you are. Know the kind of steam you need to let off to clear your head." He caressed her cheek again, unable to be this close and not touch her. "Only two options. Fighting or fucking. Which do you want?"

Heat flared in her eyes.

He'd bet his last beer she'd die before she said fucking. He was ninety percent sure that's what she wanted. He sure as hell did.

He was an ass for challenging her this way, but he'd be damned if he'd kiss her again until she begged for it. Not after what happened last time. He held her gaze another moment, letting his question hang in the air between them.

Pushing away the rush of disappointment that ballooned in his chest when she remained silent, he turned and rebuckled himself. He hadn't expected her to admit she wanted him. Had he? He could see it written on her face. Even in the dark. He'd wanted her to admit it. To admit he had some kind of effect on her. To admit she wanted him as much as he wanted her right now.

Damn her beautiful, stubborn Hansen ass. He pulled back onto the road and they drove the remaining distance in silence. It wasn't until they coasted to a stop at Prairie's one blinking stoplight that she spoke. The empty street looked like a ghost-town at this hour of the night.

"You can drop me off at my dad's."

He turned to her, glaring. "The last thing you need to be is alone."

Her lip pouted. It would be adorable if it wasn't so infuriating.

"How do you know?"

He blew out an exasperated breath. "Because I've been where you are," he bit out. "But if you insist on going home, I'll sleep on the couch. I'll just need to stop by the ranch first.

"You don't have to do that. I'm very–"

"Maddie. Stop arguing and let me help you."

Prairie's lone officer, Travis Kincaid, pulled up behind them and flashed the police lights.

Great. How long would this take to get around town tomorrow? He rolled down the window and motioned for Travis to pull forward.

"Sinclaire, what in the hell is going on?"

He leaned out the window. "You heard about Warren?"

Travis nodded.

"Got his daughter here. Taking her home to catch a bit of sleep."

"This isn't your truck. What gives?"

Travis knew everyone but was enough of an officer he always asked questions. Even from the people he knew well.

"I rode in the ambulance. Gunnar lent me the truck to get back."

"Well, get on then. See you 'round." The police car pulled forward and drove on.

Maddie crossed her arms, which looked even tinier given the sleeves of his jacket bunched to above her elbows.

"Fine. You win."

A smile split his face. "Lose much?"

She tried not to smile back, but couldn't help it. "Stop it."

"Stop what?"

"Gloating."

He shook his head. "This isn't gloating. You'll know when I gloat."

She took off her glasses and rubbed her face, her exhaustion evident in the dim light. "Look. I owe you an apology."

"Shh. Enough." He placed his finger over her lips, trying his best to ignore their softness. "I know you're not yourself. Let's get you home."

The word home slipped out so naturally he didn't even notice he'd said it until he'd driven a block down the road.

CHAPTER 7

THE PORCH LIGHT was still on when they pulled up to the Big House. It was early enough in the season the light didn't attract bugs. Soon enough they'd have to switch to citronella candles, and maybe gather around the fire pit on the back porch.

True to their word, Ben and Brodie had waited up. Considering first light for ranchers was less than four hours away, they'd all be dragging tomorrow.

Maddie sat in the cab as he walked around to open her door. She looked small and vulnerable encased in his jacket, but the look in her eye said fear and defiance.

Of course. Brodie.

He'd run interference the best he could. He hoped Brodie would know better than to be an ass tonight.

Blake helped her down and kept a hand on the small of her back as they mounted the steps to the porch. Ben rose and grabbed two beers from the mini fridge.

Brodie leaned back, a smirk on his face. "Well, well, well. Fancy seeing you here, Britannica."

Or not. If he wasn't so exhausted himself, he'd kick the shit of out Brodie right here.

"Don't be a dick, Brodie," he gritted out through clenched teeth.

Maddie placed a restraining hand on his chest, shaking

her head. Then, she marched straight over to Brodie, yanked the beer out of his hands, and proceeded to dump it in his lap.

"What the fuck?" Brodie yelped as he leaped to his feet, eyes flashing.

She stepped forward and jabbed him in the chest, although the sleeve of the jacket covered her hands, so it looked like it was the sleeve hitting Brodie. Blake barely held back the laughter threatening to spill over.

"That…was for picking on me when I was little."

"This…" She grabbed one of the beers from Ben and, pulling on the waistband of Brodie's denims, emptied the contents down his pants. "Is to remind you that if you *ever* call me Britannica again, you are reminding to the world that I am brilliant and you are an idiot. Your choice."

Ben threw back his head and laughed. Blake joined in. Maddie took the second beer from Ben, took a swig and turned to Blake, eyes flashing. "I choose fighting." She swung her glare back to Brodie, where he was rooted to the porch, his jaw clenched tight. "Don't worry. I don't expect an apology. Don't expect one from me." She took another sip of beer, her eyes returning to Blake's again over the bottle. "I think I'd like to go inside."

Blake nodded toward the door. "I'll be right in."

Holy. Hell.

He couldn't help the grinning. Never fuck with a Hansen who's reached the end of a rope. Served Brodie right.

He passed his brothers and grabbed his own beer from the fridge.

"Got yourself a live wire there, brother," Brodie muttered under his breath.

Yes indeed. He certainly did.

Ben's laughter echoed behind him. "Brodie, you'll never

learn, will you?"

The screen door slammed behind him and he couldn't hear Brodie's answer. Not that it mattered. He wouldn't forget this for a long time, if ever.

Maddie sat at the island in the kitchen spinning her beer. He leaned on the doorjamb just taking her in. Her fomerly tidy bun was messy, softening her features. His coat on her frame made her look waifish. Most people probably saw her that way, but they were wrong. There was nothing waif-like about her. Underneath those soft curves, she was strong as steel. Admiration for her warmed him.

Pushing himself off the jam, he strode toward her. "Feel better?"

She studied him carefully before finishing her beer. She shrugged.

"Let me grab my toothbrush, and I'll be right down."

Maddie nodded, pushing her glasses up.

"That's your tell, you know."

"What?"

He reached out and gently pushed her glasses up her nose. Her breath hitched. "That. You push your glasses whenever you're worried, or irritated, or nervous… like now." He held her gaze for a moment. "What are you nervous about, Maddie?"

She bit her lip. "Umm. It's late."

Chicken.

She was a big chicken.

Given the look she just flashed him, she knew it, too. He swallowed his frustration and left her in the kitchen.

Upstairs, he paused at his dresser. Her black glasses were there on a napkin he'd kept from Frenchie O'Neill's. He'd left in such a fit of anger, he'd forgotten he had them until long after he'd left the restaurant. And after their encounter in the courtyard he sure as hell wasn't going to seek her out and return them.

He grabbed them off the dresser and headed back to the kitchen. When he strode into the room, he found her hunched over the island. She turned to face him, eyeing him warily. Slowly he took the blue pair off of her and replaced them with the black. "I believe these are yours."

He studied her intently. The black looked good. Set off the eyes. But the blue was more… *her.*

"I like the blue better."

"You do, do you?" She cracked a slow smile. "What if I like the black?"

"I wouldn't be surprised. You're as contrary as your dad."

Her eyes widened, and the barest hint of hurt flashed.

Huh.

He tipped her chin up, taking in her full, sweet mouth. He could feel himself falling into them and he stopped just as she inhaled. Neither of them moved.

"You fight, Maddie," he murmured barely above a whisper. His blood sang in his ears. She parted her lips, the tip of her tongue darting out nervously. He fought a groan as his cock stood at full attention. "You fight because you'd die before you admit you want to fuck."

He could sense her holding her breath. He leaned in the barest fraction of an inch. So close their lips almost touched. "But I can tell you want to fuck." He grazed his lips across hers. Lightly, so lightly.

Her breath shuddered out little by little, only to hitch as he grazed her lips again. Time stopped. He could stand here in exquisite agony barely touching her and probably die a happy man. But he wanted more. He shouldn't. Especially right now. But he did.

He wanted hear her admit she wanted more. He pulled back the tiniest bit. She leaned in.

His cock strained against his zipper.

If he was smart, he'd walk out right now, pile her into the truck, and leave her at the edge of her family's property. Just like he had once before.

But he wasn't. She'd wrapped him in some spell that kept him rooted to the spot.

Slowly, he tasted her bottom lip. Ran his tongue slowly over its fullness, tasting remnants of her beer, and sweetness that was only hers.

Her tongue flicked and met his, sending a jolt straight to his balls. He pulled back and she leaned in. His heart slammed against his chest.

"Tell me you want this, Maddie," he whispered into her lips.

She answered with a tiny whimper.

Not good enough.

"What would I find if I slid my fingers inside your pants?"

A tremor rippled through her body.

He pulled back a little more, and still she leaned in. Her hand reached up and clutched his shirt.

"Would you be slippery and wet for me? Aching with want?"

He gently bit her lower lip, then tongued where he'd nipped. A sigh escaped her, and he breathed it in, savoring her scent.

His balls were going to explode if he kept this up.

He would kiss her, but only once. He needed one taste of that sweet, sweet mouth. He leaned into her, lips covering hers, tongue sliding in. Opening, probing, tasting.

She melted into him, her tongue gliding against his, exploring his mouth with the same tenderness and curiosity. As if it was their first kiss, not their tenth.

He stood there drowning in her, completely losing himself in her silky wet sweetness. Only when she moaned a little did he come crashing back to earth.

He tore his mouth away from hers, panting. Her eyes had glazed over. And she searched his, asking a hundred unspoken questions.

He shook his head.

"No. Not tonight. Not until you say it."

He kissed her forehead and stepped back, shaking himself.

"Truck. Now. You're going to your house."

Willing himself not to look back to see if she was following, he spun and stalked through the house to the porch. Ignoring Brodie's laughter, he crossed the porch in two steps, paced around the truck and hopped in, revving it to life.

He was an idiot. And in way over his head.

CHAPTER 8

THE TENSION IN the cab could be cut with a knife. Maddie slid a glance over to Blake. He clenched the steering wheel so hard, his knuckles glowed in the dashboard lights. She could swear he was grinding his teeth.

Would you be slippery and wet for me? Hell yes. Her insides were ten kinds of twitchy, and God did she enjoy kissing him. But that didn't mean it was the right or smart thing to do. Kissing him was reckless, impulsive, and… absolutely pointless.

The most she could ever hope from kissing Blake Sinclaire was an occasional homecoming hookup, which was totally not her style, or a broken heart. Neither were suitable options, so she'd just have to do her best to ignore the electricity zinging around her body every time she was near him.

Like now.

"Stop thinking, Maddie." His voice held a hard edge.

"What? I haven't said anything."

"You don't need to. Your thoughts are filling up the cab, loud and clear."

She blew out a breath, crossing her arms. Like he even knew what she was thinking. "Fine, Mr. I Can Read Your Mind, exactly *what* am I thinking?"

He snorted. "Fine. If you insist. You're desperately trying to compartmentalize the fact that we have serious chemistry. It doesn't fit in any of your nicely ordered life boxes." He turned underneath the Hansen Stables sign and onto the long half-mile drive.

Damn.

Add mind reading to his laundry list of attributes.

She shook her head. "Nope." Total whopper, but she'd never let him know how close to the truth he'd gotten.

He barked a laugh.

"For all your talk about poker playing, you're shitty at disguising your thoughts. I bet you lose to your cousins all the time."

Damn.

Right again.

"Nuh-uh."

He sighed heavily, shaking his head, his shoulders sagging slightly. "Lie to yourself if you must, Maddie. But don't insult my intelligence by lying to me."

Ouch.

There was so much more to Blake Sinclaire than met the eye. No wonder he was in charge of the ranch. For all her teasing him about a poker face, he instinctively got people. At least he got her.

That rankled.

She'd always prided herself on being aloof and unattached. A coping mechanism born out of losing her mom as a young girl, surviving bullying, and then fighting for a place in a male dominated field at a young age. And, with few exceptions, she could keep people at arms' length. But not him, apparently.

No.

Blake Sinclaire was worming his way deeper under her skin at every turn. And now that she was home in Prairie, there was nowhere to run.

He pulled the truck in front of her father's modest cabin. It paled in comparison to the grandeur of the Sinclaires' Big House. The porch light was off, and the house was ensconced in shadow.

She hopped out and made for the porch.

"Maddie, wait."

His voice stopped her at the top of the steps.

"Let me go first."

She rolled her eyes. "This is Prairie. No one's going to jump me."

He tugged on the sleeve of her coat. His coat, really. "Let me just make sure everything's okay."

Irritation flashed through her. "Would you stop treating me like a little lady?"

"Put your defenses down, woman," he snapped back harshly. "Do you really want to walk in the house and see everything disturbed from this morning?"

Oh.

Her anger dissipated immediately. Of course. There he went again thinking of her. And instead of registering his thoughtfulness, she'd lashed out. Her nerves were completely trashed and all she wanted was to curl up and sleep for days. But that was no excuse.

She let out a tiny sigh, nodding her understanding. "I'm sorry. I shouldn't have–"

He held up his hand silencing her in the darkness. "For fuck's sake. Will you let me help you?"

The words hung between them.

He ran his fingers through his hair, and turning, braced himself on the porch post. "Look. I get it. I've been down this road. I know what it's like to return to an empty home and the person who should be there, isn't."

She nodded mutely.

He was right.

She wasn't prepared for what was on the other side of the door.

"You've decided to stay here. Will you at least let me go in and make sure things are straightened?"

She nodded, not trusting her voice to work.

He crossed the porch, and opened the door. A second later a light blazed on, casting a beam of yellow light through the door. She heard him move down the hall to the kitchen. A moment later he returned.

"All clear. I'll go get your bag."

She crossed the porch and paused just inside the entrance, trying to imagine the scene through Blake's eyes.

The house was shabby from years of neglect. Paint was peeling next to the fireplace. The carpet, dirty and worn. The couch, lumpy. She'd never really thought about those details when she'd come to visit. But in the stark light of a solitary lamp, she could see that it hadn't been cared for in ages.

It wasn't a home. It hadn't been since her mother had died. Over the years, it had become her dad's place.

The thought hit her with the force of an atom smasher.

This wasn't her home.

Hadn't been for years.

Deep sorrow thrust upwards, coming to rest in the form of a deep ache in her throat.

Where was her home?

Where did she belong?

She swallowed hard as Blake's boots scraped across the porch. She couldn't let him see her all discombobulated like this. She'd already cried on him once this evening. She needed to pull herself together. Taking a cleansing breath, she turned to him.

"I'm sorry, it's not much. Blankets are in the closet in the hall. Help yourself to whatever you like."

He nodded. His eyes were deep pools of compassion. If she allowed herself to look at them too long, they'd pull her in like a tractor beam.

She took another deep breath. "I'm fine. Really. I'm fine."

"Okay. But if you need anything at all…"

"I know." She bit hard on her lip, clamping down on the sudden burst of emotion that filled her belly. "Blake?"

He stayed just inside the doorway, his body taut, his eyes hooded. Electricity breached the distance between them.

"Thank you."

He didn't move. Didn't step toward her, or raise his hand in acknowledgement. Just nodded, his mouth softening at the edges.

She broke the connection and turned toward her bedroom door before she did something impulsive like launch herself into his arms.

CHAPTER 9

A KNOCK STARTLED her awake. Sunlight streamed in her bedroom window, turning the dust motes to sparkling diamonds. She was still fully clothed, on top of the covers. She'd spent the better part of the night tossing and turning, nested in the warmth of Blake's leather jacket. Tumbling Blake's and her father's words over and over in her mind until they were as smooth as river rocks.

You fight because you'd die before you admit you want to fuck.

I ain't sellin'. Especially to the likes of them.

For fuck's sake, will you let me help you?

People have changed, Maddie Jane. They're proud of you.

Don't insult me by lying to me.

Would you be slippery and wet for me?

The knock sounded again. "Maddie?"

She rolled over groaning, reaching for the alarm clock to check the time. Eight-thirty a.m.

No news was good news. The doctors had been right. Her dad had made it through the night. She lay back and inhaled deeply only to be assailed by Blake's scent on the collar of his coat. It had comforted her throughout the night, like the hug she desperately needed but was too proud to ask for. But in the light of day, lying here drenched in... in *him...* was too much. It scraped at her nerves like coarse sandpaper taming wood. Left too many edges rough and vulnerable to catching sparks.

She sat up, and rubbing her eyes, reached for her glasses. After a quick hesitation, she picked up the blue ones.

A knock sounded again, and this time the door opened a crack.

"Maddie? You okay?" Blake stuck his head in, his eyes lighting as they met hers.

Had he shaved? How long had he been up?

"Sleep okay?"

She shook her head. "Nope. You?"

He smiled ruefully. "It was better than sleeping on the ground during a bison drive. But only a little."

He had definitely cleaned up. He looked entirely too composed and fresh for having spent the night on a lumpy couch.

"May I?" He pushed the door open a bit wider, and held out a steaming mug of coffee.

She couldn't help smiling. "You figured out my dad's ancient coffee pot? That thing makes terrible coffee."

"Use one just like it when we move the herd. And I promise, I don't drink bad coffee unless I have to."

His eyes crinkled at the corners when he grinned. Her heart pounded a little harder against her ribs. She stood and reached for the mug, wrapping her hands around its warmth. She ducked her head and took a sip. Silence stretched awkwardly between them.

"You can keep the coat if you like."

Her head snapped up to meet his penetrating gaze. It was hard to tell what was behind his eyes, and it made her squirm. Was he teasing her?

She should have crawled under the covers like a normal

person. Not that there was anything remotely normal about this situation. She'd never spent the night here without her dad, and now Blake was towering over her in her bedroom.

Yeah. Awkward.

The air between them grew heavy.

She handed him back the mug and started shrugging out of the coat, suddenly wanting to put distance between them. "Here." She held out the coat. "I should have given it back last night."

His eyes softened. "Keep it."

"No. Really. I'm sure I can borrow something over at Martha and Eddie's."

He studied her intently. "Don't you keep a change of clothes here?"

She shook her head. "Why would I?"

"It's your home." A note of disbelief entered his voice.

Irritation blossomed, and she pushed on her glasses. "Not."

"Prairie's not all bad, Maddie."

She rolled her eyes, dropping her arm. "The one thing you and my dad have in common. May I have my coffee back please?"

His mouth flattened, and he handed her the mug. "You need to get off your high horse about the people in this town." He spun on his heel and left, not bothering to shut the door behind him.

Why did everything with him have to be a sparring match? Or a kiss fest?

Fighting or fucking.

She took another sip of the coffee. The man did make a mean cup of coffee. Way better than her dad's.

Whatever was between them would simply have to be

ignored. She needed to get her dad sorted and then find a decent internet connection so she could keep working during her stay. The one at Martha and Eddie's was spotty and not secure, so that was out. As was the public library. They were still on dial-up. She could book a hotel in Manhattan, but that was public wi-fi. At least there she could skype her team. If she was incommunicado for more than a few days, her boss would have her head.

Squaring her shoulders resolutely, she rooted in her bag for yesterday's work clothes. First things first. She needed a shower. Taking her mug with her, she headed down the hall to the bunkhouse's sole bathroom. The shower hadn't been used. Did that mean Blake had gone home to shower and then returned? Shaking her head, she turned on the water. He was the least of her worries.

Twenty minutes later, she emerged ready to meet the day, and was met by the smell of bacon wafting from the kitchen.

Geez.

He made decent coffee *and* he made breakfast? What else was going to surprise her about Blake Sinclaire? Her dad never made her breakfast.

She paused at the threshold to the kitchen, studying Blake over the stove. He moved with the practiced ease of someone who regularly made breakfast. Broad shoulders pulled his shirt taut across his back. And his ass… Heat bloomed in her chest, leaving her breathless. His Levi's perfectly molded to his backside and left little… No. Too much to her imagination. Her pussy throbbed eagerly as she stared, captivated.

He turned and grinned as his eyes raked over her. Her flesh tingled under his gaze.

"A little overdressed for the hospital?"

Embarrassment that he'd caught her staring replaced the

warm fuzzies. "Of course I am," she said a little too brusquely. "I went straight from the Fermilab stables to the airport."

He tutt-tutted as he turned back to the skillet. "I see mornings agree with you. Sit down. This will be ready in a sec."

She shouldn't have snapped at him that way. But he just… got under her skin in the most irritating way. Like a pricker in her sock. There was no place in her life for an agitator. An outlier. She couldn't concentrate around him… couldn't *think.* She did irrational things around him like… kiss, and pour beer down people's pants.

He… set her off balance.

Made her…..*feel* things.

Blake Sinclaire was quite possibly the most challenging, unpredictable man she'd ever met. And that meant she needed to get home and back to her orderly, predictable life as quickly as possible.

He placed a plate in front of her filled with the standard country breakfast fare. Bacon, fried eggs, and potatoes. Might as well jam a needle of cholesterol right into her heart. She'd bet the last dollar in her wallet if she peeped in the fridge, there wouldn't be anything green.

"Can I refill your coffee?"

"Stop being so chivalrous."

He scowled. "Look. I know your type. You exist on too much coffee and only eat when someone waves food in your face. You've had a helluva past twenty-four hours, and I'm guessing the only thing you've consumed in the last day besides coffee were the peanuts on the plane."

So. Busted.

He stood over her, arms crossed over his chest. Her eyes drifted to the muscles pulling his sleeves tight.

"Am I right?"

She didn't need to answer because the flush was already crawling up her neck.

"Thank you. I apologize."

He pulled out the chair across from her, and sat down as she dug into her breakfast. It was good. Surprisingly so.

"Accepted." He rocked back on the chair legs. "I know this is a stressful time, but try and accept that there are people besides your immediate family who might want to help you."

"I'm a Hansen. We don't take handouts."

No need for handouts when she could survive just fine on her own, thank you very much. Being dependent on someone else was flat out dangerous.

She couldn't do it. It was too risky. Both professionally and emotionally. She'd learned that lesson in both arenas times ten from Marcus. She wouldn't make that mistake. Not ever again.

He banged the chair legs back down, scowling. "Jesus, Maddie. No one's giving you a handout."

She was clearly losing this argument, and the expression on his face said he wasn't about to let it go. So she did what any right thinking person would do. She changed the subject.

"Where'd you learn to cook like this?"

A sardonic smile lifted the corner of his mouth as he shook his head. "You can play it that way if you want, Maddie. But our conversation isn't over."

"C'mon." She propped her chin on her hand and gave him what she hoped passed for a flirtatious grin. "Who taught you to cook?"

Blake shook his head, laughing a little. "Mrs. Sanchez, our housekeeper. But I'm only good for breakfast. She preps dinner several times a week."

If she kept bombarding him with questions, they wouldn't drift back into dangerous territory. "So when did you eat?

"At about five this morning, over at my place."

"Wait. How'd you get over there?" He rolled his eyes. "On a horse. Ben rode over with a mount and we rode back together. Your cushy city life has softened you."

"I wouldn't call the hours I keep cushy."

"By choice, not necessity."

She waved a piece of bacon at him. "There's a reason I left Prairie, cowboy."

He cocked his head at her. "Let me guess. No one understood you."

She rolled her eyes at his reference to the previous night's discussion. If you could call verbal sparring a discussion. "No one could teach me." She glared at him. The way he got under her skin rankled.

He returned her glare with a steady gaze, an amused smile flicking at the corners of his mouth. "You're adorable when you're wrong." His eyes smoldered, but he wouldn't break eye contact.

She ignored the way her pulse fluttered when he sparred with her. "And you're arrogant when you think you're right."

His half smile broke into a lazy, triumphant grin. He looked like the devil himself. "Shall we get you to the hospital?"

She shook her head, pushing her glasses up her nose.

Oh no.

Definitely not.

She refused to be in confined space with him for the two hour round trip.

"If you hand me Gunnar's keys, I'll drive myself thanks. I

can drop you off on my way out of town."

He smirked, laughter dancing in his eyes. "That ship sailed at dawn, darlin'. You're stuck with me today."

CHAPTER 10

THE RIDE TO the hospital stayed largely silent. And for at least the fiftieth time this morning, he questioned his motives driving Maddie all the way up to Manhattan.

Ben had ridden over at dawn with his horse, Blaze, and together they'd ridden back for chores and a quick shower. By then it was only seven and he'd driven his truck back over to Warren's place. He didn't want her to be alone when she woke up.

It would have been easier to let Gunnar take her earlier this morning. He'd received more than an eyebrow raise when he answered the door and informed her cousin that Maddie was still sleeping.

But no.

He'd insisted on being chivalrous and said he'd bring her up later, drawing yet another raised eyebrow from Gunnar.

He pulled the truck up to visitor drop-off and shifted into park. He tilted back his Stetson and turned to her. "You go on ahead. I'll park and be up."

She pursed her lips, pushing up her glasses. "No need. You've already done enough."

Her voice sounded breathless and a little wavery. She had every right to be nervous. Warren had cheated death by the skin of his teeth.

"Did it occur to you that I might want to see Warren

too?"

Her eyes widened and she sagged, dipping her head.

Before he could stop himself, he reached out. Grazing her silky cheek with the back of his finger. So soft. She was so soft.

"Hey, you okay?"

Her face had the oddest expression. But she nodded, adjusting her glasses again. "I'm fine."

He snorted. "You keep telling yourself that."

She unbuckled her seatbelt. "Think what you want," she responded loftily, shrugging. "I'm *fine.*"

She scooted off the seat and hopped out of the truck, slamming the door behind her. He pulled the truck through and into the nearest parking spot. Why was she acting like she wanted to get as far away from him as possible? He'd done nothing but be a total gentleman. Except for kissing her in his kitchen.

He squirmed, his balls tightening at the memory of her mouth. Yeah. There'd been nothing gentlemanly about that kiss. He'd done it to provoke a response. Even though he'd tortured himself in the process. He couldn't help it. She pushed his buttons, and in return he wanted to push hers.

All of them.

He stalked through the lobby and hit the elevator button a little too hard. Hell, he'd wanted to kiss her as soon as he'd seen her in the airport. She'd tied his gut in knots the second her eyes locked with his. He should win a medal for showing restraint the way he had. And this morning too, when she was all sleepy faced and still wrapped in his jacket.

But no.

He'd walked away and made her breakfast instead.

A total gentleman.

He moved out of the elevator and started to turn the

corner into the waiting room when Martha's voice pulled him up short.

"I'm so surprised by Blake Sinclaire. We owe him so much now."

Maddie's voice murmured something unintelligible.

Martha giggled. "I just have this feeling about him..."

He stood rooted to the spot, unsure whether he should interrupt.

"Don't get any ideas, Martha," Maddie reprimanded her.

"I really don't understand all the hullabaloo between our families. I mean, Jake might have been a sonofagun, but I always liked Amelia. Was real sorry when she went."

A flash of grief pierced him. Martha wasn't the only one who was sorry. Sorry didn't even begin to describe the loss he'd felt when his mother passed.

"You could do far worse than to hitch your ride to his, Maddie Jane. He's solid, that one. Solid as they come."

"Stop this, Aunt Martha... My work is *in Chicago.*"

"The course of true love never did run smooth, dearie. Jobs can change. True love is constant. Besides, your daddy'd be mighty pleased if you settled down close by. He'd never admit it, but he misses you something fierce."

Oh no. This had to stop. He needed to rescue her from this conversation. Hell, he needed to rescue himself.

"Lordy, Auntie M, do I look like a neutrino in a particle smasher?" Maddie asked.

Blake strode around the corner unable to keep the grin off his face. "No. You are much more lovely."

Maddie turned her head, eyes filled with panic. He wouldn't let on that he'd overheard anything but her last statement. At least not yet. "Have you seen the nurse yet?"

She rolled her lips together and shook her head.

"Do you want me to come with you?"

Indecision covered her face, and she shut her eyes, taking a strong breath. He could see the wheels turning in her mind and bit back a laugh. The mothers of Prairie had been making plans for him for years, falling all over themselves for his company. And she hesitated to walk down the hall with him. But it was nice to know at least one Hansen didn't think all Sinclaires were mud.

She opened her eyes and stared directly at him.

His breath stuck in his throat.

A silent conversation took place in the span of a moment.

You're laughing at me.

Yes. I am.

Stop it.

You're beautiful.

The windows to her thoughts slammed shut, replaced with aloof detachment.

She shrugged. "Sure." She peered at him over the tops of her glasses, coming off more like a flustered librarian than anything remotely threatening. "But no talking in there, and you leave if he gets agitated."

He bit back a laugh but nodded solemnly.

"Do you want to come too, Auntie, M?" Maddie turned back toward her aunt who was watching them with open speculation.

Great.

This was sure to make the rounds at Dottie's Diner.

"Go on ahead, honey. You two see him first. I'll wait until Eddie arrives after lunch."

Maddie spun on her heel and marched down the hall, the echo of her heels clicking the only sound between them.

Keeping pace with her, he reached out his hand toward

the small of her back, catching himself just in time before he touched her. Electricity leaped to his palm, nearly making him clench his fist.

She pushed up her glasses. "You don't need to hover. I'm fine."

He dropped his hand, biting back a retort that was certain to elicit a fiery response. She was anxious, and he happened to be here to absorb it. Fine. If that's what she needed right now, he was her man. He could see her brain working on overdrive again. If it wasn't so adorable it would be damned irritating.

"Stop thinking, Maddie." He didn't bother to hide his grin this time.

She slid him a sideways glance, made an irritated little squeak, and kept walking.

Yep.

Totally adorable.

"You're still thinking, Maddie."

She stopped short and spun around, jabbing his chest with her finger.

He stepped back. She moved forward, punctuating each word with another jab of her finger. "Get. Out. Of. My. Head."

He reached for her arms, pulling her close. Every cell in his body tightened in awareness as she molded to him. Their eyes locked, and she let out a little gasp. The urge to bend his head to hers and take a quick taste of her rushed through him. He swallowed hard then stepped back, letting her go. Not here. Not now.

"No." He shook his head. "Sorry." Not really. He liked teasing her.

She pressed her lips together, eyes sparkling with aggravation.

Huh.

Had she wanted him to kiss her just then?

Not how he'd imagined getting the upper hand with a Hansen, but he'd take it.

He left her where she was and walked a few more paces to the door and held it open for her to pass. She squared her shoulders and marched through the door.

"I'm here to see Warren Hansen."

The nurse on duty looked her once over. "And you are?"

"His daughter."

"Yes. Of course." She reached for the chart, looking at her notes. "I see you were here last night. They took the ventilator out about twenty minutes ago. He's recovering nicely and he's still very weak. But you can see him for a few minutes."

The nurse nodded toward the doorway across the room. Still pointedly ignoring Blake, Maddie stepped around the nurse's station and paused in the threshold. Tension rippled through her body, and his heart went out to her. Her attitude be damned. She needed support. He stepped up behind her and brought his hands to her shoulders. Some of the tightness leached from her body.

Standing there, taking her father in this way over Maddie's shoulder, twisted something in his chest. Warren looked like shit. His color and had improved a shade over the hideous oatmeal color from the previous evening, but he still looked terrible. And frail. Like the fight had gone out of him. As if sensing them there, Warren's eyes fluttered open. He opened his mouth, a hoarse rasp escaping.

Maddie stepped forward, reaching for his hand and sinking into one of the chairs set up next to the side of his bed.

"Shh, Dad. It's okay. You gave us quite a scare."

His eyes widened as he tried to speak again. "What happened?" he rasped out, his voice barely above a whisper.

"You had a massive heart-attack, Dad. We nearly lost you. If it hadn't been for Blake..." She turned, acknowledging him with a grateful smile.

Something warm puffed up inside of him as he basked in her appreciation. God she was beautiful. He leaned against the doorjamb, and shoved his hands in his coat pockets.

Warren grunted and tried to raise himself.

"No, Dad. Don't move. You're still hooked up."

"Blasted machines," Warren rasped with effort. He wheezed, pinning his eyes on Blake.

Blake shifted uncomfortably, fisting his hands in his pockets. Their last conversation had been... intense. He wasn't seriously going to try and pick it up now? Maddie would kick the tar out of both of them if she discovered what had transpired.

"Don't...don't jes' stand there like a ninny, Sinc...Sinclaire."

Covering the distance to the bed in two steps, he settled himself next to Maddie, and stretched his hand around the back of her chair. "Near death has done wonders for your disposition, sir."

A small smile broke across Warren's face, and he wheezed out a cackle. He shut his eyes, still smiling. Even with the oxygen tube, his breathing remained labored. He raised his finger, waving it between the two of them. "Glad to see.... You two've worked things out... Maddie Jane."

Wait. What?

Worked what out?

What was the old man playing at?

"Of course, Dad. I'm here as long as you need." Maddie squeezed her father's hand reassuringly.

Warren opened his eyes again, and looked straight at him. His blue eyes, the same intense hue as Maddie's, penetrated Blake like a laser. "Our families… this fighting… So glad… over." Warren sighed shakily.

The anesthetic must have rattled his brain. Or the meds.

"Daddy?" Concern laced Maddie's voice. "Of course. Everything's fine."

"He'll be good… husband… not like… Jake…"

She stiffened in her seat. "Dad… I don't–"

Looking back, Blake could never say definitively what made him act so irrationally. It was like some unseen force propelled him to action. He leaned forward, clasped Maddie to his side, and patted Warren on the leg. "Of course, sir." His hand gripped her shoulder tightly. "I'll make her very happy. You have my word."

Ooh, he would pay for this.

In this life or the next.

Of that he was confident.

Not that he had any intention of marrying Maddie Hansen. He didn't. But maybe Warren seeing the two of them together was just what he needed to recover. And, it would buy him more time to figure out how to purchase his land outright from Warren.

Warren let out a contented sigh, his body visibly relaxing. He squeezed Maddie's hand like it was a lifeline.

Maddie shot Blake a scathing glance, but he kept his poker face firmly in place. He had to admit, seeing her squirm was just the tiniest bit entertaining. He guessed that made him an ass, considering where they were. But they'd sort this out soon enough.

She pointedly shrugged his hand off her shoulder and patted her dad. "I think we should go, Daddy."

She slid another dagger-filled glance his direction, and Blake continued to keep his face bland. Even giving her a little half-smile, as if she was the love of his life.

Oh yeah.

She would come unleashed as soon as they left.

The fireworks would certainly be interesting.

"I think you're not… yourself, Dad." She leaned over the bed and placed a kiss on his forehead. "You need rest."

Warren's eyes were already shut, a small smile still curving his thin, pale lips. "Happy… Maddie Jane… Love… you."

Warren was either overmedicated and off his rocker, or the wiliest damned sonofabitch he'd ever met. Either way, he was going to capitalize on Warren's gift. Even if he regretted it later.

He was certain to regret it.

CHAPTER 11

MADDIE TURNED ON him, eyes flashing. "You," she hissed. "Outside. Now."

She swept past him, her ass wiggling as her heels clicked on the tiles. He'd bet the farm she had no panties on.

Again.

Was this a thing with her?

It had taken all his self-control this morning to not ask her when she'd entered the kitchen wearing the same outfit as she had in Chicago. And to not touch her to find out for himself. His cock jerked in his jeans. He wanted to touch her. Badly. His mouth salivated at the thought of cupping her curves in his palm. Of finally sliding his hand between her thighs to discover just how wet she was.

Jesus.

He needed to tone that shit down fast. The last thing Maddie needed was to see him with a raging hard-on at the hospital.

As soon as the ICU doors closed behind them she stopped, turned, and marched straight back to him. Eyes flashing like a warrior Goddess.

There would be the fury he expected.

"Are you six kinds of *insane?*"

He grinned down at her. He couldn't say for sure what had happened back there. It was like some supersonic gravitational force pulled the words right out of him. And funny – but the thought of being with her, *really* being with her, intrigued the heck out of him.

"Yes… Yes. Eight, actually."

"What. Were. You. Thinking?"

Warmth flooded him. He wasn't sure. Not that he'd tell her that. He raised his eyebrows. "Payback?"

Her brows furrowed and she pursed her lips. He wanted to run his thumb over that sweet pout. She turned on her heel, walked six steps then stalked back to him. "Payback. This is *payback*? For what?

He couldn't help it. He was overcome with the grins.

She rushed on. "You do realize that the *entire* town will know before we get back to Prairie. Did you *think* about that? For even a millisecond? About the unintended consequences of your… your… spontaneity?"

He scowled at her.

Of course he had. Sort of.

He'd known she'd be pissed as hell.

"I was thinking about the dying wish of an old man to see his only child settled and happy. Don't you think he deserves that?"

Her chest puffed up in indignation and she turned and stalked away, only to stalk right back. "I have a career, you know. What do you think's going to happen if word reaches them?"

"They're going to congratulate you, like normal people do." Jesus. Was he was chopped liver? He was a catch, dammit.

A good one.

No.

A *great* one.

She opened her mouth to respond, then snapped it shut, glaring at him. The more he thought about it, the better this idea seemed. Warren wouldn't be out of the hospital anytime soon, which meant Maddie would be staying in Prairie at least a few more weeks. And God help him, he was intrigued. He wanted to get under that armadillo armor and discover the real Maddie. The passionate, irrational, emotional Maddie. He'd bet his favorite horse that when she came for him – on his mouth, on his fingers, on his cock – she'd go supernova.

He took a step closer, his boots coming toe to toe with her little pointy shoes. Forcing her to tilt her chin. "Know what? Last time I checked, you were not the center of the universe."

"What's that supposed to mean?" she snapped like a polecat, her anger rolling off her in waves.

"I mean, your father is an old man who just had a major health scare. Maybe, just maybe you should think about someone besides yourself for a change. Did you see how happy he looked in there? When have you *ever* seen him happy like that? You, Maddie. Yes *you.*" He held up his hand when she opened her mouth to object. "You are the person most precious to him… his *pinch point.* He wants nothing more than to see you settled and happy. Are you so cold you'd deny a sick old man a bit of happiness?"

Emotions flickered through her eyes as fast as clips in an old silent movie. Outrage. Guilt. Fear. Love.

She scowled, then shook her head.

Was he an ass for pressing her this way? For pushing her until she practically broke?

No.

He wasn't.

He was right about this. Right about his instincts. She

might be a super scientist, but he was no schlump, and it was high time she took other people into consideration. He leaned into her, reaching to caress her soft cheek with this thumb. "You're like an unbroke filly. You buck and run the second you get scared." He let the iron enter his voice. "Dr. Hansen, you're about to learn what it means to be a team player."

Who was she to impugn him? He was a Sinclaire for chrissake. His family started this community.

"I know all about teams."

"Do you?" He raised his eyebrows. "I don't think you do. You're a team player only when it benefits you. Your goals. Your ideals."

She gasped, puffing up her chest. From this vantage point, he could see her luscious cleavage contained within the vee of her shirt. Every time she gasped like that, her tits pushed upwards a little more. He tore his eyes away before it became obvious and concentrated on a blob of paint on the wall behind her.

He continued, talking to her as if she were his younger brother. "You don't like being in a position where you're dependent and out of control. Guess what? Neither do the rest of us. But that's exactly the situation you're in. So it's time to sink or swim, darlin'."

She opened her mouth to respond, her eyes still flashing wildly. Then snapped it shut, crossing her arms, pushing her breasts up even higher. Thank God she was glaring at his face, because his dick would not stand down.

"Fine." She worried her bottom lip with her teeth. After a moment, she glazed up at him, eyes softening a fraction. "You're right."

Of course he was, but how much had it cost her to admit that?

She speared him with a heavy look. "But as soon as he's back to himself, you'll tell him we broke it off, and I go home."

She'd given a fraction of an inch, but he'd make it a mile by the time this charade was over.

"So the cold scientist does have a little compassion."

Hurt flared in her eyes. She looked away. Then back to him, the determined fire back in place.

"I'm not cold." Her voice was low and thick with emotion.

He raised his eyebrow skeptically.

"I'm not," she defended. "But I am pragmatic. Every problem has a solution. You… you keep… *pushing.* You fail to understand emotions cloud the possibility of finding the right solution. Solutions are found in facts, not feelings."

She glared at him mutinously, certainty and self-righteousness radiating off her in waves.

It tugged at him. There was a passionate, loving woman inside her. He was certain. One even stronger than the woman in front of him. He'd figure out a way to mine that. He'd put his cock on ice if necessary. Let her make the moves.

He snaked his arm around her, pulling her flush against him. "That's where you're wrong Dr. Hansen. You can't make the right choice without emotions. And I aim to prove it to you."

CHAPTER 12

"YOU OWE ME a bottle of twelve year Redbreast if Dottie knows about this," Maddie said.

She refused to look at him. Instead, she continued to stare out the window like his sister Emma did as a pouty teenager.

"Give it up, Maddie. I'd buy it for you anyway. All you'd have to do is ask."

She snorted.

Dottie must have been keeping an eye out, because before he he'd set the emergency brake, she'd bustled out the front of the diner and around to where they had parked in the side lot.

Blake knew word traveled fast, but this must be a record. From Warren, to Martha, to Dottie… that meant the story was likely to be fairly accurate.

Dottie waited, bouncing on her toes, dishtowel in hand, practically bursting with excitement.

He should buy her two bottles of Irish whiskey for what she was about to endure. As soon as he opened the truck door, Dottie was there, beaming from ear to ear. She helped him and enveloped him in a squishy hug.

"After all this time. I just *knew* you'd be perfect for each other."

He refrained from rolling his eyes. Dottie loved to gush. How many years had it been since she'd seen Maddie?

Dottie grabbed his hand and pulled him around the front

of his truck, opening the passenger door herself. "Maddie Jane, you are a vision!"

She reached into the cab and pulled Maddie down into an enormous hug.

The glare Maddie shot him over Dottie's shoulder was hotter than a branding iron. It burned him all right, but not in the way she probably hoped.

"You owe me," she mouthed silently. He bit back a laugh.

"I always knew you two'd be perfect for each other," Dottie rattled on. "Ever since the day Cassie came home all those years ago and told me how Blake rescued you."

Dottie stepped away, giving Maddie a once over, then pulling her back into a hug. "You a big fancy doctor, and your knight in shining armor just waiting for you the whole time, under your nose."

Maddie narrowed her eyes at him, as she cleared her throat. "Umm. Yes. We're…we're so happy?" Her voice broke as Dottie thumped her on the back. "But I'm actually a–"

"I bet your daddy's fit to split. This is just the thing to make him pop up outta that bed in no time."

"Yes… yes, uh, he approves." She smiled faintly, extracting herself from Dottie's embrace.

He turned his head to hide the shaking from his laughter. This was so much worse than he'd expected. Unintended consequences. Maddie had a point. He hadn't thought this part through. Not that he'd admit to it ever. Not even hogtied and roasting on a spit.

"Come here you two luvvies." Dottie pulled them both into an embrace, her face glowing with joy and anticipation. "Now when were you thinking for your nuptials? It's been so long since Prairie's enjoyed a wedding. And now our two oldest families." She sighed beatifically. "Destiny."

Maddie's eyes were like saucers. Even this was a little much for him. He cleared his throat. "We're waiting until Warren is out–"

"Of course you are." Dottie gave them both a little squeeze. "As soon as Warren's home, you'll have the wedding. Yes?"

Maddie squeaked, quickly covering it by coughing. Blake swallowed nervously. He'd owe Dottie an explanation later. Clearly, she was swept away with the excitement of news.

Dottie finally released them and stepped back, wiping her hands on her apron.

Maddie pushed on her glasses, then pressed her hand to her cheek. To the average onlooker, the pink flush creeping up her neck would indicate she was overcome with excitement.

But he knew better.

She was pissed as hell and trying to think two steps ahead of everyone else at the diner. He had to admire her cool in a crisis. If there was one thing Maddie did brilliantly, it was think fast and not panic.

"Dottie," she asked. "Tell me how your girls are." She inhaled and smiled, the cool facade of professionalism once again in place. It was a marvel to behold. Especially when he wasn't trying to dig under it.

"Sure thing, sweetie." Dottie herded them across the parking lot to the front door.

"Cassie's a helicopter pilot over in Afghanistan right now. We're so proud of her. Then Lydia is in New York City right now working for a shoe designer, and of course her twin Lexi's just down the road in DC working as a lobbyist for some environmental group. It's close enough they sometimes get together. And my baby, Carolina, is just about to receive her degree in physical therapy." She beamed proudly as she held the door open for them. "I'm sure they'll be thrilled to fly home for your ceremony. You can catch up then."

The smile didn't quite reach Maddie's eyes, but she nodded her assent.

A white hot flash of possessiveness puffed up inside him again. He reached for her and pulled her close, laying his claim for everyone in the diner to see. This might be temporary, but she was his. For now. And he wanted there to be no doubt in anyone's mind about that.

As soon as they'd crossed the threshold to the diner, Dottie clapped her hands.

"Listen up, everyone. We're gonna have a country weddin' real soon. I'm pleased as punch to introduce to you the future Mr. and Mrs. Blake Sinclaire."

He winced inside. He would be ten kinds of surprised if Maddie ever consented to change her name. Not that he cared about things like that. Besides, this was all a sham. And he had more important things to worry about, like how he was going to convince Warren to sell him his land back when it seemed like he'd just given into his demands.

If Maddie ever had an inkling that Warren had considered trading her like a cow, she'd flee to Chicago and that would be the end of everything. She'd never speak to either of them again.

"Well, well, well," an acid voice dripped from the Formica counter that ran the length of the room.

Maddie stiffened in his embrace. Kylee Ross, sitting on a stool in a pair of too tight red jeans, turned and glared at the two of them, pale blue eyes sparking venomously.

"If it isn't little Britannica, come home to lord it over the peons of Prairie."

"Hello, Kylee," she replied evenly, with just the barest

hint of steel in her voice. "So glad to see you've… made something of yourself."

"I've made more than you'll ever know." She turned her glare to him. "And you'd do well to remember that…"

He shook his head the merest fraction at Kylee. More unintended consequences. Kylee was rarely at the diner. Her presence here this morning was bad luck. Plain and simple. But if he didn't tread carefully, this whole thing would bite him in the ass. The best thing to do would be to smooth things over as quickly as possible.

He gave Maddie an extra squeeze. "Ladies, how about you retract the claws and shake hands."

Now both women glared at him.

"What?" He looked between the two of them. "Don't you think it's time to let water flow under the bridge?"

Maddie pushed her glasses up her nose, but remained silent, glowering at him.

Kylee stood, sauntering closer to Maddie, her lips slicing her face in a sneer. "You always thought you were so smart. So much better than us. And now look at you. Stealing one of Prairie's own? It's not enough for you to live off of some old man, you have to come home and screw our cowboys?"

His fist clenched and he forced himself to open his hand. "Enough, Kylee."

He wouldn't tolerate her airing dirty laundry in public like this. That he'd ever let himself get involved with her was one of his biggest regrets.

Kylee turned her glare to him. "And you. You think fucking Warren's daughter is going to get you your land back? He hates you."

Maddie vibrated next to him. The flush creeping up her neck and the hard line of her mouth the only indicator that

Kylee's words had hit their mark.

"Kylee Ross." Dottie's voice boomed from where she stood back by the coffee pots. She flung her dishtowel on the counter, and leaned on it with both hands.

The low level buzz in the diner fizzled into awkward, expectant silence.

"I know your momma raised you to have better manners than that. You put a zip on that mouth of yours right now, or you will not be welcome back in here. You understand?"

Kylee pressed her lips so thin a piece of paper couldn't breach them. But she stood her ground, animosity pouring off her in waves.

Maddie removed his hand from her side. Sliding him a glance filled with disappointment and anger, she stepped back. "Please take me home. I'll wait outside."

She turned, the staccato click of her heels the only sound echoing through the diner as she stalked out, head held high.

Christ.

That could have gone better.

He stepped toward Kylee, lowering his voice just enough that the other diners wouldn't hear. "Pull a stunt like that *ever* again, and so help me God I'll–"

"You'll *what,* Blake? Turn your back on me? You've already done that." Bitterness laced her voice.

"Don't start, Kylee. I'm done with your games." He turned and hurried after Maddie.

CHAPTER 13

NO TEARS. SHE would not give that… that sorry excuse of a subatomic particle the power to make her cry. She was a grown woman. She'd outgrown small town pettiness.

She leaned back against the cab of the truck. The dust would mess her skirt, but she didn't care. A little dirt was nothing compared to the thrashing she'd love to give Kylee Ross's face.

That was *absolutely* the last time she'd allow Kylee Ross to penetrate her armor. Kylee was a speck of dust on the outhouse of the universe. She threw her head back, laughing bitterly.

Clearly her father had done nothing to dispel the rumor that she was a doctor living with an old man. She didn't even know how that one had started, but it galled her not one member of her family had bothered to correct it. And they wondered why she wasn't interested in moving home?

The distinct crunch of Blake's boots sounded on the gravel as the pointy toes of his Tony Lamas entered her field of view.

"Maddie."

Shame settled, hot and heavy in her gut. The years of public humiliation pressing on her like a millstone. She put her hand up. "Don't…" Any more tenderness and she would disintegrate. She couldn't compartmentalize when he touched her, and she was done feeling sorry for herself where Kylee was concerned. "I'm fine."

She whirled, yanking open the door to the cab, and stopped short. There was no dignified way for her to get into the cab without his help. And she wasn't willing to rip her skirt to prove a point.

His arms engulfed her, pulling her back against the hard planes of his chest.

"Wanna talk about it?" His breath tickled her ear, sending sparks skittering straight to her nipples. He had to have felt her reaction against his arms. How could she concentrate on anything in his proximity?

She shook her head. "I do not."

"Are you sure?" He planted a kiss at her temple.

She couldn't relax into him. Couldn't let herself. If she admitted she needed him, relied on his comfort more than she already had, he'd only see her as a helpless female in need of rescuing. The only thing she needed rescuing from were the emotions zinging through her chest like a Tesla ball.

He sighed and pressed another kiss to her temple, then helped her into the cab and walked around to the driver's side. She risked a glance as he stood silently, holding the door open for a moment before he hopped into the cab. That was a mistake. His gaze penetrated to the darkest part of her soul. How did he get in her head that way? With a look?

He pulled out of the parking lot and drove the whole length of town before he broke the silence. "Great job fighting back there." His voice dripped with sarcasm.

Indignation swelled in her chest. "You don't understand."

"You're right, I don't. You don't hesitate to fight me. You poured a beer down Brodie's pants for chrissakes. What hold does she have over you?"

"She doesn't." She adjusted her glasses, shrugging.

He snorted. "You don't fool me for a second, Maddie." She squirmed under the piercing gaze he shot her direction as he slowed the truck to turn onto Sinclaire land. "Time to cowboy up, darlin'."

"I think you should take me back to my dad's. I can stay there."

His low tut-tut of a chuckle scraped across her awareness, firing the neurons she was desperately trying to reassert control over.

"Are you looking to add fuel to the speculation fire?" He glanced at her again, not bothering to hide his amusement.

This was *not* funny. She needed space to think… and bring her senses to heel. She pushed her glasses up her nose. "You don't have to laugh."

This time, his laugh was full throated and rich, as sweet and burned as toffee sliding over her tongue. The taste of him flooded her mouth, heightening her agitation.

"Because you sitting there all puffed up like an indignant prairie chicken protecting her nest isn't funny."

He pulled the truck up the long gravel drive between the Big House and the barn, and slowed to a stop. He turned to her, stretching his arm across the back of the cab.

"I recommend we keep this going in front of my brothers. Brodie doesn't know how to keep his mouth shut."

Great.

She was in too deep now to back out. Her father better make a damned speedy recovery for the pain and suffering she was about to endure. A tiny part of her relished the idea of a co-conspirator, but she shoved that little part back to the recesses of her brain. This charade was certain to bring nothing but disorder and chaos to her orderly life. She needed to concentrate on the task at hand and get back to Chicago as soon as her dad was in the clear.

"You need to understand right now that I have no intention of being a ranch wife. With or without a ring on my finger." She swung her hips around and eased herself out of the truck without waiting for him to help her. She moved to the porch steps, waiting for him to join her.

"I don't cook," she said when he reached her. "Not even oatmeal."

He smiled hopefully at her. "Does that mean you're willing to stay here?"

Damn. Did he have to look so adorably mischievous? For a split second, she held in her minds eye a tiny boy with the same naughty grin. Oh no. Most certainly not. She hadn't fantasized about children since... She forced the thought away. Those days were over.

"Don't worry." His voice held a note of expectation. "Our family housekeeper, Mrs. Sanchez, helps with meal preparation. She also helps with laundry. You don't need to lift a finger if you don't want to."

She narrowed her gaze. "I can do my own laundry. But, do you have secure high-speed internet? That's a deal breaker."

He stepped up the porch and opened the door to the house.

"Come with me." He extended his hand.

Her hand itched to hold his. A thousand grasshoppers started jumping against her ribs. She could barely breathe.

He rolled his eyes at her hesitation.

"Come on, Maddie. Take my hand. It's not dangerous."

The body attached to the hand certainly was.

Bracing herself against the sensation that would envelop

her, she tucked her hand into his. Her arm electrified and currents of awareness shot across her body. She'd just have to turn off her brain when she touched him.

His hand engulfed hers completely. Surrounded it in warmth and strength. A longing swept through her, the likes of which she hadn't felt since she'd been a silly, naive teenager in Boston. She had to pull it together quickly. If she wasn't careful…

He led her upstairs, turned and opened another door to a second set of stairs. They climbed to the top floor. The room spanned the length of the house, with dormers facing both east and west. Against the west wall stood a large oak desk centered between two low book cases. The perfect vantage point to see the Flint Hills in all their glory.

"This is your office?" Of course it was. She needed to get her head examined if she continued to state the obvious.

He nodded, flashing her another grin, releasing hundreds of butterflies in her belly. "Complete with secure, lightning fast internet. Fastest you'll find in Prairie. You can join me at any time."

"Stop with the charm already." She prided herself on being impervious to charms. She would have to do better at resisting.

He pulled her close, his eyes twinkling. "You'll know when I turn on the charm, Maddie."

She held her breath, as her pulse started to race wildly. Was he going to kiss her? He couldn't kiss her. That was a bad, bad idea. Too bad the rest of her body felt differently.

She slipped her hand from his, stepping back and nervously scanning the rest of the room. A large leather sectional had been pushed against the far wall, a mini fridge next to it. In the center stood a pool table. Interesting. A man attic.

With a gorgeous view.

"I think I should sleep up here for the time being."

He cocked his head, raising an eyebrow. "Afraid?"

"I usually work late into the night. I might as well stay up here and not disturb anyone."

"You mean hide out here."

She stared at him in disbelief. "Surely you don't think that because we're pretend engaged I'm going to sleep with you?" The hungry light that entered his eyes did not inspire her with confidence. It did, however, set her pussy quivering in anticipation.

"If people close to us are going to buy this, we need to act like we're in love."

She crossed her arms stubbornly, covering her suddenly achy nipples. "But why should I have to pay the price for your crazy scheme?"

They stood, eyes locked in battle, electricity arcing between them.

His eyes raked over her like a wolf about to devour its prey, as a slow smile curved his lips. Did that make her dinner? The throbbing emanating from her clit said *Yes, please.*

She blinked first and dropped her hands. "Fine. I'll stay here, but I'm *not* sleeping with you."

"You don't have to be worried about the price, sweetheart, because I'll be sleeping on the floor."

He stepped into her space. So close her nipples practically grazed his chest. So close she had to tilt her head, inhaling his scent as she did so. Desire settled in the pit of her belly. She swallowed, but refused to let him see the effect he was really having on her. She wouldn't give him the satisfaction of knowing the kind of power he could wield over her.

He dipped his head close, so his lips hovered a fraction

from her ear. All she'd have to do is tilt her head.

"What are you afraid of, Dr. Hansen… Madison?" The way her name rolled of his tongue sent a flood of liquid to her core. She clenched her thighs. God help her if she opened her legs even a fraction. "Falling in love?"

Her breath hitched as warmth ballooned up, hardening her nipples and making her head buzz like she'd inhaled helium. She locked her knees, not giving a millimeter.

"Be honest, Maddie. If not with me, at least with yourself." His breath heated her blood, slowing it down. Her limbs began to feel heavy and languid. "You're afraid of your feelings."

He reached up and trailed a finger down her cheek… down her neck… tracing the collar of her blouse… down the vee to the top button. She trembled uncontrollably, her breath coming in short gasps. She bit hard on her lip to keep from moaning, but she was too late to prevent the somewhat choked sound that escaped.

His lips broke into a smile against her ear. Damn him. He was toying with her. She swallowed hard, focusing on having a thought that did not have to do with body parts.

"I… I… am not," she hissed, as his finger began the reverse trail up her collarbone.

"Liar." His tongue flicked at her ear. She flinched at the jolt of electricity to her aching clit.

"There's… there's… no room in my life for love," she rushed out.

He stiffened, but didn't stop his one finger assault of her collarbone and neck.

"So the tears and anxiety for Warren… just mild familial concern?"

Ouch.

She deserved that.

"Yes… *no*… it's not like that. Of, of course. He's my dad. B-b-but I'm talking about romantic love. It-it overrides common sense. It's just people giving into their hormones. That's all."

His other hand captured her hip, sliding dangerously close to her ass. She rolled her hips involuntarily, and his lips curved against her a second time. She shouldn't have done that. She could feel the last vestiges of her control fraying and flying away with every caress.

"So, this… electricity… between us…" He continued his exploration of her backside, his hand sweeping over her ass. There was no doubt now that he knew she had no panties. None whatsoever. "It's just raging hormones. Nothing more?"

She let out a ragged sigh. Her tongue lay thick in her mouth. She couldn't speak.

He tilted her chin. "Look at me, Maddie."

She raised her eyes. His hazel depths showed raw hunger and fierce determination.

Expectation thrilled through her. Heat spread through her veins and settled at the top of her legs. Her pussy throbbed in a silent dance of anticipation.

He raised his eyebrow, his lips so close she could breathe him in as he spoke. "So this…" he grazed his lips across hers. "Is nothing…" he grazed them again, this time his tongue flicking over her seam. "But a chemical reaction…"

"Yes," she breathed. *No.* More like a nuclear meltdown. Her pussy drenched in readiness, she parted for him, unable to stand against the waves of unabashed lust crashing over her. She shut her eyes in surrender.

"Look at me, Maddie." There was no dismissing the rough command in his voice, and her eyes widened. "I call bullshit."

His lips covered hers. Slowly. Sensuously. Pulling things from her, laying her open. His fingers drove into her hair, pulling apart her bun, as his tongue rode over hers, probing and taking.

His other hand clutched the fabric of her skirt, raising it inch by torturous inch. Soon his fingers would graze the lace of her thigh highs. Her body thrilled at the thought. He pressed her close, deepening their kiss, his tongue relentlessly swirling and probing, demanding she give back with equal measure.

Something unlocked inside her, releasing a flood of longing, and she leaned into him, clutching his corded arms beneath her palms. Need swirled up into her brain, blotting out all thought, everything but the sensation of his mouth and his hands working her over.

His fingers tightened in her hair as his other hand traced the inside of her thigh along the lace of her stockings. Oh God, he was so close to the spot she wanted him to touch. She shifted, widening her stance, easing his access. Finally, after what seemed like an excruciating wait, his fingers slid the length of her slit.

She cried out, knees shaking.

"Jesus, fuck, Maddie," he groaned into her mouth. "Do you always go commando?"

He slid his fingers back down her opening.

"Only… one… pair…"

"Jesus, you talk too much."

His fingers swept the length of her pussy again coming to rest on her clit, covering it with her desire. Her hips bucked and she cried out, riding the rising hurricane of sensation building within her. If he did it again her brain would explode.

He ripped his mouth from hers and stepping back, removed his hand from between her legs. His chest heaved as his eyes met hers, a mixture of lust and anger.

"This." He waved his hand between the two of them. The scent of her arousal on his fingers invaded her awareness. "Just chemistry? That's all it is… right? Just chemistry."

His lips flattened and he shook his head, turning and stalking off through the door, leaving her struggling to bring her arousal under control. Her brain moved at a snail's pace. Was that all it had been? Just some crazy chemical reaction?

But that moment.

That shift inside her.

That hadn't been a trick of the mind.

And it scared her to death.

CHAPTER 14

BLAKE SAT NURSING a beer on the front porch as Maddie pulled his truck between the Big House and the barn. She'd been pushing herself too hard this last week. Hell, they both had. Sleeping in the same room but not touching had become a nightmare.

Every night had been a battle of wills as to who would fall asleep first. Every morning, a contest to see who would rise first and vacate the room fastest. He wanted more than anything to sweep her into his arms and crush every barrier she'd erected between them. But he refused to make another move. He wouldn't beg for a woman's affection.

Ever.

Even if that woman was supposed to be marrying him.

The cab door slammed, and she came around the front, pausing warily when her eyes met his. Even from this distance, he could see the worry lines that had etched themselves into her face over the last several days. Exhaustion seemed to pour off her body.

Damn.

How much of that stress was because of him? Because of the situation he'd created? If he was half a man he'd let her go right now and figure out some other way to get Warren to sell. But he wasn't. There was too much of Jake in him. Even though that knowledge galled him, it helped him keep his life in perspective, and the women at arm's length.

Present company excepted. He couldn't get enough of her. Hell, just seeing her now, her hair free from its usual tidy bun, he grew half hard. He stood, turning to the mini fridge to reach for a beer. The last thing she needed was to see him with a woody.

He cracked the beer, and turned, offering it. "Come sit a spell. You look wiped."

She gave him a small smile, pushing up her glasses, and moved to join him on the heavy porch furniture. She was still wearing the blue ones. Interesting. He probably shouldn't read too much into it, but it secretly pleased him she hadn't switched back to the black frames.

The late afternoon air lay heavy and still, pressing down on them. A sure sign of bad weather soon. If not tonight, then tomorrow. They'd already had three severe storms in the last week, one of which had dropped a small tornado that took out an old barn about six miles east of here.

"Thanks." She took a sip, then pressed the bottle to her head and leaned forward, balancing her elbows on her knees.

Unable to resist, he reached out and draped his arm across her shoulder. She stiffened slightly at his touch, but didn't shake him off. Deciding not to take offense, he massaged at the knot in her neck.

She groaned and rolled her shoulder into his fingers.

"Rough day?"

"You don't know the half of it." She took another pull on her beer. "I met with Gary Anderson today and the director of the lab at K-State."

"Oh?" He stilled. He'd just been yanking her chain in Chicago.

"Yeah. You were right when we talked with him. And I

figured as long as I was in town..."

Something warm and prideful bubbled up inside of him. That was a step forward – admitting he was right.

She continued. "And with my luck these days, he'd find out I was in town and dissed him, and that would be a professional discourtesy."

He deflated a bit. So her motivation had nothing to do with him. "How's your dad today?"

She groaned and dipped her head. He continued to work the knots in her neck and shoulders.

"Dad's ornery under the best of circumstances. He's just a bear now. He thinks he should be home already and hauling hay."

He laughed quietly and settled himself a bit closer. "So thoughts of our pending matrimony did nothing to soothe the savage beast?"

She slid him the stink eye. Good to know she was still irritated about that.

"Funny you should ask. He's hell bent on us setting a date. And where's my ring?" She flicked her left hand at him and glared. "As soon as he's out of the hospital, you need to set things straight."

As soon as he had the title to his family property back, he'd be happy to. The only thing this arrangement had been good for so far was a pair of blue balls and a need for blood pressure medication.

"Know what you need?" *Besides a thorough fucking?* He continued to massage the knot in her shoulder, working his thumb over the hardest part. She was wound tighter than a spool of baling wire, and equally dangerous.

She shrugged, taking a sip of her beer and waiting for him to continue.

"You need a ride."

Her eyes widened and she shot up. "*What?*"

It should be illegal to have this much fun yanking her chain. "Get your mind out of the gutter, darlin'. I've already told you that's your call. Come ride the fences with me this afternoon. I need to see if the storms have caused any damage."

"Oh." Her cheeks pinked, and her hand flew up to adjust her glasses. He swore she looked the tiniest bit disappointed. He drained his beer, tossing it into the growing pile of recycling at the edge of the porch.

He stood and offered his hand, giving her yet another chance to reject him. She was skittish as an unbroke filly. And he'd learned over the last several days that over time and with patience on his part, the smallest gestures would be welcomed. First the hand at the door, then the hand holding. Mostly for effect, but she'd settled into it. Same with the little kisses he could get away with now in mixed company. And every now and then he'd caught her staring at him. She played her cards close. Who wouldn't, living with a man like Warren? She'd learned from the best.

She took his hand and stood, letting him lead her down the little hill to where the great stone barn stood. The hundred and twenty year old barn was a remnant of a bygone era, when limestone and timber were plenty. When neighbors helped neighbors build, and the designs were meant to last generations. It was one of the last barns of its kind in the Flint Hills. Sixteen feet of limestone, topped with a timber roof that looked like the underside of a ship. It had withstood generations of fierce Flint Hills weather.

They'd both need a shower later with the humidity and heat so high. The visual of soaping her back made his balls ache. And unconsciously he squeezed her hand. She squeezed back, sliding him a tiny smile.

He paused at the large double doors that comprised the entrance to the barn and heaved the bolt across, opening the door. They stepped into the cool interior. Limestone was a great insulator, and one of the reasons his four-legged farm hands were always in top form. He never had to worry about them getting heat-stressed in the brutal summer conditions.

"This way." He took her hand again, pulling her along, and stopped in front of a roan quarter horse with a white star. "This is Blaze. I raised him from a foal."

Maddie reached out and offered her hand, letting him nuzzle her. Her smile lit up the barn like a Christmas tree. "Aww whad a sweetums you are…" She cooed as if she was talking to a baby.

She turned to him, eyes bright. "Do you have any treats?"

"Does Santa have reindeer?" He reached into a bucket just outside the stall and handed her a few.

"Aww. You're such a handsome boy." She oohed and ahhed, and Blaze pricked his ears forward, clearly loving the attention. Aww hell. Blake's heart melted a fraction at the interaction. He should have brought her here sooner. Of course she loved horses, she was a Hansen.

He'd allowed himself to become jaded over the years. There hadn't been a serious girlfriend since before the summer from hell. And the women he saw on the road thought ranching was a quaint activity. They weren't interested in horses unless it was to pose in a selfie or show off an outfit. The last woman he'd seen gush over a horse was his sister, Emma. And that had been years.

"Don't let Blaze monopolize your time. Let me introduce you to your mount." Anticipation at her reaction threaded through his gut. What would she think when she saw Iris? He brought her to the next stall.

Inside stood a beautiful Palomino. Maddie gasped and turned, eyes wide and full of shock. "Is this...?" She trailed off.

He nodded. "One of Hansen Stables finest. This lovely mare is named–"

"Iris." She finished.

How did she know?

She giggled nervously, shaking her head. "You're not going to believe this, but I have her sister with me in Chicago. Daisy."

"I don't understand."

She rolled her eyes. "Of course you don't. You don't raise horses."

How did she always manage to turn the conversation? This was supposed to be his surprise.

"You might know cattle and bison, but you don't know the first thing about horses."

"I know plenty," he sputtered. "I raised Blaze."

"That's one horse. I grew up around Palominos. And, I happened to be present the day Iris and Daisy were born. Twin foals are highly unusual, surviving identical pairs a statistical miracle." She scratched Iris's nose and offered her treats from the bucket.

"Of course you were." He rolled his eyes, disappointment swelling.

She studied him intently. "You're upset about this. Why?"

Maybe because he thought she'd see he respected her family. Maybe because he'd thought it would make her feel the tiniest bit at home on his ranch. Maybe because for an insane second, he'd thought it would be nice to surprise her.

He needed to rip a page from her book and keep his emotions under wrap. He needed to quit thinking around her. Jamming his thoughts down, he ignored her question, and opened the stall door, stepping in to snap a leader line on her halter.

"Let's get these beauts saddled up." He slid a sideways glance her way. "I assume you know how to do that?"

She pursed her lips and guilt quickly settled in his ribs. He didn't need to be an ass because she'd stolen his thunder.

"I can manage." She cocked her head, the glint in her eye clueing him into her level of ire. "Unless you prefer to ride bareback?"

Not with his balls in the condition they were. "No thanks. Gotta protect the family jewels."

"Just what I thought."

"What's that supposed to mean?"

She sauntered past him, hips swaying seductively as she headed toward the tack room. She peeked back over her shoulder, a naughty twinkle in her eye. "Manly to a point, but when the chips are down…" She raised her eyebrows saucily, then turned and kept walking.

Damn her for baiting him that way. Little vixen with the saucy mouth begging to be kissed. He would not let her stand here, in *his* barn, and question his manhood. Not when his balls were ready to explode in frustration.

He followed her into the tack room and handed her a bridle. "You know what your problem is?"

She rolled her eyes as she passed. "Let me guess, you're going to enlighten me."

"You've never been with a real man. Those scientists you spend your time with don't know the first thing about fighting or taking care of women." He followed her back down the aisle.

"So real men are Neanderthals?" She narrowed her eyes at him then went back to adjusting Iris's bridle.

"No. We're gentlemen. But we're stronger. Firmer. We keep things going." He opened the stall and walked Blaze down to outside the tack room.

She made a growly sound in the back of her throat as she followed suit. A sound that sent electricity straight to his cock. He'd love to hear it in the throes of ecstasy, not just when he'd irritated her to the breaking point.

"What you're saying is that the town *buckle bunnies* want nothing more than a caveman who fights and bosses them around? In and out of bed?"

"We're cowboys not cavemen."

She followed him down the aisle. "Are you yanking my chain, or do you seriously believe this trash you're spewing?"

Both. He shrugged and grinned. He handed her a saddle pad and placed his on Blaze. Then tilted his chin toward the saddle she'd need.

Her voice rose. "What about brains? What about friendship? What about respect? What about love?" She sputtered, giving the cinch a firm yank.

"You have no room in your life for romantic love. Isn't that what you claimed the other night...*Madame Scientist?*"

She opened her mouth to argue, then snapped it shut, glaring at him as she untied Iris.

Ha.

Let her stew on that for a minute. He'd settle for the sparring, but it wasn't enough. Not by a long shot.

He tucked some tools and two pairs of gloves into the saddlebag and led Blaze out of the barn with just a little more swagger than was polite. He twisted the reins over the corral fence and went back to shut the huge oak doors after Maddie.

He called after her. "You can't have it both ways." She glared at him as she walked Iris over to join Blaze. "Don't be a sore loser, Maddie."

"Are we going to ride or stand here and argue?"

"You can change the subject, but this conversation isn't over."

He adjusted the cinch a final time and mounted up. Maddie followed suit. Swinging Blaze around, he headed out for the main north-south fence line. If there was damage from the high winds, this is where they'd see it first.

They rode up the short rise to the west of the Big House then turned north along the barbed wire. Even on the hill there was barely a breeze, as if the prairie was holding its breath waiting for a shift.

He was waiting for a shift. How long would they continue this dance? How long before she finally admitted he was right? That feelings mattered? He couldn't let this go. Didn't want to. He was going to get to the bottom of this with her. One way or another.

He slowed Blaze, waiting for Maddie to catch up. His gut tightened at the sight of her. She rode with the ease of someone who'd been on horseback before she could walk. In the late afternoon sun, the tension evaporated from her face.

Time to take the bull by the horns. "Have you ever been in love?"

The anguish that flashed on her face as she registered his question spoke volumes. So she *had* been in love. She averted her eyes, studying the horizon.

They rode on, the silence punctuated by an occasional meadowlark.

When she finally glanced sideways, her cool professional

mask was firmly back in place. "I don't believe in love."

"You did."

The only acknowledgement she gave that he'd guessed right was the way her hand suddenly clenched the reins. Anger, hot and possessive, toward this unknown male who'd broken her to pieces, shot through him. The kind of anger so hot he wouldn't hesitate to pound his face to a pulp.

"Who was he?" He ground out.

Her eyes widened in surprise.

"I swear, I will beat him."

She rolled her eyes, but a tiny smile curved her lips. "See? Neanderthal."

"Call it defending your honor."

"My honor doesn't need defending."

"Like hell it doesn't," he growled.

"Look. It doesn't matter. It was a long time ago."

"What happened?"

She sighed, giving him an exasperated look. "Nothing but a teenaged misunderstanding and a painful lesson learned."

"Maybe he was just an asshole and not worth a second thought."

Her eyes were pools of deep sadness. So deep his soul ached for her. If the universe ever presented him with an opportunity to deliver karmic justice with his fist, he would not hesitate.

"Maybe I needed to learn the only thing you get from love is hurt."

His gut twisted. Given his own history with love, part of him agreed. Yet the bigger part of him knew there was more. "Love is what separates us from the animals and the robots, sweetheart."

That earned him a small smile.

"Logic keeps you safe. It keeps you orderly. Ask any drunk in a bar fight. It wasn't logic that cocked his fist."

"So you're saying a world with no emotion would be better?"

"It would be simpler… more predictable."

"And we might as well be wolves hunting bison. What about compassion? What about forgiveness? Isn't that love?"

She hesitated, worrying her lip. "It's not the same."

"Bullshit. You can't have it both ways." Frustration from the past several days roiled in his gut. There had to be a way to break through the fortress she'd erected around herself. God*dammit*. He clenched his jaw as he spotted a post that needed righting.

He spurred Blaze on ahead and swung off when he reached the downed post, still hot under the collar.

She pulled alongside.

He tossed a pair of gloves to her.

"Here," he bit out. "I need your help."

The barbed wire had captured the branches of a small oak. Enough that it had acted like a sail in the winds, and pulled the post out.

"Move the branches off the wire, and set them down on this side of the fence," he barked, not feeling very patient.

She moved without comment.

He grabbed the portable shovel from the saddle bag and began digging. The hole would need to be reset. He'd have to send Brodie and Ben out with the post hole digger tomorrow, but this would do for now.

His spade hit rock almost immediately. That was the problem. The hole had been too shallow.

"God*dammit,*" he bellowed.

"Can I help?"

"No." He glared at her, emotions spilling over. "You're like that Goddamned limestone, Maddie. Immovable." He grunted, trying to use the shovel as a lever to move the rock. "You think you have your life all planned out. Predictable and compartmentalized. But it doesn't work that way. Life requires you to *feel,* dammit."

He drove the shovel into the ground. "You think you don't need anyone, and by God, maybe you don't. Maybe you're the one exception in the whole human race who gets to go through life, *completely…*" he shoved it in again.

"*Independently.*" He jammed his foot down.

"*Without.*" He heaved back.

"*Needing.*" He tossed the dirt.

"*Anything.*" He shoved in the shovel, pausing to glare at her.

Her eyes were wide and sorrowful.

"The rest of us mortals? We need people." He jammed his foot down again. "It may hurt. It may suck, occasionally. But that's life, dammit."

He groaned loudly, heaving back. This fucking rock wouldn't budge.

"You need a longer lever and a better fulcrum."

He glared at her, letting her feel the full weight of his anger.

"If I use a fulcrum, I will break the shovel. I need a crow-bar. Any other words of brilliance, Madame Scientist?" Sarcasm dripped from his voice.

Her head popped back as if she'd been slapped.

"I was just trying to help," she muttered quietly.

"You want to help, Maddie?" He was shouting now. "Then start by feeling. Something. *Anything.*" He wiped the sweat beading across his forehead. He pulled his phone out of his pocket, dialing Ben.

Goddamned voice mail.

"Ben, you and Brodie need to bring a crowbar and a posthole digger to number 27 along the main north-south line. Put this on your list for first thing. *And don't forget a fulcrum.*" He couldn't resist.

He stalked to the saddlebags and replaced the tools. "It's time to leave your ivory tower darlin', and come down to earth with the rest of us." He pinned her with a hard look. "You're not the only one who understands basic physics, and you're damned well not the only one who's ever been hurt."

But she might be the only one who'd ever responded by locking herself up and throwing away the key.

Reaching down, he lifted the reins over Blaze's head, and remounted. Spinning Blaze around, he set off for the ranch without a backward glance.

CHAPTER 15

MOMENTS LATER, MADDIE trotted up beside him.

He risked one glance at her. Her face swirled with emotions. That was a start. He was done talking for the moment. Instead he let the rhythm of the horse settle into him, slowly replacing his angry outburst with resigned calm.

By the time they reached the stables, he was fairly certain he could sleep in the same room with her again. By the time he'd gotten Blaze cooled down and put up, he knew he could look at her again without clenching his jaw.

He stalked to the tack room, not bothering to ask her if she needed help. He slammed the saddle on the rack, and set about cleaning it up. He'd be damned if he'd offer her anything right now. Except a spanking. His lip curled at the thought. The vision of her bare-assed and rosy from his palm stiffened his cock instantly. Just as fast, he dismissed it. He wanted, no he needed, her to ask.

"His name was Marcus." Her voice was heavy and thick, as if speaking was a struggle. He kept his focus on cleaning the saddle, sensing it might be easier if he didn't turn around.

She sighed, and her boot scuffed the floor. "I was eighteen. He was a postdloc from Switzerland. Very glamorous. Very aloof."

His hand clenched around the rag, but he forced his movements to remain calm. If he went ballistic now, he'd just scare her off.

She inhaled a ragged breath, then exhaled in a whoosh. "I… ah… fancied myself in love… H-he was my world. He was smart. Brilliant, really. And he had this way of making me feel special. He was also my research supervisor." She rushed the last bit out.

Bastard.

Motherfucking bastard knew better than to take advantage of a girl that age. What the hell was Warren thinking, letting her go off to college at sixteen? Jesus. He might as well have put a target and a neon sign on her back saying 'shoot me'.

"We… weren't together long. Only enough months for him to compile then steal a research project I'd been working on after hours and present it as his own."

He spun around, outrage on her behalf soaring through him. By God, he'd go caveman on this Marcus's ass if they ever crossed paths.

"And you let him get away with it?"

Her eyes, her beautiful sapphire eyes were stricken. "I-I-I reported him to my advisor, but he'd gotten there first, and lodged a complaint against me accusing me of being a lazy intern. The project was my own and separate from the one I was assigned to help with. So it became my word against his."

She blinked, grimacing, and gave a tiny laugh. "The worst was when I-I barged into his office, and… and, he was screwing my lab partner. The only other woman in the program."

He wanted to punch his fist through a wall. Through this guy's face. But that wasn't an option. Especially not in a limestone barn.

"When I asked why, he looked at me like I was an idiot,

and… and he said we never loved each other. That we'd had a-an understanding. That everybody knew sex was only chemistry, and that, and that… I needed to grow up." The last part came out in a whisper.

His gut twisted. Hard.

She glared at him. "Don't look at me like that. Don't feel sorry for me."

"You work with this guy now?" He didn't give a shit if she heard the anger in his voice. This guy was scum.

She shook her head. "He's a director at CERN now… like Fermilab but in Switzerland."

"Because of your research."

She shrugged. "Hard to say."

"Somebody should have been there to defend your honor, Maddie. I would have."

She laughed bitterly. "That's very sweet of you, but we both know the world doesn't work that way."

Truth. The question remained. How did you respond to the shit life dealt? "So did you go on a fucking spree?"

Her cheeks pinked, and she cracked a tiny smile, shaking her head. "You would ask that."

"Well, did you?"

"Umm. Negative."

"So…ah, what about…?"

"The next one?" Her eyes fixated on a spot on the floor, the pink deepening to crimson.

She took a deep slow breath and glanced up timidly. Realization dawned.

Shit.

There hadn't been a next one.

"You're kidding."

She shook her head.

Something went hard inside him. He'd never been so pissed off at another human being. Except perhaps Jake. Oddly enough for similar reasons.

"Why give him the satisfaction?"

She shrugged. "It wasn't that so much. It was just easier not to bother unless I felt close to someone…" She faltered. "I-I work really hard. You have to as a woman in this field. And I didn't want to mix work and sex again, and I just didn't meet other people."

"For *ten years?*" Christ, that was a lot of tension to carry. No wonder she was strung so tight.

"After awhile, I just stopped thinking about it."

She was like a tree that had been struck by lightning and only grew on one side.

"What about now?" Pressure built in his chest as he waited for her answer. It shouldn't mean so much, but it did. The flush crept back up her neck.

She straightened her shoulders and looked him in the eye, her eyes steady and clear. "I want… I'm ready…" She swallowed crimson to her ears. "Don't hurt me, Blake." Her voice came out ragged and breathy.

His gut clenched at the raw emotion on her face.

Jesus.

What the hell was he supposed to do with that?

He dropped the rag and reached her in two strides, pulling her into his arms.

"Nothing to be afraid of, sweetheart. I promise. I'd never hurt you."

He had no business making promises like that, but he didn't care. She was in pain and he'd say anything, *anything* to show her she was not alone. He cupped his hands around her cheeks, tilting her face up, covering her mouth with his.

He started softly. Tenderly. But the emotion was too great to hold back. He crushed her to him, probing the sweet recesses of her mouth, his hand drifting down and cupping her ass, grinding her into his length, demanding she respond in kind.

Her hands slipped up and gripped his shoulders. "Blake, I–" she panted.

"Don't worry, sweetheart. Let me take care of you."

He kissed down the column of her neck, exposing her collarbone, nipping and sucking. That fierce, possessive part of him bloomed as her body melted into his.

He wanted to claim her.

To right an enormous wrong.

To show her how things could be, how things should be, between two people.

Angling her back, he ran his tongue from the top button of her shirt to the hollow of her neck, up her throat, before taking her lips again. She opened immediately, this time her tongue joining his in time to the rolling of her hips.

His cock strained at his zipper. That would have to wait. Right now was about her. Continuing to kiss her, he unbuttoned her shirt, bringing his hands to the gloriously smooth skin underneath.

God. She was so perfect, so smooth, so strong. How could anyone throw her away like garbage? He growled in his throat as he deepened their kiss. Right now, in this moment, he would make her forget everything. Including her own name.

Sweeping his hands up the silky expanse of her back, he quickly unsnapped her bra, slowly moving underneath to explore the newly exposed skin.

He flicked this thumbs across her nipples, hardening them into tiny, perfect buds. She groaned into his mouth and clutched harder at his shoulders.

"You're so perfect. So beautiful." He muttered as he tore his lips from her mouth to explore the hollow under her ear with his tongue. He pushed the lace out of the way and tilted her back so he could bring a bud to his mouth.

Her breath came in short gasps as he flicked his tongue back and forth across the hardened peak, finally sucking it in and rolling his tongue around it. She fisted a hand through his hair as he moved to do the same with the other. Goosebumps raised across her torso.

"Oh, Blake…ah…" she sighed.

"Let go, darlin'. Let it all go," he breathed across her collarbones.

He should take more time. She deserved better than a tack room tryst. But this would at least take off the edge. They could get to the main show a bit later.

He ducked his finger inside her waistband, running it against her skin to the button of corduroys. "You're wearing panties." He grinned.

"I… ah… wear them most days," she rushed out. "Every day, really. Except two."

"Make it more," he commanded. "You drive me crazy when you leave your panties off." He pulled her hips to his, grinding his straining cock against her. This fucking-not-fucking was exquisite torture.

His thumb flicked open the button and unzipped her pants. He glanced at her and met her eyes, glazed and hot, staring back at him. She licked her lips in anticipation.

"You want me to touch you, Maddie? Make you come?"

The pink on her cheeks deepened at his words. She swallowed. "Yessss," she hissed quietly.

Savoring her consent, her satiny soft skin, he slid his

fingers under the lace of her skimpy drawers. His knees practically buckled at the first touch of silky wetness he knew he'd encounter.

"God, you are so fucking hot." He plundered her mouth, moving his tongue in time with his finger. Slowly pulling her creamy liquid from entrance to tip, bringing his finger to rest on her nub. Her hips bucked wildly and she gasped as he slowly circled her clit. "You like that, hon? Tell me you like it."

She groaned in answer, swirling her hips on his finger. He slipped a finger inside. So wet and tight. Goddamn, if his balls didn't explode it would be a miracle. Slowly he began to pump her channel, resting his palm against her clit, letting her creamy essence flow across his hand.

"That's it, baby. Just ride it out." He flicked his finger inside her, searching for the spot that would send her through the roof.

She was glorious like this, all swollen and flushed, with her hair wild from the ride. Nipples tight and pink from his tongue. Widening his stance so he could balance against her bucking, he pulled her close, covering her mouth, pulling her sweet lip between his teeth. Her breath came in quick pants, punctuated by staccato cries as her movements increased in intensity.

Suddenly, her eyes sprung wide open and she grabbed his face, pulling his mouth down to meet hers. She kissed him, sucking his tongue into her as she groaned loudly into his mouth. Her walls clenched, rippling against his fingers, as she rode him through the orgasm, her body shuddering uncontrollably.

The ache in his balls made his head hurt, but he kept his focus on her, helping her to squeeze every ounce of pleasure from the moment. He rained kisses across her face, murmuring endearments as she slowly came back to earth.

With regret, he removed his hand. He could keep his hand inside her, pleasuring her, all day.

"Better?" He nuzzled her ear.

"Um. Yeah… Yeah."

Her response shot through his veins like ice.

He leaned back, studying her. Had she been faking?

She gave him a tentative smile. "I, ah, liked that."

"You liked it." She damn well better have liked it. She seemed like she had.

"Well it was definitely better than masturbating…"

Hurt flamed to life in his chest as he stared at her in disbelief.

"You haven't been with a man in ten years and this is your best response… *It's better than masturbating?*"

"It's my honest response." She ran her hands through her hair. "I'm trying." Her eyes looked panicked.

"Tell me you felt something."

Jesus, she *had* to have let herself feel something?

Her eyes widened with shame and sadness. "Yes. No. I don't know… Oh God, Blake. I'm so sorry… I don't know what's wrong with me…" She yanked up her pants, zipping them and rebuttoning her shirt. "I think I'm broken and I can't be fixed. This… us… I don't know what you were thinking." She gasped, a tiny sob hitching in her throat. "I'm sorry." She spun and fled, leaving him standing in the middle of the floor.

What the fuck had just happened?

He stalked to the threshold, but she'd already slipped out the door. Hurt and rage rushed through him like a tornado, spotting his vision. He kicked the door as hard as he could, forgetting momentarily about the large iron doorstopper that permanently held the door in place.

"Gah." Blinding pain seared up his foot, sharpening his vision. "MOTHERFUCKER." He kicked the door again, this time avoiding the doorstop. The second kick hurt as much as the first, but he didn't care. Let it hurt. It hurt less than his heart right now.

Only one other time in his thirty-two years had he been this angry. That incident was permanently etched in his brain. He'd made too many mistakes in life because of that anger. He wasn't going to let that happen this time. He clenched and unclenched his fist, letting the adrenaline run its course and fade away.

When his heart rate finally settled, he grabbed a brush and limped over to Blaze. No broken bones, but it hurt like hell. Brushing Blaze seemed to calm him like nothing else. A good lay would calm him, but that wasn't anywhere in his future. Not for a while at least.

He ran the brush down his neck, tuning into the rhythm of his breathing, letting the familiar, comforting scent calm him. Letting his mind wander as the habit, long ingrained in his muscle memory took over.

Maddie was a conundrum. A paradox. Unbroke filly didn't begin to describe her. Abused? Abandoned? Shit. He should talk to Ben. Ben would know what to do. He had a psychic way of coming up with perfect solutions every time.

He shut his eyes, envisioning her fearless and strong. He knew in his marrow that woman was locked away inside her.

Blaze nickered, as if he sensed someone. Ben? He had the uncanny ability to show up when he was most needed.

He scanned the door, startled from his thoughts. A bright haired woman stood silhouetted in the entrance holding a chubby dark haired child. He blinked, hard, shaking his head. Hell and damnation. He hadn't just seen that. There was nothing there. His heart thumped wildly in his chest, buzzing his ears. He shook his head, returning his focus to Blaze's withers. He couldn't shake the feeling that someone else was in the barn with him. A shiver passed down his spine.

Shit. Ben was the one with their great-whatever-granny's sixth sense. Not him. Despair and hope warred within him. That vision had as much chance of coming to pass as lightning striking him in a tornado shelter. But still, hope ended up on top.

CHAPTER 16

MADDIE LAY CURLED up in bed by the time Blake came in. As soon as she heard his footsteps on the stairs, her heart started pounding. The door opened quietly and he paused at the threshold. The single light on the bedside cast the room in a soft glow, but not enough that she could read his eyes, even with her glasses on.

He stepped into the room and shut the door, his eyes not leaving hers. His mouth remained in a hard line, but he didn't speak. His presence did nothing to calm the agitation that had stayed with her since she'd fled the barn. She was a hot mess. She knew it. But how could she stop the rollercoaster of emotions? She was just hanging on for dear life.

He crossed in front of the bed, unbuttoning his shirt. He moved like a panther, keeping her in his sight, ready to pounce at the first sign of weakness. She held her breath as he threw his shirt into the laundry basket. She'd seen him shirtless every night for nearly a week now, and her breath still caught at the way his taut muscles rippled in the lamplight.

Every night for nearly a week he'd proceeded to brush his teeth, then flop to the floor with nothing but a blanket. The thought of him sleeping there, at her feet, after what they'd shared, ate at her.

He glanced at her periodically as he went about the nighttime routine she'd memorized her first night with him.

First, he'd throw his shirt in the laundry, then it was teeth and washcloth. Lastly, his boots, and then his jeans. Always with a glance at her, daring her to comment. So far, she hadn't.

And tonight… what could she say after her behavior in the barn? Hell yes, his hands had been better than her own. But she'd been so discombobulated it had come out all wrong. Yet another sign she wasn't remotely relationship material.

Her tongue lay heavy in her mouth. She screwed up her courage to say something as he left the bathroom.

"Blake…" The buzzing in her ears was so great she couldn't hear her own voice.

His eyes burned into her. Scorching her soul. "I-I'm so sorry. About everything. I-I liked it a lot better than masturbating." Her chest burned with the admission, as she felt the flush creep up her neck to her cheeks.

She wiped her hand across her eyes. "You really don't want to marry me. I'm a hot mess… I'd make you crazy."

He smiled tightly. "You've already done that, sweetheart."

The shuttered expression in his eyes twisted something deep in her. She'd hurt him. The realization stunned her. It made no sense. She couldn't wrap her head around the idea that she had the power to hurt someone. Especially Blake. If she could hurt him… that meant…

Oh God.

She needed, no – she wanted to make this right. Even if it scared the shit out of her. The last thing she wanted to do was hurt him.

She patted the empty space next to her, entreating him with her eyes.

"Lie next to me? Please?"

His expression instantly became guarded. She couldn't blame him. She'd kick herself out of the house if she were him. Fake engagement be damned. He nodded once, keeping his eyes locked with hers.

Slowly, he undid the buckle of his belt, pulling it through the loops and tossing it on the bench under the window. Oh lordy, was he stripteasing her? Even in the dim light, she recognized the carnal hunger in his eyes. Her stomach dropped as butterflies tickled her insides. He undid the buttons of his jeans with short, swift movements, letting them drop to his ankles. There, as obvious as the moon in the sky, was his enormous erection, prominently jutting out of his boxer briefs.

Her mouth turned to sand. Instinctively, she knew. All she needed to do was reach out and touch him, and he would be hers. And yet… the fear of jumping in with both feet messed with her logic. Fear was an irrational response to a logical set of circumstances.

Circumstances indicated sex with Blake was the next logical step. And evidence from the barn showed it would not suck. Not in the least. He gave great orgasms. So why was she afraid? Her heart slammed against her ribs as the answer floated in front of her.

She liked him.

A whole damn lot.

She shut her eyes, letting the weight of the realization sink in. Liking Blake opened up a Pandora's box of messy thoughts and emotions she was too tired to dissect. They would keep until morning, when she could examine everything with fresh eyes.

She patted the pillow again, and removed her glasses. "Come on. Maybe we'll sleep tonight."

He nodded, and kicked out of his jeans. He stepped around, and pushing the light off, slipped into bed beside her.

Something shifted in her again. Like a key turning in a lock. Blake stretched out next to her, wrapping his arms around her. He place a kiss on her shoulder, dropped his head and shut his eyes.

For the first time in a week, she slept.

CHAPTER 17

MADDIE STARTLED AWAKE. The phone buzzed insistently next to the bed. Flailing for it, she brought it close, checking the time. Seven-thirty. Blake had slipped out and let her sleep. She'd risen early with him the mornings he'd slept on the floor. She couldn't sleep with him so close, and she hadn't wanted to come across as a princess. Besides, she was having trouble working at the hospital. Her dad was a big spoiled baby. And early mornings at the Big House were quiet.

The phone buzzed again. Martha. Her heart dropped. Not again? No. The hospital would contact her first if something happened. But what if she'd been asleep?

"Martha? Everything okay?" She couldn't keep the edge of panic from her voice. Or her heart from banging relentlessly into her ribs.

"Tell me you're not already on your way to see Warren."

Shaking the remaining fog from her head, she sat up. "No, no. I usually work here until eight or nine, then drive in."

"Well, not today, honey. Eddie is gonna relieve you a spell. Boys are covering for him today."

"Great. Tell him thanks." She hated it, but relief surged through her. The mental drain from babysitting her dad had stretched her thin, and she was getting behind on her research.

"Don't go filling your calendar though. Dottie and I have plans for you."

Warning bells sounded. The two best friends were up to no good.

"I'd love to, but I really need to catch up on my research. Raincheck?"

"Not this time, Maddie Jane."

She recognized that tone. The one that meant no arguing whatsoever.

"But I promise we won't monopolize your whole day. Just the morning. Now, be shoe shined and ready to go at nine. We'll pick you up."

She couldn't say no. Martha was a second mother to her. Especially since hers had died so young. Growing up on a horse farm full of testosterone hadn't been easy. Martha'd been the one to make sure she washed her hair and taught her how to walk in high heels. She and Uncle Eddie had helped her apply to MIT at fifteen, even though they'd cautioned her against it. Her dad had been fit to be tied. Wouldn't talk to any of them for a week when she announced she would attend college the following fall. Saying no to Martha was out of the question.

"I'll be ready."

Promptly at nine, a carload of women turned up the long drive between the Big House and the barn, honking and hanging out the windows. Relieved Blake wasn't around to see this, she smoothed the pair of jeans she'd borrowed from Emma's closet. They were too long, but she'd rolled them up past her ankles and paired them with her heels. They'd work in a pinch.

Opening the door, the women practically fell out like a clown car at a circus. "Hen Party," they screeched, their raucous laughter bouncing off the limestone. Her heart sank to the tips of her toes.

Noooo.

No. No. No.

She plastered on a smile, hoping that her face didn't convey what a horrible idea this was.

Millie Prescott, the lovely woman who ran the organic grocery, had joined them and was holding an open bottle of champagne. What was she doing here? Millie was about her age, but they didn't know each other very well. She'd been homeschooled growing up, because her parents had played the county fair circuit. Prairie had been their home base, and their little farm had been one of the first in the area to go organic. Last she'd heard, they'd planted three acres of champagne grapes, and were trying to bottle it.

Oh lordy, if that was the champagne…

Next to Martha was Gloria McPherson, the organist at First Lutheran, holding plastic cups. She'd never seen Gloria crack a smile ever. And here she was holding her sides with laughter. Had they dragged her into an alternate universe? Worse, were they drunk?

Dottie bustled up with a glittery plastic tiara that read "*Bridezilla*" attached to a piece of white tulle. For a wild moment, she considered making a run for it to the barn.

No. Way.

She drew the line at the crown.

She had to preserve her dignity.

Before she could protest, Dottie placed the tiara on her head and Gloria pushed a plastic glass of champagne into her hands. "Do you like it? I ordered it off Amazon."

She nodded, keeping the smile in place. As long as no one took a picture.

Millie stepped up shyly. "Congratulations, Maddie. I'm so happy for you."

As much as she wanted to run and hide – in the barn or in the man-attic – she couldn't. She'd grin and bear it and thank her lucky stars Blake and his brothers were out in the middle of the property today, checking on the herd. She'd never live this down if they saw her like this.

She took a sip of the champagne, keeping her face neutral. Not bad in a box wine kind of way. Jamey would dismiss it immediately, but it was better than she'd expected.

"Mmm. Delicious. Is this from the grapes I heard your family's planted?"

Millie smiled, a look of relief passing over her face. "Yes, it's our very first bottling."

Martha beamed from behind Millie's shoulder. "Dottie and I decided to ask Millie to help with your wedding. She's good at pulling things together. We've bought up the entire first vintage to serve at your reception."

She choked on the champagne she'd been about to swallow, ending in a fit of coughs. This wedding was spinning out of control too fast. She had to talk to Blake tonight about coming clean to everyone. She couldn't lead them on this way. Not when everyone was so excited.

"That's lovely." She plastered her smile back on. "I'm thrilled. But we haven't set a date yet."

"Don't worry. Eddie called about an hour ago, he thinks Warren will get to come home next weekend. So we could set the wedding for two weeks from then. Won't it be perfect?"

No. It would be a disaster.

Getting married in less than three weeks' time was impossible. She and Blake barely knew each other. They hadn't even discussed children. Or their favorite colors.

She shook herself mentally. Why was she thinking like marrying him was even a remote possibility? It wasn't. Blake was a gentleman, he was smart, and so, so hot. And she liked him. God, did she like him. But he was perfect for someone else. She was not marriage material. For him or anyone else. And she refused to become a rancher's wife.

She opened her mouth to protest, and the picture of them – the three older women, and the younger one, smiling brightly with joy and expectation – slammed into her heart. Was she so hardened that she would destroy all of this in a few words? This would all fall apart soon enough. May as well wait until it all comes out at once. Guilt roiled in her stomach, churning the champagne.

Dottie clapped her hands, bringing silence to the little circle. "Ladies, it's time to get this bridal show on the road. But first Millie, pour out the rest of that champagne and let's toast our girl."

Millie poured the remains of the bottle into the plastic cups and passed them around.

Dottie lifted her glass. "To Maddie, the brightest star in the night sky. You've made Prairie proud, and we wish you all the happiness."

She couldn't take a sip. The lump in her throat prevented swallowing. "This really isn't necessary."

"Maddie Jane, this is Prairie tradition. It's bad luck if we don't." Dottie took a sip from her cup, then handed it to Martha. "Driving," she winked.

Maddie looked to Martha for help. Martha just patted her cheek and gave her a squeeze. "Don't think you can escape, Maddie Jane. Hope will get this, too."

"As will every one of my girls," chimed in Dottie. "Even if we have to fly to Afghanistan to do it."

"You can call us the Prairie Posse," Gloria added, waving her fingers. "Sprinkling joy and laughter wherever we go."

Maddie laughed nervously. Longing for Jamey shot through her. Stuff like this was right up Jamey's alley. But she hadn't yet had the nerve to tell Jamey about her supposed engagement.

The women hustled her to the car, and she found herself squeezed in the back between Millie and Gloria. Dottie spun the car around and they started down the long driveway.

"Where to?"

Martha turned around from the passenger seat. "Dottie's put together a nice little brunch for us, and we have a few surprises in store." She grinned wickedly.

This was a new side of Martha. She'd only ever known Martha the ranch wife. Martha the counselor. Martha who ran the domestic side of Hansen Stables with an iron fist. This Martha, who giggled like a teenager, who joked and laughed, was a revelation. They all were.

She turned to Gloria, who was practically bouncing in her seat waiting to talk. She couldn't quite reconcile the memories of Gloria banging out 'This Little Light of Mine' in the church basement during Sunday School with the vibrant, mirthful woman next to her.

"What is it Gloria?" Martha asked. "Are you about to wet your pants or do you have something to tell us?"

"Both." She giggled.

"Well spit it out. And Dottie, drive faster. But don't get us a ticket. If Travis pulls us over, she'll tinkle."

"He is rather cute though. Don't you think?"

Huh. The older women of Prairie, ogling the cops. Maddie pressed her lips shut to keep her own giggles down.

"I'll keep lookout," offered Millie.

And they were delinquents, too.

They sped across the back roads and in twenty minutes were pulling onto the Grace ranch. Significantly smaller than the Sinclaire and Hansen spreads, Teddy Grace only ran a few hundred head of cattle a year. But their farmhouse, clear on the other side of town, had been lived in by Graces since the Civil War.

As the front porch came into view though, her heart flopped and she bit back a groan.

They had gone all out.

The porch had been decorated in pink and white hearts. The pillars wrapped in white satin. The extent of the women's scheming became evident as they exited the car and made their way up the wide steps.

The table the Graces used in warm weather, and where Maddie remembered doing homework after school on occasion, was covered in white with a large bouquet of pink carnations in the center. Mini bouquets of white and pink carnations flanked the centerpiece.

Dottie's best china and silver had been laid out, the chairs draped with tulle, three bottles of champagne sat in a bucket on the floor, and three large white cakes were placed on a makeshift sideboard in front of the picture window. The sideboard had also been draped with tulle and flowers.

It was the most hideous thing she'd ever seen.

The furniture version of a gaudy, over decorated cupcake.

It pulled at her heartstrings.

Until she noticed the neon pink condom wrappers at the center of each plate. And the pink penis glitter tossed over the tablecloth. And the pink penis balloons hanging at the ends of the porch.

"Martha?" she tilted her head in question.

She giggled. "We know these bachelorette parties you kids throw these days include genitalia. So we thought you'd enjoy it."

Her smile froze in place. *Keep smiling.* She had to keep smiling.

"Where did you-?" She stopped. She didn't want to know.

Gloria piped up. "Isn't the glitter cute? I got it all on a website called Adam Eve Toys." She grinned like she'd discovered a hidden treasure chest. "They send you a gift package."

Maddie raised her eyebrows, certain she didn't want to know, but that Gloria was going to tell.

"Do you think I should get one for Teddy?" Dottie asked as she unwrapped the champagne top.

Gloria's eyes grew big. "Oh yes. It had a vibrator, and feathers, and warming lube. I haven't felt this relaxed in ages."

The inevitable flush started creeping up her neck. Maddie didn't know whether to laugh or hope for the earth to swallow her whole.

Dottie twisted the cork off with a loud 'pop'. "Maddie, men can't abide a prude. We've all had children. We understand and enjoy the mechanics. Well, except Millie here. She doesn't have children."

"But I know all about the mechanics," Millie clarified. "My parents used to play the Oregon Country Fair in Veneta. People would have sex in the bushes all the time. I was curious, so I watched."

"You watched?" Maddie's mind went blank. She had just heard it all.

Gloria patted her arm. "Close your mouth, dearie, you're catching flies," Why weren't these ladies as surprised as she was?

"Well, sure," Millie answered. "You all grew up around animals having sex. People are animals..." She shrugged, taking the glass that Dottie offered her. "I was always fascinated by the people getting oral sex."

"Why is that?" Maddie asked faintly. She never even had discussions like this with Jamey.

"They always looked so ecstatic."

The older women nodded their heads enthusiastically in agreement. Gloria smiled like an angel in a Christmas pageant. "Oh it's the best."

Maddie kept smiling and nodding. What else could she do? Blake had done more to her last night than Marcus ever had. Not that she'd ever disclose that to anyone. Not even Blake. She must have woken up in a parallel universe this morning. That was the only answer for this craziness. Maybe someone at Fermilab had finally managed a tesseract, and it had gone wildly, spectacularly wrong.

Dottie tut-tutted, narrowing her eyes. "You'd be as enthusiastic as the rest of us if you've had it."

Gloria gasped, her eyes widening. "Oh heavens, you're not still a virgin, are you?"

"No... *no.*" She took a resigned breath. "I'm not a virgin." She gulped the remaining champagne, letting the sting of the bubbles focus her scattered thoughts.

Martha had talked about sex with her when she was a teenager and had insisted she go on the pill before she moved to college. But never in the history of the human race had she expected to have a conversation like this one.

"Well you march straight up to that man of yours when he gets home this evening and demand he have you for dessert."

This time, she couldn't stop the laughter. "I'm sure he'll

be thrilled." The image of Blake's head between her legs shot a bolt of anticipation straight to her pussy. And knowing him, he'd make sure she was extremely satisfied.

"He better be," Millie huffed. "The last thing you want to saddle yourself with is a man who takes, takes, takes. In the bed and in life."

Dottie began to unwrap another bottle. "In all seriousness, honey pie. I've raised four daughters, and every one of 'em have heard me say this. Best to be up front with your needs, otherwise you'll have a hornet's nest under the sheets later."

Millie chimed in. "My ma always said if you can't say it, you got no business doin' it."

Maddie shot Martha a silent plea, but her aunt just raised her glass and grinned broadly.

Great.

She was at the mercy of a gaggle of horny middle-aged women who thought they needed to dispense sex advice to a twenty-eight year old. The day could go nowhere but up.

Dottie popped the second cork. "I think Maddie Jane needs nourishment right now. She's sustained a bit of a shock."

Millie's eyes flashed concern. "Oh dear. What was it?"

Gloria laughed, an earthy musical sound Maddie was sure she'd never heard. Ever. "Keep up Millie, dear. Maddie's just learned that our bodies don't turn off the second we finish having children." She winked at her. "Sex wasn't, and never will be, a chore. Always something new."

Oh mercy, the temperature on the porch must be a hundred and rising.

"Millie, Gloria," Dottie called. "Help me bring out the bacon and biscuits." The women disappeared inside, and

Maddie moved to refill her glass.

"Martha?" She raised the bottle.

Martha nodded and held out her glass. "I hope this is okay, Maddie Jane. You're the first one of our daughters to get married. We wanted to do something."

She pulled her aunt into a hug. "I'm completely mortified, but honored you consider me one of your daughters." Tears pricked her eyes as soon as the words left her mouth. Her mother had died when she was so young, that the grief only surfaced occasionally. It was more of a constant dull ache in the recesses of her soul.

Martha hugged her tight. "You are, sweetheart. You always will be. And my advice? Do whatever you can to keep the sex as hot as you can for as long as you can. My secret for a long and happy marriage."

"I did not want to know that."

She chuckled. "I know honey. But you *need* to know it."

The screen door burst open and the women brought a country feast to the table, complete with biscuits, bacon, hash browns and eggs.

"Sit, sit." Dottie ordered. "You're queen for a day, Maddie Jane."

"Don't you mean Bridezilla?"

The women laughed. "You're the furthest thing there is from a Bridezilla, sweetie pie." Martha assured her.

Maddie took a biscuit and passed the bowl.

"So when's Blake getting you a ring?" Dottie eyed her left hand.

"He's got it under control." The lie slipped easily off her tongue. It wasn't exactly a lie. Blake always had things under control. Living with him for a week had taught her that he was steady under pressure and kind to his brothers. Solid. Just like Martha said.

Gloria chimed in. "Wasn't he supposed to do that first?"

She shrugged. "Blake doesn't stand on ceremony, and frankly, neither do I."

"A match made in heaven, then." Gloria beamed her approval.

"Now how did you two meet again?"

Shit. Shit. Shit.

They'd never confirmed a story.

Not even once.

"I work at Fermilab in Chicago. They keep a bison herd, and Blake consults with the wranglers."

That was the truth. Just so long as they didn't ask for juicy details, she was okay.

"Ooh, see? It was meant to be," cooed Dottie.

"Fate brought you together," added Millie.

Dottie stood to clear the dishes. "Ready for cake? I made three kinds for you to taste, I'll make whatever you like."

"Umm, shouldn't Blake be here?"

Martha rolled her eyes. "Oh sweetie. Learn this now. I guarantee you, that man is more interested in you than cake. He won't care."

She didn't really care either. This whole morning had been an exercise in futility on their part, and once it came out they weren't marrying, she wouldn't be able to show her face in town for a long time, if ever. Visions of herself as an old lady living in a cold apartment surrounded by cats, floated in her eyes.

Dottie cut three narrow slices and placed them in front of her. "Left to right, my great grandmother's vanilla-rose cake, chocolate with chocolate, and lemon pound cake."

She speared a fork into the first one. The cake was light

and fluffy with a hint of vanilla and the scent of rose. Jamey would like this one. The others were equally delicious. Shaking her head, she put down her fork.

"Dottie, why not do all three? Nothing fancy. A layer of each. Or whatever you prefer. People will love any of these."

"Of course, dear. Whatever you think."

Too late, she realized she hadn't delivered proper praise. "They're delicious, Dottie. I love them all and can't decide."

Plastering on the smile again, she took another bite of the rose. No doubt about it, Dottie was a master baker. Too bad she'd be the only one to appreciate her efforts in wedding cake. A pang snaked through her, settling in her chest. She'd never fantasized about being married. When other little girls were playing bride, she rode horses and watched the stars until dawn. She'd never fantasized about a boyfriend, or what it would be like to kiss, or even fuck. Of course now she fantasized about Blake every 7.3 minutes, but she'd already established that he turned her into an irrational, nonfunctioning blob of feelings.

She was so screwed.

Dottie opened the last bottle of champagne and passed it around. In spite of the irony, Maddie had enjoyed herself this morning. She'd seen a side of these women who'd been a constant in her life that she never believed possible. The champagne wasn't awful, and the morning had taken her mind off her dad. A win all around.

"Thank you so much for this. I'm very touched. You've made being home… nice. Really nice."

Dottie's eyes filled with warmth, and leaned over enveloping her in a huge hug. "Oh sweetie pie. I know you had a hard time as a kid, but you know we love you to pieces, right? We're all so proud of you."

A little broken piece shifted back into place inside her. Dottie echoed what her father had been telling her for a long time. Maybe now she could believe it?

"We're not quite finished, Maddie Jane." Martha patted her arm with a twinkle in her eye. "We're waiting for one more person."

As if on cue, a beat up old pick-up turned into the Grace drive. She didn't recognize the truck, but she'd been gone so long, that didn't mean much.

Another young woman hopped out of the cab, with a basket thrown over her arm.

"Emmaline's here." Gloria clapped her hands.

"Emmaline?"

"Yes. Her family moved here after you went to college. She's the best seamstress west of Kansas City. Makes me a new Easter dress every year."

Warning bells started ringing again.

Oh no.

A seamstress could only mean one thing.

Two hands covered her eyes. Millie's? Or Gloria's?

"Ladies? What's going on?" She wasn't sure she could handle any more surprises today.

"Come with us Maddie Jane, we have a surprise." "Oooh we can't wait." "You're going to love it." "You're gonna be so beautiful." They all talked at once as they helped her out of her chair, and slowly moved her into the house.

They walked her through the living room, up the stairs in the center of the house. Whose room were they taking her to? Cassidy's was second on the left, Lydia and Lexi's, second on the right. Caro's was third on the left. They kept moving down the hall. To the end. Of course. The master bedroom. They were taking her to Dottie's room. Why?

They marched her to the center of the room. Unless Dottie'd moved it, she was standing in front of a full length mirror.

"Ready sweetheart?" Martha's voice caught.

"As I'll ever be."

The hands were removed and in front of the mirror hung a satiny white dress with a long vee neck, long sleeves that puffed just slightly at the shoulder, a tiny waist and a skirt cut on the bias.

She gasped. She'd never seen it in person, but recalled it from pictures.

Martha clasped her. "What do you think?"

"It's stunning."

She'd never fantasized about a wedding dress, but if she had, this would be it. She took off her glasses, wiping the finger prints off, and replaced them, so she could inspect it more closely.

"Do you recognize it honey?"

"Yeah….. This was great-grannie Minerva's wedding dress."

The lines were simple. Efficient. Graceful. In short, it was perfect.

"I told you the story?"

"Yes. When I told you I wanted to apply to MIT. You said she'd been at Bletchley Park when she was nineteen. And that she'd been sworn to secrecy."

Martha repeated the story. "And that she'd met grandpa Ollie during the war. They fell in love in London, but it wasn't until after the war she came to Prairie when your grandfather was a baby."

Tears pricked her eyes a second time. But not for joy or gratitude. This time, hot, sticky regret burned her eyes so she could barely see. She stopped a sob from leaking out. These women had showed her a possibility for her life she'd never imagined. And offered her the wedding dress of a smart, strong ancestor.

She hadn't thought about Minerva in years. Not since… not since she decided to quit romance. How had Minerva and Ollie made things work? In an age when women had few options? They'd died before she was born, but Auntie M always lit up with love the few times she mentioned Minerva and Ollie.

Was Blake the type of man who could stand next to her? Not shy away from her career goals? Longing pierced her heart, making her catch her breath. The loneliness of the last twelve years pressed down on her. She'd toughened up after Marcus. She'd had to because it was her only option for survival. For moving forward. Returning to Prairie simply hadn't been an option.

A hard knot formed in her throat. If she'd organized her life differently, maybe she could have the fairy tale and the happily ever after, but that was not her story. Her story and her future lay in the study of stars and little else. The bitter reality of it all tore her up.

Emmaline knocked on the door. "Mind if I step in?"

The ladies cleared a path for her.

The young woman held out her hand. "I don't think we've met. I'm Emmaline. This is a lovely dress. Are you ready to try it on?" She surveyed the older women. "I've made dresses for some of you, but rest assured, on a restoration piece like this, I take the utmost care, and I make as few cuts as possible." She turned her gaze to Martha. "Are there any other women who might want to wear this?"

Martha nodded.

"Tell me about them."

"Well, Hope is a few years younger than Maddie Jane, but a little bit taller, and a little bit more... willowy."

"Okay... so how much taller?"

Maddie knew, because the last time she'd seen Hope they'd teased about this. "She's five feet nine inches, but she's leaner than I am."

"Great." Emmaline searched in her basket for a piece of marking chalk. "I promise anything I do to the dress will ensure you'll be able to use it again if you choose."

The women nodded expectantly.

"Ms. Hansen–"

"Please. Call me Maddie." She liked this young woman. And the respect for history she brought to her work.

"Fine. Let's put it on, and I'll see how it fits.

Martha removed the dress from the hanger, and ushered her toward the old fashioned changing screen in the corner.

Inside, she quickly doffed her clothing and slid the silky satin over her head. When she couldn't reach any more buttons, she stepped out. The collective gasp from the women told her everything she needed to know. She stepped in front of the mirror and stopped breathing.

On top, the dress fit perfectly. It accentuated all her curves, and was simple enough to suit her. The only issue was the length. She was significantly shorter than her great-grandmother, and the bottom would have to be hemmed.

Martha gathered her hair, and Dottie placed the ridiculous Bridezilla tiara back on her head, but even with the humor, the sentiment was obvious. She would be a lovely bride.

If she only had a real groom.

Anguish speared through her. Learning that her beloved

research had been stolen had been heartbreaking, but it didn't hold a candle to this. How could she lie to such earnest, loving, hopeful women? And stand here in a dress that belonged to the woman who, if she'd been living, might have been the sole person who understood her? God, she was such a hypocrite. At least Hope stood a chance of actually wearing the wedding dress someday.

Emmaline crouched at her feet, working at the hem.

"Don't… don't cut the material. I want Hope to wear this too."

Emmaline nodded and continued her pinning. In a few moments, she had finished her adjustments. But instead of turning up the bottom, she'd added ruching at the sides to maintain the integrity of the hemline.

The end result was spectacular. A vintage dress that perfectly enhanced her curves. For a suspended moment, Maddie felt the presence of the woman who'd worn the dress. The brilliant mind that through some twist of dimensions was a kindred spirit to her own. Goosebumps skittered down her body and words raced through her head. *I won't let you down. I won't let you down. I won't let you down.*

CHAPTER 18

MADDIE'S STOMACH FLIP-FLOPPED as Blake pulled his truck into the Trading Post parking lot. She had a bad feeling about this. As the town's only hang-out with a dance floor, the Trading Post was always crowded with locals. And while she knew things were different, childhood insecurities pounded at her.

Blake's hand on the small of her back propelled her forward into the din, setting off a chain reaction in her body that left her frustrated and on edge. She suspected the same for Blake. Each morning, he'd been grumpier than the last.

"You'll be fine, Maddie. You can't hide on the ranch forever."

"One person in my brain is enough, thank you."

He snorted and led her to a table in the corner.

It was loud inside, so she slid in close. Blake turned, his lips grazing her temple. Her pulse rocketed. Of course he had to go and wear the delicious spicy aftershave he'd worn in Chicago. The scent alone melted her panties.

"Irish Whiskey?" He quirked a smile and signaled for a server without taking his eyes off her. His eyes held a challenge. Would she take it? Was she game?

"Two Irish whiskeys," Blake asked when the server arrived.

"No scotch?" This was a surprise.

"Not tonight."

He leaned in, his lips brushing hers in the barest of kisses. Her lips tingled where they'd touched his and a bolt of lightning zipped straight through her. At this rate, her panties would be drenched in… about thirty-five seconds. That's what she got for sleeping next to him for more than a week, but not touching him. The lightest kiss and she was ready to jump him in public.

"Well, well, isn't that sweet?"

Disdain dripped out of Kylee Ross's mouth. Why hadn't Blake mentioned she worked here? She turned and speared him with a look. "Could you have at least warned me?"

His eyes widened.

"Do you not know anything about women?"

"Oh he knows plenty about women. I'll be happy to tell you how much," Kylee interjected, her meaning quite clear.

A stab of jealousy rocketed through Maddie. Hot jealousy so intense, that for a moment she wanted to rip Kylee's face off.

Huh. The strength of her reaction surprised her. There wasn't time to analyze her feelings now. It was time to shake off Kylee Ross once and for all.

She straightened her glasses and sat a little taller in the booth. She was engaged to Blake for a little while longer. And no one, *especially* Kylee, was going to slam Blake that way.

Maddie put on her frostiest smile. "I already know everything." She lied boldly, raising her eyebrows for emphasis. She might not know yet, but she would. Most definitely.

Blake shifted, suddenly interested in the neon sign across the room.

Good. He damned well better be uncomfortable. "And, for the record, Blake and I have no secrets. So if you can't handle bringing us our drinks, I suggest you send over another server."

Suck it, bitch.

Kylee's jaw opened and snapped shut.

Before she lost her nerve, Maddie pulled Blake's face toward hers and kissed him. Hard. She opened her mouth and flicked his lips with her tongue, practically groaning when he immediately opened, and his hand tightened on her shoulder. Their tongues slid together, but he let her control the kiss. Something that turned her insides into an inferno. Somewhere in the back of her brain, she registered a catcall, and reluctantly she pulled away. Kylee was gone.

Blake's low chuckle washed over her.

"Impressive, Maddie."

She pushed her glasses back into place and glared at him, hot as hell and fire still in her belly. "So. You want to tell me all about Kylee Ross now or later?"

He shifted again and looked at his hands. He was hiding something and she was going to make him squirm.

"There's nothing to tell."

"Really? The evidence says otherwise."

He shrugged, suddenly interested in a dent on the table. "You know small towns. Old history. No big deal."

"Well, it seems like it is to her."

"That's not my problem." He shifted again in his seat, looking around the bar.

She would *not* be jealous. Blake Sinclaire was not worth the emotional energy jealousy took. Was he? God. The realization hit her. They'd probably dated. She had no right to be irritated that Blake had an ex in town. It wasn't like he was celibate his whole life. He probably had more than one. The thought twisted in her belly. It was her own fault she wasn't more experienced. She usually scared men off as soon as the small talk ended and they realized she was smarter than they were.

A different server returned with their drinks. Younger and cuter than Kylee, and her eyes raked over Blake as she placed the drinks on the table.

"Here you are," she said cheerfully, bending over just a little bit too long.

Blake tried valiantly not to look at the cleavage on display. She'd give him that. But she entwined his hand in her own as she gave the girl her fiercest look. The girl blushed and scooted away.

She grabbed the whiskey and took a big gulp, allowing the burn to diffuse the anger that still roared inside her. Blake reached for her left hand.

"I should get you a ring."

Her heart pounded in her chest, and she pushed at her glasses. "Does it matter?"

"Of course it does."

She would not cave. She would not cave. "Don't change the subject, cowboy. You're still avoiding answering me."

He sighed deeply and raised his eyes to hers, conflict swirling in their depths.

Damn.

Her heart sank.

Double damn.

Whatever history he had with Kylee, he wasn't willing to come clean just yet. Disappointment knifed through her, settling in her gut. She withdrew her hand, taking another gulp of whiskey to deaden the ache that threatened to overwhelm her.

"How many other secrets are you keeping, Blake?"

For the merest of seconds, panic flew through his eyes, only to be replaced by the same impassive, shuttered expression.

So there were more. *Silly Maddie.* He had zero obligation to her. Technically, he wasn't even her boyfriend.

"Sinclaire finally let you up for air, Maddie Jane?"

A half empty beer bottle slammed on the table. She glanced up to meet the laughing eyes of Axel and Gunnar. Oh boy. They had trouble written all over their faces. "How many beers have you had?"

"Enough to know it's time for a few rounds of pool." Axel gave her hand a little tug. "Come on. You owe us for babysitting Uncle Warren. We've got a table reserved."

"Come on, Maddie." Blake was already pulling her out of the booth. "Do you play?"

She shrugged. "A little." This could not end well for any of them.

Gunnar's arm snaked around her shoulders as they made their way to the back where the tables were lined up.

"Don't worry." Gunnar spoke low in her ear. "We're not going to rough him up."

She tilted her head up to spear him with her severest look. "You better not."

Where Blake's laugh was rich and low, Gunnar's was more melodic and earthy. His laugh had always put her at ease. "Do you think that look can scare me, Maddie Jane? I've endured worse from Ma."

"Look, just don't make a scene, okay?"

"Fair enough. But now that I have you alone, I want to ask you a few questions."

Uh oh. This was it. Her jig was up. She pushed her glasses up her nose. Gunnar could always tell when she was lying.

He'd put the fear of God into her too many times when they were kids. Conditioned her to the point she'd blurt out the truth before he even asked. Anything to avoid his nuggies. She swallowed, and forced herself to smile brightly.

"Of course. Anything. I'm an open book Gun, you know that."

"I will nuggie you if I think you're lying."

She didn't doubt that for a second. "No need."

His eyes narrowed as he maneuvered her around a couple. "Why are you marrying Blake Sinclaire?"

Did he have to be so direct? It was a horrible Hansen trait.

"You don't waste time, do you?"

"Not my style. Are you going to answer my question?"

And tell you he sweet talked me into a fake engagement? Or that he was so hot I didn't want to say no? The admission surprised her. Was that why she'd agreed to this crazy scheme? Because deep down she'd wanted to?

No.

Absolutely not.

"Dang, Mads." Gunnar rolled his eyes. "Your shit eating grin says it all."

Did it? Lucky her. One bullet dodged. "Any other questions?"

"Yeah. Wanna tell me why you never even told us you were dating him?"

"What is this, the third degree?"

"Pretty much." He tucked her further under his arm. "There's a lot that doesn't add up, and I mean to find out."

"Why? What's the point?"

"Just lookin' out for my cousin."

"Just looking for a way to stick it to a Sinclaire is more like it."

His eyes narrowed. "Look, Maddie Jane. If you're happy, I'm happy. But why marry a Sinclaire? Especially when for the last twelve years, all I've ever heard from you is that your life is in Boston, or your life is in Chicago. You barely come home for the holidays. And now when Uncle Warren drops over you're back? And engaged?"

Damn he was good. She shrugged. "He asked, I said yes. End of discussion."

"We'll see about that."

CHAPTER 19

BLAKE TRAILED AFTER Maddie and Gunnar, disliking the way he seemed to be grilling her. Protective instincts kicking in, he quickened his pace. He didn't care that Gunnar was her cousin. He'd pound him to next week if he upset Maddie in the slightest.

"Hold up there, Sinclaire." A hand landed on his shoulder, and Axel caught up with him.

Great.

Were they tag teaming tonight?

His balls were ten kinds of agitated already, thanks to the incredible kiss Maddie had laid on him. If Axel wanted to pick a fight, he'd go there. He certainly wouldn't be fucking tonight. Or the next night. Or any night soon.

"What do you want?"

He'd lost sight of Maddie and Gunnar, and he didn't have the patience for bullshit tonight. Not with Kylee here, too.

"Just wondering what your intentions are with Maddie Jane."

He didn't like it, but he respected it. Hell, if Emma'd shown up out of the blue, engaged, he wouldn't hesitate to do the same thing. Hansens were stand-up. Even if he didn't like them.

"Entirely honorable." Mostly honorable.

"Because if they're not… If we find out different… we'll be waiting for you in the tall grass."

He nodded. "Understood." He didn't doubt it for a second.

Axel moved to pass him, but Blake stuck out his arm, stopping him. "And just so you know. You're *going* to see us kissing. Better get used to it."

Axel chuckled low, respect showing in his eyes. He tipped his Stetson. "I think we've reached an understanding. Buy you a beer?"

He nodded. Axel slipped through the throng to the bar while he made a beeline to the table, and Maddie.

Slipping a hand around her waist, Blake pulled her close. "Everything okay?"

She turned her face to him, eyes stormy behind her glasses. Everything was not okay. "What's wrong?"

"Nothing. Just the usual first date activities. Deflecting probing questions from Gunnar, wondering if I'll meet any other exes, and whether you'll tell me about them."

"Are you jealous?" He couldn't keep the smile off his face. "That's an irrational feeling for a scientist."

Before she could respond, he swept his lips over hers, savoring her sweetness for the tiniest second. "Don't worry." He murmured in her ear. "I like you more. *Lots* more."

Gunnar grumbled behind him. "Who's up first?"

Maddie eyed him with a glint, adjusting her glasses. "Blake and I go best of three. Then we can team up."

"Are you sure, you wanna do that, sweetheart?" Concern slipped into his voice. "How often do you play?" He played pool all the time, and had won more than his fair share of drinks at the table.

"Enough to know which end of the stick to use."

So she was going to take out her frustration at the pool table. Fine. Maybe he'd let her win the first round. "Feeling sassy, huh?"

"You might say that."

"What are we betting then?"

She skewered him with a look so hot, his balls tightened. "Winner gets to ask the loser any question they want. Loser has to answer." She narrowed her eyes. "And no evading."

Huh. Not what he expected. But he was game. Everything would change tonight if he won. No turning back. Not with the question he suddenly had in mind. He stepped toe to toe with her, forcing her to look up. "That's a pretty confident wager, darlin'. You sure about this?"

A hint of a smile played at her lips. "I'll give it the old college try."

He tilted her chin and swept his lips across hers, savoring her taste. It didn't matter they were in public. He could drown in the sweetness of her mouth.

"I'll look forward to collecting my winnings later," he murmured against her lips.

"Play or get a room, Sinclaire." Her cousins stood scowling on the other side of the table, arms crossed.

"Just setting the terms of our little wager." He handed her a stick. "Ladies first."

She strolled to the end of the table and began racking the balls. He could have sworn she put an extra swing in her hips as she stepped away from him. And as she bent over the table, his mouth went dry. He reached for his glass on the high top, not taking his eyes off her.

She glanced up at him, a flirtatious smile on her face. "Be gentle with me, it's been awhile."

Blake's gut clenched at her innuendo. He was already half

hard just watching her. How in the *hell* was he going to stay cool enough to focus if she kept doing that?

"Ready to go down?" He grinned back mischievously.

She bit her lip and pushed her glasses up her nose. The telltale flush pinking her cheeks. "I confess I have an unfair advantage," she acknowledged, gazing up at him through her lashes as she covered the cue with blue chalk.

"Yeah?" He sidled up to her, running his hand over her hip.

She smelled great, too. That aroma of violets and hay drove him wild. Gunnar coughed loudly. He didn't care. She stepped to the table getting ready to break. She looked over her shoulder at him and winked. His cock jumped to life.

So that's how she was going to play it.

Just as she was ready to break, he leaned close. "I'll be asking you my question naked."

She made a sound in the back of her throat, and the cue slipped off the ball, ruining the opening shot.

She glared at him. "No fair."

"Two can play that game, darlin'."

She adjusted her glasses, and pinned him with a steely gaze.

"Fine. This is war."

He tilted her chin, stealing a kiss. "Fighting or fucking. It all comes down to fighting or fucking. You decide."

Her cheeks flushed pink. He couldn't resist. He stole another kiss, savoring the whiskey still remaining on her lips.

"If you two are going to kiss every two seconds, then let us have the table," Axel hollered.

She kept her eyes locked on his. "I'm just warming him up, Axe."

Giving him a seductive smile, she trailed a finger down his

shirt, hooking it just inside his waistband. The movement sent an ache straight to his balls.

"So… I've decided."

Holy. Hell.

Lust churned in his gut. These days on tenterhooks had to end soon. He'd explode from wanting.

"Decided what?" He asked thickly, his tongue suddenly sticking to the roof of his mouth. They weren't talking about the game anymore. They couldn't be. Her tongue flicked out, wetting her lips. His cock jerked and he choked back a groan.

"To let you win."

Sweet Jesus. He wanted to get this game over as quickly as possible and sashay her back to the ranch. This fighting or fucking standoff ended tonight.

She handed him his stick, and God help him, the only thing he could think about was her hand wrapped around his cock.

She grinned, a triumphant gleam in her eyes. "Your turn, cowboy."

He covered her hand with his. "Don't play me, Maddie." Desire roughened his voice. "This ends tonight."

Her eyes softened a fraction, and she stepped back, breaking the electricity arcing between them.

She leaned her hip on the table, still smiling. "Play on."

He stalked around the table, looking for his best shot. Gunnar and Axel stepped back, sipping their beers, entirely too interested in the game. If he was a gentleman, he'd have taken the harder shots and left her with the easy ones. But he was through being a gentleman tonight. He sunk three before missing.

She sunk one ball, then missed her shot, setting him up to take two more.

She brushed by him, scoping out her next shot, then leaned forward, wiggling her ass. He clenched his fist to keep from palming it in front of her cousins. She turned to study him, a slow smile curving her mouth.

"I hope I'm not distracting you."

He stepped close so her cousins couldn't hear. "Keep this up, and I won't be the only one naked."

Hunger flashed in her eyes, even as her cheeks flushed. She turned and missed her shot.

Ha.

He finished the game, calling the eight-ball. Gunnar and Axel saluted him from across the table. He moved to join them, taking a sip from his beer.

Gunnar poured out the remains of the pitcher between the four glasses. "Maddie Jane's out of practice."

"Yeah." Axel leaned against a pillar, munching on a chip. "Usually she puts up a better fight. You must have her wrapped pretty hard around your finger, Sinclaire." His voice held a hint of challenge.

"That a problem?" He fought the surge of adrenaline that went straight to his fist.

Gunnar answered thoughtfully. "No… no. She needs a strong hand."

What was it with all the Hansen men treating her like a piece of livestock? He clenched his fist, but for different reasons now. "She's not one of your horses."

Gunnar snorted. "Don't be an idiot, Sinclaire. Every woman is as unpredictable as a broomie. But once you figure 'em out, they'll gentle." He slid him a glance. "Maybe even take the sugar you offer."

He held up his hand. "Enough. I get it."

Maddie rejoined them, taking a sip of her beer. "Ready to

lose?"

"Whatever you say, darlin'." He admired her pluck. Even if he was about to kick her ass.

"You break this time?"

He nodded. This would end quickly. He struck the cue ball forcefully, sending the balls scattering. Nothing sank, but a few were close. Maddie took the easiest shot, sinking one. She missed her next shot.

He sunk two.

All the easy shots were gone. She circled the table, brows furrowed in concentration.

He slid next to her, stroking her side. "No way you'll make that shot, hon. Try for fourteen in the corner." He might as well help her. The ten was an impossible shot.

She shot a glance sideways, challenge in her eyes. "Are you trying to tell me how to take my shot?"

He put up his hands.

She smiled tightly. "I didn't think so."

She took the shot and came surprisingly close. But now the ball blocked his shot. He'd either have to shoot her ball in with his, or he'd have to look for another shot.

She leaned her hip on the table, watching him circle.

He missed his next shot. She made hers.

They both quieted after that, circling, shooting, sometimes missing. Soon there were two balls left. Her ten ball, and his six. He'd have to separate his ball from hers, but risked sinking it in the process.

She slipped up next to him, chalking her cue.

"Tough shot. Think you can manage?" She pursed her lips, eyes twinkling behind her glasses.

"I've managed worse."

"Good. You won't mind if I watch how you do it? I'd like

to improve."

Warmth ballooned in his chest. He tilted her chin, leaning in to graze her lips. "For luck."

He bent, lining up his stick with the ball. Just as he shot, she caressed his ass, giving him a little squeeze. He jerked, glancing the stick off the cue, and sinking her ball.

He spun, pulling her tight. She shook with laughter. "Vixen. You'll pay for that." He took her mouth, not caring who saw, bringing his hand up to caress her check as his tongue slid against hers. Whoops and catcalls from the cousins registered in the back of his brain, but he didn't care.

Ending the kiss, he leaned back, gazing down at her. "That was a dirty trick."

Her lips tilted up, and she pushed her glasses up her nose. "All's fair, cowboy."

"Fine." Grim determination mixed with hot lust. His voice turned hoarse. There was no turning back tonight.

"Fine. Double down then. Winner gets to ask any question, and call the shots in bed."

She inhaled quickly, eyes widening in anticipation. She slowly worried her bottom lip between her teeth, then licked the spot she'd bitten.

"Okay…" She smirked. "Winner take all." She turned, hips swaying exaggeratedly, and strutted to the end of the table.

The ache in his balls increased. Tongues of fire licked through his belly. They needed to get out of here fast. She deserved better than a heated fuck in the darkened corner of the parking lot, but that was what it would turn into if she kept torturing him like this.

She glanced up when she finished racking, a dangerous glint in her eye.

"Ready?"

He lifted his chin and crossed his arms. Her first break hadn't been very good. But he'd distracted her.

She broke with a firm stroke, sinking a solid and a stripe.

Not bad.

She circled the table sizing up her shots, choosing the eleven in a side pocket. Easy shot. He'd seen how she played the first two games. She'd take the few easy shots, and then he'd take over. He'd take no quarter. Their game ended tonight.

She hit two more, then aimed her stick at the thirteen. Ha. No way. It was partially blocked by another ball, making the only angle available all wrong. "Good luck with that."

She gave him a look of challenge, and bent, eyebrows furrowed in concentration, tongue sticking out. At least she was putting on a good face. She shot. The cue ball glanced off the rail, hitting the side of the thirteen, sending it right into the corner pocket.

Triumph glinted in her eyes. "Like that?"

"Lucky shot."

She shrugged and smirked.

There were two more stripes on the table, but there was no way she'd sink either of them. Warning bells started ringing when she sunk the nine by sending the cue ball into a solid with just enough backspin the solid stopped while the nine hit its mark.

She eyed him shrugging. "Lucky shot." Her hip knocked into his as she brushed by him to set up her next shot. She aimed the stick, letting it slide between her delicately arched fingers. A fierce light shimmered in her eyes when she glanced up again. "So's this one."

Burning realization hit as she sunk her final ball with the

ease of a pro. But she didn't stop. She went after the rest, calling ball after ball, moving around the table like a queen. Sinking impossible shots with ease.

Damn if it wasn't the sexiest thing he'd ever experienced. And now she'd be calling the shots in bed later tonight. His cock twitched in anticipation.

"Sinclaire, I do believe you've been schooled." Gunnar saluted him with his beer.

Axel shook with laughter. "Maddie Jane, you know it's not nice to run the table like that." He handed her drink over after she replaced her stick.

She'd played him hook, line, and sinker. He'd been foolish to underestimate her. He turned to Axel and Gunnar. "You knew."

Gunnar chortled. "Welcome to the family, man. She schools everyone at least once. And when she's pissed, look out. It's brutal."

"I'm right here, you know." She rolled her eyes, taking a sip.

"How'd you do that?" he asked, trying to keep the shit-eating grin off his face. "I've never seen anyone run a table like that."

Maddie shrugged and giggled, adjusting her glasses. God he loved her laugh – all husky and sweet.

"Physics. It's just angles, velocity and rotation"

As if.

"I used to win spending money in college playing pool. In fact, that's how I first met Jamey." She glanced up at him, apprehension flitting across her eyes. "You're not mad?"

"I'm impressed," he assured her, putting his arm around her shoulders, and kissing her temple. *And very turned on.* "Promise me you'll show me how to make those combo shots when we get home."

He caught Kylee out of the corner of his eye, balancing a tray full of beverages in one hand and three beers in the other. She paused, a smug smile on her face. A flash of understanding hit him, but he was too late. Even as he moved to protect her, Kylee tripped and dumped her tray onto Maddie. She shrieked in surprise as beers and sodas poured down her shirt. To anyone else it would have looked like an accident, but he knew better.

Rage prickled at the corners of his vision. He turned to Axel and Gunnar, who'd managed to avoid the spill. "Quick. Go grab some towels from the bar. Maddie, honey, are you okay?"

Hurt and humiliation flooded her eyes, but she nodded.

His heart shredded.

Kylee Ross was a vindictive, manipulative bitch. He'd put an end to this, one way or another. Even if he got hurt in the process.

"Oh… sorry." Kylee giggled, her eyes glittering. "It's so crowded. Someone bumped me and I lost my balance."

Maddie pressed her lips together, accepting the towels Gunnar handed her.

Blake stepped up to Kylee. "What the fuck, Kylee?"

She turned on him. "What do you mean, what the fuck? It was an accident, Blake." The venom dripped from her voice.

"Like hell it was."

Fred Turner, the Trading Post's owner, pushed through the crowd. "What's going on here?"

Kylee pointed at Maddie, glaring at her. "*She* wasn't looking where she was going and backed right into me. It's her fault."

"Bullshit," Blake exploded.

Kylee put her hand on Fred's shoulder, softening her voice. "Of course it wasn't me Fred. You know I can't afford to take any drinks out of my paycheck." She slid a sly glance back to him. "You know I need every penny for Simon. He's eating me out of house and home right now."

Fred pressed his lips together, sweeping his gaze around the group. "I don't want any trouble with my help. Just make sure the drinks get sorted out so my till doesn't come up short."

"Come on, Fred." Gunnar stepped forward, but he held up his hand. "It's crowded tonight, and I don't have the time to play detective. No trouble, hear?"

They wouldn't get anywhere with him tonight and Kylee knew it. She shot Blake a malicious smile and turned, following Fred back to the bar.

"I'm going to the ladies to try and clean up," Maddie mumbled, slipping through the crowd.

Blake shot a glance at Gunnar. "Make sure she's okay? I'll settle up."

He threaded his way through the crowd and waited at the bar to pay the tab. Including the spilled drinks. No sense in causing another scene in front of Maddie. Or poking Kylee. She had the upper hand here at the bar and she knew it. He'd been wrong to bring Maddie here. He should have been more sensitive to her concerns. But he'd wanted her to stand up to Kylee, to see that Kylee and her kind had nothing on her.

He caught Kylee threading her way through the crowd again, and stalked over, pulling her elbow and moving her to a corner by the jukebox. "I don't know what you're playing at, but this stops. Now. Maddie's never done anything to you."

She glared at him and tugged her elbow back. "Except

exist. We had a deal, Blake," she snapped.

"It's long dead, and you know it." Why couldn't she leave well enough alone? At some point the whole lurid story would come out. He could just feel it. What would Maddie think of him then? Between Kylee's sneering innuendos and Warren's ultimatums, he was neck deep in quicksand.

"I don't think so." She narrowed her eyes at him. "I need more money."

"Like hell you do. What are you spending it on? More cigarettes? More booze?"

"I hate to interrupt this little tête-à-tête," Maddie glared at both of them, eyes angry and full of hurt. "But I'm going to go home with Gunnar and Axel." She turned on her heel and threaded away through the crowd.

"No. Maddie, wait."

Disappointment and anger stabbed through him. Anger at Kylee, anger at the Hansens, at Warren, at this whole fucking situation that was bound to blow up in his face if he didn't tread carefully.

He'd hurt her feelings. He could see it all over her face. He was an ass. He scowled at Kylee, who stared back, a triumphant light in her pale eyes.

"We will discuss this later. You do anything to hurt her again you'll have me to answer to. Understand?"

He turned on his heel, hoping to catch Maddie. This evening was blowing up in his face.

CHAPTER 20

BEN AND BRODIE were waiting on the front porch when Blake stepped out of the truck, slamming the door.

"Heard about the incident down at the Trading Post."

"Which one?"

Brodie handed him a cold beer from the fridge.

"How Britannica schooled you."

"Don't call her that, Brodie."

"Also heard Kylee managed to make a scene."

Ben nodded his agreement, taking a long pull on his beer. "Why is it she always manages to get your goat, brother?"

"Yeah," chimed in Brodie. "You know she's a user, Blake. Don't even know why you talk to her."

Blake let out a long breath. "Hard not to in a town this size. The point is, I don't think she'll be bothering Maddie anymore."

"I rode out to check the south pasture," Brodie volunteered. "We noticed signs of a coyote pack down there."

"Saw that too when I was out earlier today. They shouldn't bother the cows. We still have a few weeks before they start to calve. We'll have to watch closely then."

Ben spoke up. "I'm more worried about the flooding. The water's high down by the homestead."

Blake raked his hands through his hair trying to shift gears.

"Warren's neglected our land. And he's not going to be able to do much when he gets home. Why don't you two start clearing out the underbrush down there."

"Don't you think he'll go on a rampage if he knows you've been down there?"

"I'll talk to Maddie about it."

Ben studied him, taking a long pull on his beer. "You make some kind of a deal with Warren?"

He hated that Ben could read him like a book. Even as a little kid, Ben had always been startlingly perceptive. Always seeing the unspoken truth. It made him believe the stories about their great, great, great grandmother's sixth sense.

"No," he lied, refusing to meet Ben's eyes. "No. Just being neighborly."

"Liar. You were never interested in being neighborly with Warren until you and Maddie hooked up."

Blake looked at him sharply, senses suddenly on high alert. "What do you mean?"

"It doesn't take a scientist to figure out what's going on. You go see Warren about buying our property back, next thing you two've gotten engaged."

Shit.

Was it that obvious? If Ben figured it out, who else had? He took a sip, concentrating on the cool liquid, and pointedly ignoring Ben's musings.

"Yeah, and you've turned into Prince Charming, spending all that time at the hospital. You didn't have two kind words to say about Warren until he had his heart-attack," Brodie accused.

Damn.

It was two on one now. Once Brodie got involved, he'd hang on with the tenacity of a bull rider in the national finals.

Blake shrugged. "Pure coincidence. Nothing more." He took a sip of his beer for emphasis.

"Looks more like you're a puppet and he pulled the strings."

He silently cursed Ben's sixth sense.

So what? Even if Ben figured it out, he'd play it cool and wouldn't meddle. Brodie was the one that could sink him. He was a hothead and would spout off at the wrong time.

Ben narrowed his eyes, pinning him with his gaze. "So is marrying Maddie his price for the property?"

Blake choked on his beer. "Hell no." He wiped his mouth.

"What I can't figure out, is how you convinced her to marry you so quick." Brodie grabbed another beer out of the fridge.

He grinned at his brother. "Got the goods, man."

"Come on, Blake. We might not have the big MBA, but we're not idiots."

"What can I say? We fell in love."

The lie stuck in his throat. He felt dirty even saying it. Like it betrayed whatever it was they did have, even if it wasn't quite love.

"You don't know the first thing about being in love," Brodie said. "The only thing you've ever known how to do is break things."

Blake glared at Brodie, clenching his fingers around the bottle, tamping down the temper that flared deep inside at the accusation. "You don't know what you're talking about."

Brodie didn't have the least bit of understanding about how complicated things were. Of the messes he'd fixed. Of how he'd fought to keep them together when Jake was off the rails. The phone calls at college from mom, asking for food money. How he'd bought ramen at the local gas station and sent her his money so the rest of them could eat. His whole life, he'd done what needed to get done to keep the family and the ranch intact. Agreeing to marry Maddie was a continuation of that, nothing more. And when she was gone, once again, he'd be the one left to pick up the pieces.

"I think it's time you saw to the horses."

Brodie glared back at him, clenching and unclenching his fist. "Dismiss me if you like. But this is not over." He turned and stalked toward the barn, leaving them alone in the twilight.

"Don't let him get to you," said Ben, reaching into the mini fridge for another beer. "He's always this way when he hears about Kylee."

"It's been twelve years. Maybe it's time to get the fuck over it."

"Maybe. But you can't help him do it. He's got to figure things out on his own."

Blake nodded. "He can be as pissed as he wants, but he needs to stay focused on things around here. I have enough to worry about without babysitting him."

"Easy there, big guy." Ben reached out and patted him on the shoulder. "You've got bigger fish to fry right now." He grinned. "Gunnar said something about you fetching Maddie when you were ready to do the proper amount of groveling."

"Groveling, huh?" Well he deserved that. He could see he'd hurt her, standing there arguing with Kylee. And he felt like an ass. But there was too much on the line to confide in her until after he got the deed to the property.

"Don't go down the rabbit hole, Blake. Go apologize and start fresh. No need to carry on the worst of dad's behavior."

Blake's eyes shot up. Ben's eyes bored into him. He hated

it when Ben did that. It was like Ben crawled into his brain and set up camp. All the bluffing in the world wouldn't put him off. "Want to say more about that?"

"Nope. No need to. You know exactly what I mean."

He did. Jake Sinclaire was never wrong. He didn't recall ever hearing his father apologize to his mother. Not once. Quick to anger, he'd ruled with an iron fist, the other holding a bottle of Jack Daniels.

Growing up, all of them had felt the sting of his discipline more than once. Thankfully, his little sister had been spared most of it. But the Hansens had always been the recipients of the worst of Jacob's ire. It had only increased when he'd lost the land to Warren in a poker game.

Ben stood and stretched. "I know you hate apologizing. Just go sweet-talk her." His brother pinned him with a stern gaze. "Ma always said you catch more flies with honey."

He didn't like where this conversation was going. The last thing he needed was Maddie uncovering his closely held secrets. Laying him bare. It was bad enough she was already under his skin in the worst way. Forming an emotional attachment would only make things worse when they inevitably ended things. And things would end. The best he could hope for would be that they ended on friendly terms, and maybe they could see each other again the next time he visited Chicago.

"Since when are you the expert on women?"

Ben raised an eyebrow. "It doesn't take a rocket scientist to figure out a woman. Just need to pay attention to the signals."

Gunnar had said much the same thing. What the hell was wrong with him that he couldn't figure her out? That she had him jumpy and on edge, and practically dying of want? He *had* listened. He'd given her space. Was letting her call the shots. And the more he did that, the more she proceeded to confuse him.

"Don't brood too long, brother. Nothing good ever came from brooding." Ben squeezed his shoulder and took off toward the barn. Blake stayed on the porch, watching the fading twilight, thoughts swirling around him like fog in the river bottom. He kicked his feet off the porch wall and leaned forward, resting his chin on his fingers.

Groveling.

Hell if he'd ever grovel in front of one Hansen, let alone a group of them. When had he ever needed to apologize? Never. He just didn't do it. A thought struck him like a blow to the head. How like Jake.

Bullshit.

He was nothing like his father. He'd done nothing wrong. It wasn't his fault Kylee had her undies in a bunch about Maddie. And it wasn't his fault that Maddie'd gotten pissed off. Hell, he'd tried to set things straight and got blamed in the process. He was the victim here. He'd head to the Hansen's and bring Maddie home all right, but one thing was certain.

There would be no groveling.

But something needled at him. If he charged over to the Hansen spread and dragged her home like a caveman, she'd blast him up one side and down the other. Not that he'd mind terribly. He loved it when she got all sassy and smart with him. Loved the way her sapphire eyes blazed with fire. The way her mouth moved.

His breath caught in his throat as the realization startled him.

He liked her.

A whole lot.

Hell, who was he kidding? He was nuts about her. And before things had gone off the rails tonight, he was fairly certain she liked him, too. And was finally willing to let go with him. He shifted in his seat as he grew uncomfortable. God, it didn't take much. Just thinking about her.

The memory of his vision in the barn hung over him. Taunting him.

The only thing standing between the two of them was the creek.

And their families.

And his secrets.

CHAPTER 21

MADDIE SAT PUSHING her food around the plate. Coming home with Gunnar and Axel had been a mistake. A huge mistake. She'd have been better off sulking back at the Big House, away from the pointed questions of her cousins. But at least she'd been able to raid Hope's closet for a change of clothes.

There was something ugly between Blake and Kylee. She was sure of it. She'd use her question from their bet to get to the bottom of it. As for the rest of their deal… all bets were off until he came clean. She simply couldn't be with someone who wasn't straightforward.

No matter how much she wanted him.

"Maddie Jane, what's got into you? You look like a prairie chicken ready to go on a rampage."

Her head snapped up. Did every man in Prairie sound alike? "Let it go, Axe." Underneath the table, she clenched her fists in frustration.

"You're funny when you get all riled up."

"Kylee did it on purpose didn't she?" She turned to Gunnar.

"Ah hell, Maddie Jane, I'm not sure he's a good idea."

"Excuse me?"

Gunnar finally looked at her, his eyes serious.

"You're too good for a Sinclaire."

She rolled her eyes. "And you know best who's good for me."

"Of course." Both of them nodded vigorously, widening their eyes at her like she was an idiot.

"And that is?"

Axel crossed his arms and leaned his chair back on two legs. "Not some pansy scientist."

"So anyone with brains is out?" Unbelievable. They sounded just like Blake.

"Well… he could have brains," Gunnar conceded.

"How very big of you."

"But he has to be able to ride a horse."

"And protect you in a fight," Axel added.

Mother of God. Why did every man in her life have to be a walking, talking, testosterone factory?

"And Blake doesn't measure up how?"

Axel brought the legs of his chair back down with a thud. "He's a Sinclaire. That's enough."

"Well maybe you need to start looking at him differently then." She could not believe she was defending him to her cousins. Maybe *she* needed to start looking at him differently…

Nope.

No way.

He was a sex magnet.

A very handsome sex magnet.

Like the black hole of sex magnets.

That was all. He didn't love her, and she certainly didn't love him. He'd just bamboozled her senses. She needed to remember that. And he kept secrets. She refused to be with someone who kept secrets.

These… these feelings, were clouding her judgment.

Interfering with rational, logical thought. She'd do well to remember she was heading home in a few weeks and that this chaos would become a distant memory.

"Maybe he needs to stop being an ass first," Axel returned.

"Who's calling who an ass?" Blake stepped into the kitchen, his eyes riveted on her. Gunnar and Axel pushed back their chairs and stood as one.

Oh God. The generations of animosity were about to come to a head. Maddie stood too; ready to throw herself between Blake and her cousins. If fists started flying in the confines of the kitchen there'd be hell to pay with Martha.

"Sit down." She pinned Axel and Gunnar with a glare. "This doesn't concern you."

No one moved. The tension crackled between the men.

"Forgive us if we don't pull out the welcome wagon," Axel spoke tightly.

"Shut up, Axe. He saved Dad. And you just welcomed him to the family a few hours ago. I say he's welcome."

Gunnar crossed his arms over his chest, glaring at Blake. "Why you here?"

"A little birdie said I might find my lady here."

My lady. If she wasn't so irritated at him, she'd think it was cute. His eyes didn't move off her. Heat curled up from her belly, drying her mouth. She swallowed, refusing to look away. Her tongue flicked out to wet her lips. Lust flared briefly in his eyes.

Ooh…

So he liked that, did he?

"Outside," he said gruffly, nodding toward the back door.

Axel stepped in front of the back door. "Anything you need to say can be said right here."

"Would you stop already with the pissing contest?" She'd

had enough. "I'm not a fire hydrant."

Blake's eyes were still on her, radiating an intensity that half scared her, half turned her on. Scared her because she couldn't read his intention. Turned her on, well, for obvious reasons. Like he was so hot she'd incinerate if she stayed standing there.

"No. You're definitely not a fire hydrant." A wry smile flashed across his face.

With a grunt Axel stepped aside. Tearing her eyes from Blake's, she turned and stepped through the door. He followed, shutting the door firmly. She moved to the railing, keeping her back turned.

"Turn around Maddie." There was no mistaking the command in his voice. Slowly she turned, hugging her arms. His face was half in shadow underneath his Stetson. The glare of the porch light threw his features into strong relief. His eyes seemed hungry. Predatory, even. She braced herself on the railing waiting for him to speak.

The silence stretched between them.

"I don't know what you thought you saw back there, but there is *nothing* between me and that woman."

"I know."

"Then why did you leave?"

Jealousy stabbed through her at the memory of the way he looked at Kylee, as if they shared a secret. But she couldn't tell him.

Wouldn't.

The last thing she wanted to do was appear insecure and untrusting.

"Because." She bit her lip, emotion lumping in her throat.

Dammit.

She couldn't do it. Couldn't give him the upper hand by

admitting she was jealous of whatever was still left between them. "Because, I'm not going to stick around and watch you coddle your ex, while I was the one wronged."

There. That would show him.

"What did you want me to do, Maddie? Punch her? You know I'd never do that to a woman. Not even her."

That took the wind right out of her sails. Her shoulders sagged. He was right. She'd wanted to punch Kylee in the face and wished she'd had the courage to do it.

"So here we are again, Maddie." He stepped closer so that she had to tilt her chin to maintain eye contact. "We can stay here and fight in front of your family, or, we can go home and fuck. Which will it be?"

Her mouth went dry. "Did you really just ask me that?" He had nerve. He cracked a smile, and for the first time in days, it went all the way to his eyes. She hated it when he smiled like that. No. She loved it.

It made her insides gooey.

Would she do it?

Could she do it?

Tell him she wanted to go back and rip his clothes off? The image of him naked in nothing but his Stetson floated before her. A shot of hot arousal soaked her panties.

"Well… if you keep your hat on." She reached her hand inside his coat and toyed with the top button of his perfect shirt. She wanted to wrinkle the heck out of it.

His hand came down on hers, trapping it in place. Electricity jumped between them.

"But first you have to have to make good on our bet and answer any question I ask."

"Of course. Anything." He leaned in to nuzzle her neck, sending little thrills down to her nipples.

"You'll answer?"

He lifted his head and pinned her with a gaze so intense her knees shook. She could drown in his eyes. Swim in them like they were a galaxy of stars.

"I'm an open book. Ask me anything."

She swallowed, holding her breath. Anticipation and anxiety set her nerves tingling. She pulled away and leaned back on the rail. "Kylee Ross. I want to know what you're hiding about Kylee Ross and why she hates me when she doesn't even know me."

His eyes shuttered and he shrugged noncommittally. "I don't know the answer to the second part of your question. She's just a very unhappy person. As for the first part, that's easy. Not much to tell."

As if. She tapped her foot. "I'm waiting. Spill it."

He jammed his hands in his pockets. "Twelve years ago. I was twenty and in school at K-State, Brodie was sixteen. She and Brodie had dated on and off. Brodie was really hot for her."

"And?"

"During one of the 'off' times, she came up to K-State and fooled around and got knocked up and Brodie found out. Ended badly for everyone."

She narrowed her eyes.

She'd expected something more dramatic, like Brodie had caught Kylee with one of his brothers. But not something so… typical for a teenage romance. Maybe no the pregnancy, but it happened sometimes. Bottom line. Kylee had simply moved on. So why the drama and animosity?

He shrugged. "In some ways he's never let it go."

He opened his mouth, and for a split second, looked like he was about to say more. Then snapped his mouth shut and nodded once.

Something didn't add up.

She nudged his boot with her toe. "Any other secrets? I mean it Blake, it all comes out now."

He swallowed, looking like he'd just eaten a whale. "Nope." He shook his head, and reached for her hand, twining his fingers in hers. "Scout's honor."

Liar.

Her heart sank to her toes. So he didn't trust her. Whatever his secret was, he was still holding onto it with two fists. Not that it mattered a whit. They weren't really getting married. They had nothing between them but a bunch of crazy sexual chemistry bouncing between atoms. Was she willing to give him the benefit of the doubt? Was she willing to risk being hurt down the road?

"But you know my big, dark secret…"

He brought her fingers to his lips, before capturing the tips of two of them in his mouth, sucking on them lightly. The movement acted like tinder for the sparks spiraling through her.

"Your secret's safe with me."

She laughed nervously, covering her disappointment. Maybe she needed to analyze why she wanted so badly for him to confide in her.

"What about the rest of me?" A tremor shook her voice.

He turned her hand over, and brought his lips to her palm. Tingles raced up her arm to her nipples, hardening them to achy points. He ran his tongue over the hollow in the center of her palm. She locked her knees to keep them from buckling. Couldn't feel her fingers from the buzzing. Her pulse thrummed wildly.

He raised his eyes, raw lust glittering in their depths.

"If you were smart, Maddie Jane," he rasped, voice rough with desire. "You'd run while you can."

Her tongue flicked out to wet her lips, "I think you said that once before… What if I don't want to?" She couldn't keep the breathiness from her voice. Waves of anticipation rippled through her. Desire roared in her ears, thrumming with a vibration that tensed every muscle.

"Then let the wild rumpus begin."

He pulled her close and brought his lips to hers, running his hands down her sides to cradle her ass.

Her need finally breached rational thought, and she looped her hands around his neck.

There was only this.

Only now.

She groaned in the back of her throat, shifting forward to press herself against him. He ground his cock into her, sending a thrill to her core.

"Blake," she murmured against him, rocking her hips into his.

The back door swung open.

"If you're gonna suck face like that, do it on your own property."

He groaned and tore his mouth from hers, leaving her lips numb. He looked back over his shoulder, but she knew who was there.

Gunnar and Axel stood smirking in the doorway.

She decided to have a little fun with him, and skittered her hand down his chest so it came to rest right underneath his balls. She gave them a little squeeze. He whipped his head back around, pinning her with a ferocious look. Whatever issues lay between them, one thing was certain. He wanted her as much as she wanted him.

"Thanks for dinner, boys," she called out over Blake's shoulder. "We'll see you around."

"We expect you for Sunday dinner, Maddie Jane."

"We'll be there." She squeezed him again, trying not to laugh. Grabbing his hand, she tugged him toward the back steps, into the dark. "Did you ride or drive?" she asked, once they were out of earshot.

He twined his fingers with hers. "Rode. Blaze is tied up down by the paddock."

"I heard the boys talking about the rains. Isn't the creek running too high to cross?"

"Not on horseback, although after the rain later tonight, we'll have to keep an eye on it. Any significant amount and it will be impassable for a spell."

"How can you tell?"

"That it will rain? The science of my nose."

"Are you making fun of me?"

A laugh rumbled in this throat. "A little. But seriously, when you've lived here your whole life, you can just tell. Or maybe it's great granny's sixth sense."

"What do you mean?"

"Our ancestor, Pascal St. Claire, married a Pawnee woman who'd run away from a reservation. The story goes she used to get visions. So anytime we guess right about something, it's because of granny Stands With Eagles."

They reached the paddock where Blaze stood patiently.

"Can he carry both of us?" She placed her foot in the stirrup and waited for him to help her up.

"No problem." His hands lingered a moment on her ass. They were so close to where she wanted them to be, wanted him to be, that she nearly hurled herself right over the other side when he boosted her. Grabbing the pommel, she righted herself and leaned forward, giving him room to settle behind her.

He hoisted himself up and snaked his arm around her, pulling her close to his chest, his hands splayed across her side. She gave a little sigh as she leaned back into him, enjoying the feel of him.

He wheeled Blaze around and headed in the direction of the creek. Darkness enveloped them as they left the compound. Even at half-full, the moon dimmed the smaller stars, casting a silvery light over the landscape. Coyotes yipped in the distance. They rode in comfortable silence surrounded by the sounds of night frogs and the occasional owl.

"You know this was why I became a physicist." She casually pointed to the sky. "I found an old telescope in the attic, and Uncle Eddie brought me out here one night when I was probably six or seven and showed me the Orion Nebula. I was hooked."

"Maddie. Stop talking."

She shifted in the saddle to glance up at him quizzically. His eyes glinted down at her. His lips were so close, if she stretched her neck, she could kiss him.

"I'm not going to devour you. I've already said, you call the shots."

A thrill ran through her.

"I-I was just talking. I'm not nervous."

He snorted. "Of course you are. You never make small talk."

"I can't help it if my hormones go bonkers around you."

"So you're admitting you like me?"

"No. I'm admitting my body likes you."

"Cut the crap, Maddie. You like me. If you didn't, you wouldn't give a shit about Kylee."

He had her. He was right. And *that* terrified her.

He lowered his head. "It's okay, Maddie. Because I like you, too. A lot."

Her stomach dropped to her toes. He couldn't be serious. Could he? She felt like she was on top of a rocket about to launch, but she had no oxygen. He'd just sucked all of the air out of her lungs.

His hand tightened around her middle.

"In fact, if you could admit that, we might get somewhere beyond sexually frustrated." He nuzzled her neck. "I see the heat in your eyes when you think I'm not looking. I feel how you tremble when I crawl into bed next to you."

"I can't believe I'm saying this because... this whateveritis... chemical explosion... is melting our brain cells. But if you want this... us... to mean anything, then I need..." She let out a frustrated sigh. "You have to be willing to be honest."

Blake's silent laughter rumbled against her back. "Are you saying you want *whateveritis* between us to mean something? Doesn't that imply more than chemical reactions? Doesn't that imply *emotions* are involved?"

"Not exactly," she hedged. He was right, and she hated it.

"Isn't that the pot calling the kettle black, Doctor feelings-are-irrational-Hansen?" His breath tickled in her ear.

She let out a rickety sigh.

"For a scientist, sometimes you're dense."

She rolled her eyes. "Speak plainly, Blake. It usually helps."

"You talk this great talk about feelings being irrational, and you're right; they are. You can fight to stay in control, but the person you're hurting the most is yourself."

Okay, she'd deserved that after her little speech. She swallowed the knot of fear that had lodged itself in her throat.

To not be in control was to be vulnerable. To be vulnerable was to be weak. To be weak meant people like Kylee and Marcus ate you for dinner and spit out the bones.

"You can't have it both ways, Maddie. When is it going to sink into that brilliant mind of yours that love is messy? You can't love anyone and be in control. Love is messy and unpredictable. Look at the evidence in front of you."

She twisted back to study him. His face obscured by shadow thanks to the moonlight and his ever present Stetson.

Deep down, some part of her wanted this. Wanted it to mean something. Something more than just super hot amazing mind-blowing sex. She turned forward and took a deep steadying breath.

This was it. The moment where all her timelines collided. If Dr. Who and the TARDIS materialized right in front of her, she'd jump into the unknown without a second thought.

Wasn't this the same?

Jumping into the unknown?

And just like Dr. Who, she even had a companion to hold her hand.

"You're thinking again, Maddie."

She sighed heavily. "You don't want to know what I'm thinking."

"Try me."

The challenge was obvious in his voice, but he let the silence draw out between them.

He massaged her side in lazy circles. Everywhere he touched, jolts of electricity zinged straight to her core. And when combined with the movement of the saddle against her clit, she wasn't sure she'd make it to the barn. Orgasming on horseback would definitely be a new milestone for her.

For the final time, she jammed the fear down into the sole

of her boot. And jumped.

"Fine." Her voice no longer sounded like her own. "If you must know… I was, I was… questioning whether or not I could make it back to the barn without…without having an orgasm," she finished hotly.

Immediately, Blake stilled. Silence crackled between them.

Flames of embarrassment licked up her neck. "Say something," she whispered after what seemed like an eternity.

"Jesus," he rasped. "That's the hottest thing you've ever said to me."

He pulled her tighter against him, his fingers diving under her waistband searching for her skin. "Did you really mean it?"

His voice was low and hot in her ear. She nodded, not trusting herself to speak. A thrill of exhilaration roared through her. What else could she tell him? Emboldened by his reaction, she continued.

"When you put your lips on my neck like that, it makes my nipples hard."

This time he groaned. He moved his hand to palm her breast, his fingers searching for and finding her taut nipple. He pinched it gently, sending a bolt of lust right to her core. She threw her head back onto his chest, reeling from the sensation.

"Unbutton your shirt," he commanded.

"D-do my other nipple."

He sought her other nipple and rolled it between is thumb and forefinger. Wetness pooled at her crux, heightening the friction of the saddle. She clenched her thighs, squirming in the saddle.

"Jesus, Maddie. Your mouth is so fucking hot. Keep

talking to me."

"Wait until you feel the rest of me."

She unbuttoned the top button of her shirt. Then the second. His breathing was becoming more labored. She placed her hand over his, circling her nipple, reveling in his quick intake of breath. Quickly, she undid the rest of the buttons, exposing herself to the night air.

His hand was instantly inside her bra, the rough pads of his fingers scraping against her buds. It was her turn to gasp. The cool night air coupled with his hot hands, sent spirals of pleasure through her limbs.

Her hand reached for the button of her jeans.

"Put your hands down my pants, Blake. I want you to feel how wet you make me."

He jammed his hand into her pants, forcing the zipper down. Twining his fingers, he pushed her thong out of the way until they came to rest on her very wet clit.

"Holy hell, woman." He stroked into her wetness, bringing his finger back up to swirl around her clit. His movement sent sparks shooting out and she rolled her hips encouraging him to do more.

The horse started and picked up his gait. Tearing his lips from her neck, he brought the horse to a standstill.

"God, Maddie. I want you so bad my balls are going to explode. But we're making Blaze nervous."

"Then get me off this horse."

Feelings be damned. He had had finally breached her defenses. She wanted him so badly she couldn't see straight. She'd regret this later. She knew it. But she had no rational thoughts left. She needed him and couldn't think beyond doing whatever it took to get him inside her.

CHAPTER 22

BLAKE DIDN'T NEED to be told twice. He'd never been more turned on in his life. And no one had ever turned him on more than her.

He looped the reins around the saddle horn and slipped off Blaze. Turning, he helped her down, then immediately scooped her up into his arms. Her shirt fell open, exposing her skin and lacy bra to the silvery light. He placed a kiss at the base of her neck. She hummed in the back of her throat.

He scanned around for a place to set her down. They were about a hundred yards from the river, and there wasn't much cover save for the trees at the edge of the bank.

She laughed low.

"Put me down, Blake."

"Wait. Here?"

"Where else? The trees are too far away."

His cock was like steel in his pants.

"I swear to God if you keep talking like that Maddie, I'm not going to make it."

She laughed quietly again, and drew a finger down his jaw. "So my mouth turns you on, does it?"

He dipped his head, needing to taste her.

"I love your mouth," he murmured before capturing her in an open mouthed kiss. She responded immediately, and slid her tongue against his. Demanding. Taking. A moan erupted from the back of his throat, and he deepened their kiss, drinking her in like she was water in the desert. She shifted in his arms and pulled off his Stetson so she could run her fingers through his hair. Every nerve in his body fired with unbridled lust.

Giving into the sensations, he sank to his knees, pulling her with him. The damp earth barely registered. Her hands were everywhere. Tugging at the buttons of his shirt, splaying across his collarbones.

She pulled her lips from his, dragging her tongue down his neck, nipping and sucking. "Your jacket. Take off your jacket."

He shrugged it off, and laid it on the ground. His fingers went to the remaining buttons on his shirt, but she stopped him. She finished the job, then pulled it off, laying it next to his jacket.

His skin skittered with goose bumps, but whether it was from the night air, or her lust-filled gaze, he couldn't tell. She pushed him back onto his clothes, and straddled his hips, grinding herself into his hard length.

He hesitated, waiting for her next move. What had gotten into her? Maybe the moonlight had made her crazy. Whatever it was, it was fucking amazing, and it made him unbelievably hard.

She leaned over him, her hair falling in a curtain, sheltering them from anything but each other. Slowly, she came closer and caught his lower lip between her teeth. Biting gently, she sucked. A throaty groan stuck in the back of his mouth, and he reached up to cup her ass. He had to hang onto something or he'd explode.

She worked her mouth down his neck, stopping to suck at the base of this throat, moving her tongue over the hollow.

She wiggled her ass in his hands, settling into him.

"Blake," she murmured, her voice thick with lust. "You make me crazy hot. This is all I've thought about for weeks. Ever since you first kissed me."

Molten craving rushed straight to his balls and he ground his hips into her in answer. He couldn't breathe.

"Fuck, Maddie, I can't take this."

"Oh." She sat up, taking both her hands and her mouth off him. She shimmied out of her shirt, and removed her bra. Her nipples were taut and dark, an exquisite contrast to the shimmery white of her skin in the moonlight. Slowly, she brought her hands up and ran her fingers back and forth over her nipples. He dug his fingers into her ass as he stared, mesmerized.

"Should I stop?" A small smile played at the corners of her sassy mouth.

His mouth went dry. "No," he croaked. "No."

She swayed over him like a Goddess, like a siren of the prairie, her hair falling in silvery waves in the moonlight. Every cell in his body tensed. In that moment his entire world tilted.

He would do anything to keep her.

Say anything.

Be anything.

She held him completely in thrall.

He burned to be inside her, to feel her softness underneath him. More than that, he yearned to empty himself fully, completely into her. Without pretense. Without holding anything back. The weight of the realization pressed down on him. Shocking him. He didn't know whether to be eager or scared shitless.

"You are… everything," he murmured reverently, brushing her hands away from her breasts, so that he could take her into his hands. He cradled her weight, thumbs flicking over and around her nipples, glorying in how they tightened, in the emotions flickering across her face. Everything seemed sharper, more intense.

She moved to unfasten his belt, her hands fumbling for the button of his jeans. She tore his zipper down and in one fluid movement freed his cock from his shorts.

Fireworks shot off behind his eyes as her hand settled around his length and began to slowly move up and down, squeezing and releasing. Her other hand dove farther inside, reaching to cup his balls. With the same rhythm she pulled and stroked.

"Jesus, Maddie, where did you learn to do that?" he gritted, his hips rocking in response to her ministrations.

She laughed low. "My imagination. Curse of a scientist. Insatiable curiosity."

Shit. He could think of a thousand scenarios he'd like to be curious about with her.

"You like to be curious?" His breath came in pants. At this rate he'd shoot off long before she was satisfied. He had to contain himself.

"I was born curious, Blake. It's why I'm a scientist."

He risked a glance at her. Hooded eyes, glazed with unapologetic hunger, stared back at him. And a satisfied grin covered her face. God he loved her.

His breath caught. Everything stilled.

He loved her.

That wasn't possible.

But it was as certain as the moon overhead.

He was hopelessly in love with Maddie Hansen.

He shut his eyes, unable to look at her. The realization

laid him open. Bait for the wolves. He mentally scrabbled for purchase, trying to undo the thought. But there was no taking it back. He'd given that thought life, and now it was in the universe.

Growing.

Expanding.

Her tongue darted out, encircling the head of his cock.

He was lost.

There was no mast to lash himself to. The siren song had completely captivated him. Bewitched him. There was nothing left to do but ride the wave of ecstasy she was offering him. He was helpless in her hands.

Emotion bubbled up, thick and hot. He could no longer tell the difference between love and lust. It swirled in his body like a tornado. Ripping through him and leaving behind only devastation.

She took him fully into her mouth.

Her sassy, hot, mouth.

Her tongue swirled around the underside of his cock as she applied just enough suction to set his nerve endings on fire. She burned him. When she was through, he'd be nothing but smoke and ashes.

He fisted his hands in her hair, a waterfall of moonlight, and rocked into her, letting her take him to the stars.

"Maddie, I…I… you have to let me."

He was incoherent, riding a galaxy of sensation and emotion.

She hummed as she took him even further into her hot, wet mouth. Her hands were everywhere, stroking lightly first his chest, then his hips, then pulling on his balls.

It wasn't supposed to be this way. He was supposed to be calling the shots. He was supposed to incinerate her with his kisses. And yet, the closer she took him to completion, the less he cared.

The more he only wanted this moment.

This feeling.

This drowning.

This completion.

With her.

White-hot fusion centered in his balls. His whole body tightened, and for one blissful moment, time stopped.

He exploded outward with the force of a supernova, crying her name into the darkness. Wave after wave assaulted him and she drank him in until he was tossed, helpless and spent, at her feet. Tears pricked his eyes as he lay there, in nothing but moonlight, utterly shattered.

Maddie crawled upwards and nestled her head in the crook of his arm. He couldn't speak. Didn't trust himself to. So he kissed the top of her head, and pulled her close. That he could do. A feeling of awkwardness pressed up as the fog of his orgasm began to clear. How do you move on from a religious experience? Where did he go from here? He couldn't handle this. This riot of feelings she'd unleashed.

"Maddie?" His voice stuck in this throat.

"Mmm?" She made lazy circles on his belly with her fingers. He liked that. The caressing. This feeling of closeness.

"I… uh." He cleared his throat. He shouldn't talk. Talking always got him in trouble. "Thank you for that… I… uh… that was amazing." He kissed her head again.

"Mmm. I enjoyed it too."

"Really? Women like that?"

"Well I can't speak for other women." She turned her face to his, her eyes inscrutable. "But I love to see you come apart like that." She grinned, continuing the lazy circles with her hand. "It's pretty heady stuff."

Coming apart. If only. That didn't even begin to describe what had happened. If only she knew. He didn't know how to tell her. Wasn't sure he ever could. But he could show her. He shifted against her, running his hand over her side.

"I think I sidetracked us."

"No. I think *I* sidetracked us." She giggled. A sound as silvery and magic as the moonlight. She bewitched him.

"Well, whoever's at fault, the fact remains that you're not done. And I wouldn't be a gentleman if I left you hanging."

She smiled coyly. "What are you saying?"

"I'm saying turn about is fair play. Lie back."

He shifted over her, and helped her scoot to the center of the shearling so she wouldn't hurt herself on the hard ground. This wasn't exactly the ideal place for a tryst, but he sure as hell wasn't getting back on Blaze until they'd had their fill of each other.

Her hair fanned out around her, and he plucked a dried leaf from its end, wrapping her lock around his finger.

"Like spun gold in the sun, like silver in the moonlight. Are you a sorceress, Maddie?"

She gave him a smile like the Mona Lisa. "Keep talking like that and I'm going to accuse you of being a poet."

"I thought women liked poetry."

"Only if it's sincere."

He leaned close, planting soft kisses at her temple. "Oh I'm sincere, all right," he murmured. "You're a sorceress. You've tangled me in your web, and I can't escape."

She turned her head, eyes full of question. "Do you want to escape?"

Shit.

There was that Hansen directness again. A lump formed

in his throat, silencing him. He held her gaze, hardly daring to breathe. He swallowed down the anxiety that darted through him.

He shook his head once. "No." Again with more conviction. "No. I don't want to escape."

The smile she gave him was genuine and open. Satisfaction swelled through him. She liked his answer.

The electricity arced between them, and she twined her arms around his neck. "Then come closer." She drew his mouth down to hers, and he let himself fall into her.

Even after drinking him in, it was her sweetness he tasted, not himself. Slowly, he dipped his tongue into her mouth, marveling at how he never tired of kissing her. Each time his tongue slid against hers, swirled and explored the soft recesses of her delicious mouth, he wanted more.

More of her.

More of them.

He needed this to be good for her. Strike that. He wanted to blow her mind. Wanted to take her to heights she'd never visited. He caressed her lightly, fingers barely touching her satiny skin. Goosebumps raised under the pads of his fingers.

She shivered and smiled into his mouth, sighing.

"Tell me what you want, Maddie."

"Suck my tits."

Holy. Hell. Boldness for the win.

A surge of awareness charged through him. For the time being, he ignored it. This was about Maddie. "My pleasure." He shifted lower, bringing his mouth to hover right above her already taut nipple. He drew his finger under the curve, letting his thumb graze the bud.

She breathed in sharply.

Slowly, he brought his tongue to her breast, circling, but

not touching her nipple. He blew on it, pleased to see it tighten further. He glanced up at her.

Utter delight played across her features. Her lips were open, a tiny smile playing at the corners of her mouth, her eyes.

"Maddie, look at me."

She opened her eyes, naked want flaring in their sapphire depths. Her tongue flickered out to wet her lips. Jesus. Every time she did that he wanted to stop what he was doing and dive into her mouth again.

"I want you to see me making love to you."

Her eyes darkened in surprise. Damn, he was losing his edge. He'd never once referred to sex with her as 'making love'. Maybe that's because it never had been. This was different. Butterflies swept through him, lodging in his chest. This ranked up there with the first time he'd seen a naked lady in one of the ranch hand's titty magazines. This meant something.

She reached out and caressed his face. An act of simplicity that carried such weight and launched the butterflies all over again.

He swirled his tongue over the swell of her breast, before returning and finally taking her nipple into his mouth and sucking. Hard.

She gave a little sigh and began to roll her hips. "God Blake, I love that." Her breath came in shallow pants.

He couldn't resist. He had to suck on her lower lip. He palmed her breast, rolling the nipple between his fingers, while he returned to her mouth, capturing her lower lip between his teeth.

Instantly, her hands were in his hair, encouraging him. Drawing his mouth back to hers. He sucked on her tongue, inviting her farther into his mouth, and was rewarded with a groan coming from the back of her throat. He loved that sound. It sent waves of pleasure through him, settling and tightening in his balls.

He dragged his mouth away from hers to bring it to her other breast, so he could repeat the process of slowly devouring every inch of her body. His tongue swirled around the nipple, and he gently scraped his teeth along its length before blowing on it.

She moaned and arched into him. Somewhere in the distance an owl called. Being outside like this heightened his awareness. Intensified everything. Brought every detail of her body into sharp focus.

"More," she pleaded.

"Demanding, aren't you?" He moved his mouth back to the first nipple, sucking and swirling, scraping it gently.

"Yes-s-s-s." Her fingers clutched at his hair. "You wouldn't have it any other way."

No. He wouldn't. He moved his lips down her belly, flicking circles with his tongue, pausing to trace her belly button and to suck on the soft flesh there.

Placing his hands under her hips, he gave her pants one hard yank and pulled everything down to her boots, exposing the rest of her to the cool night air, and his hot gaze.

Her knees fell open as if in invitation. Her engorged pussy lips glistened in the moonlight. He licked his lips in anticipation.

She giggled nervously. "God, Blake. You look like a wolf ready to devour a meal."

He wiggled his eyebrows at her. "Oh, I intend to feast."

He moved his hands to her hips, running his thumbs over the bone as he settled himself to one side. He drew a finger down her inner thigh, enjoying how her leg muscles clenched in response. How much pleasure could he give her before she cried his name in ecstasy? He was sure as hell going to enjoy finding out.

He moved his fingers to her folds, slipping inside her slick heat. Her hips rose to meet his hand. He drew his fingers up her slit, spreading her juices around her clit, but not touching it.

Slowly, reverently, he brought his mouth down to her mound. Her musk floated up to his nose and he breathed in her essence.

Home.

This was home.

This moment, this vision of her laid open before him, bound him to her. Branded him as hers. There was nothing he wouldn't do for her.

He brushed his lips across her mound, alternating first the flat of his tongue against her softness, and then making circles with the tip of his tongue. Tasting all of her. Savoring her flavor.

She rocked her hips up, and he skimmed his finger down again through her folds, dipping into her wetness.

A cut the quiet. Whose, he didn't know. It just as easily could have been his as hers. He kneeled closer, dropping his gaze to take her in.

Her pussy glowed in the moonlight.

So ready. For him.

So wet. For him.

The enormity of the realization took his breath away. Pure love welled up inside of him, pricking his eyeballs again.

"Maddie, you're beautiful… So beautiful."

"Blake… Ahh." Her breathless voice tugged at him.

Slowly, he lowered his mouth to her folds. Tasting her as if she were fine wine.

Her hips bucked on contact and she gasped loudly.

"Oh God, Blake. You feel so good."

"Tell me more, Maddie." He spoke into her folds, letting his breath vibrate over her.

"That. OhmyGod, *that.* Do it again."

"You mean like this?"

"Yes, yes. The ladies were right."

Ladies? What was she talking about?

As if she read his mind. "The party… Prairie Posse ladies said this was the best," she panted between little high-pitched sighs. "OhmyGod, they were right."

Prairie Posse? What the hell was she talking about? He laughed into her folds, buzzing her clit. She clutched his head closer.

What else could he tell her? "I love your pussy, Maddie." He placed his lips over her clit. "You taste like heaven."

Her hips took on a rhythm all their own, which he tried to match with his own movements. He took the flat of his tongue and slowly licked from her clit to the opening where her ecstasy flowed out like honey. He lapped it up, diving and swirling in time to the rolling of her hips. He worked his way back up, diving into her folds, tasting. Loving.

Her clit stood at attention, and he circled first in one direction, then the other, finishing with the flat of his tongue sliding over the very point. Finally, when it seemed like she couldn't take much more, he placed his lips over her bud and sucked.

Gently.

Slowly.

"Blake. Oh, ooooh. Blake." Her cries penetrated the

deepest part of his soul. Triumph bubbled up, as he kept sucking and using his tongue to help her ride her waves.

Yearning stirred in his balls. He had to give her more. To prolong this moment, this… whatever it was that was happening in the moonlight.

He lifted his head to take her in. Sweat glistened across her body, only serving to make her appear more magic.

"Maddie." His voice sounded rough to his own ears. "I want you."

Her eyes, dark pools of lust, captured his.

"I want you more than I've ever wanted anything… anyone." A wave of emotion lodged in his throat. He couldn't speak.

"You have me."

When she smiled and reached for him, it spilled over. He couldn't contain it. His lips met hers, and he plunged his tongue into her mouth, tasting, taking. Giving. He had to be inside her. Now. He had to give her this… this whateveritwas that was pouring from him. His body couldn't contain it.

He pushed his pants down, his cock thick and hard again. For her. There had only ever been her. In his whole messed-up secret-filled life, there had only ever been her. He moved over her and stopped, the head of his cock hovering outside her entrance.

She gazed up at him, hands twining around his neck. It was more than he could take. This emotion that hunted him down like he was nothing more than a scared rabbit.

He stared at her in wonder. There was humor behind the heat in her eyes. And something else. Something deeper. Something that arrowed straight into his soul and lodged itself there.

"What are you waiting for?" Her breathy voice and expectant half-smile did cartwheels in his chest.

"Maddie…I… I…"

She tilted her hips up and brought a finger to his lips. "Shhh. Don't talk."

His heart squeezed.

He kissed her gently, savoring the contour of her mouth as he slowly entered her. Little grunty noises came from the back of her throat as she wiggled her hips while her tongue slid over his, and it took everything he had to not thrust hard and deep.

To prolong this moment.

This wonder.

Goddamn, she was tight. And so fucking hot. And wet. The squeeze on his shaft when she clenched him for the first time made his breath catch. So. Fucking. Good. He pushed deeper until he was fully sheathed and enveloped in her heat.

He lifted his head so that he could see her eyes. He had to see her eyes. Wanted to see her reaction as he slowly pulled out and slammed home.

He reached up and grabbed one of her hands, twining his fingers with hers and bringing them to his chest.

"I want to watch you, Maddie."

Her eyes widened, but she held his gaze.

Steady and clear.

He slowly pulled out again, and thrust home. Her tongue flitted out, wetting her lower lip. A little moan escaped, as she rolled her hips again.

"Blake…" She bit her lip, but held his gaze.

With every breath, with every slow delicious thrust, his heart filled with wonder, and yes, love. He put every ounce of love he felt for her into his movement.

She matched his rhythm, clenching and unclenching his

shaft, and rolling her hips in a way that sent his eyes rolling into his skull.

"Is this good for you?" he grunted. His voice thickened with emotion. "I want this to be good for you, Maddie."

"Oh God yes, Blake." Her eyes widened. "I… you're… yes, oh, yes."

She shut her eyes and arched her back, her body shuddering underneath him. Her pussy convulsed around him, driving a bolt of lust straight to his balls, and igniting a white-hot fire. And still, he forced himself to move slowly. Although it was getting harder with each thrust to not give in to the urge to plunder her mercilessly and completely.

She opened her eyes, her mouth shaped into an O. She clutched at his shoulder, her fingernails digging into the flesh. "Blake, oh… oh… don't… stop." Her hips rolled wildly and her breath came in nothing but pants.

The tightening in his balls reached critical mass, and he began to thrust more forcefully. Her walls tightened around him, rippling, and a groan burst from his throat as his own orgasm erupted like a meteor exploding across the night sky.

"Maddie."

His cries mingled with hers. He shut his eyes tight as the fireworks in his heart exploded with his body. *Iloveyou, Iloveyou, Iloveyou, Iloveyou.*

CHAPTER 23

THE TABLE AT the Hansen house was loud and noisy. Martha passed Maddie a plate piled high with roasted chicken and green beans. Instead of her traditional biscuits and gravy, she'd made a big salad from the corner garden. Martha had pulled out all the stops to welcome Warren home. Even their cousin Parker had come this evening. He was a local firefighter and medic who worked most Sundays. When he had extra time, he also helped out at Hansen Stables.

Warren was moving on his own, but his color was still pale. And his tall frame looked frail next to the big young men.

Parker peered at her over the mashed potatoes. "Boys were trying to explain to me what you're doing in Chicago."

She took another bite of juicy chicken before answering. "Well, it is rather complicated."

"She spends her time looking in telescopes with sissies from fancy schools," Warren interjected crossly.

"Glad to see your tongue has recovered, Dad. Dinner wouldn't be the same without it." Why did he always have to put her on the defensive where her career was concerned? She turned back to Parker. "I work at a lab that studies particle physics." She squeezed Blake's hand under the table. "It also happens to have a buffalo herd."

"Bison." Her cousins corrected in unison.

"Geez, Maddie Jane. If you're going to marry a rancher, at least get the lingo right," Axel teased. Martha didn't allow cursing at the table.

"Mumbo jumbo," Warren muttered under his breath.

"Dad." She didn't bother to keep the edge out of her voice. "I'm very proud of the work I do. Our research is leading to huge advances not only in quantum field theory, but in practical applications. It's being used to develop life saving medical devices."

Out of the corner of her eye, she saw Blake lean forward with interest. The little movement warmed her to her toes. "I actually spend more time with my head bent over mathematical equations and models than I do peering into a telescope. Although I love nothing more than looking through a telescope."

She smiled over at her uncle. "You remember when I found that telescope in the attic and you brought it down and set it up for me?"

He nodded. "You were a little bit of a thing."

"Yeah. I think I was six. At any rate, I knew that day that I wanted to be a scientist."

Martha reached over and grabbed her hand. "We're so proud of you too, honey. And so happy you're coming home."

"Well, I do have to get back to the lab soon. There's a project I'm working on, and I don't have the equipment to finish it here."

Warren's head popped up. "What do you mean yer leavin? You just got here."

"I've been here too long, dad. And given your condition, I can't afford to get fired."

"Yer place is here. With your man."

Warren narrowed his eyes and swung his gaze to Blake,

who met his gaze straight on. She admired how he handled himself around her father. Most people, other than the ones at this table, were afraid of him.

"Dad, I'm not going to get into this with you here. You don't know anything about what I do. And where I do it is my business."

"And his." He tilted his head at Blake.

He was as stubborn as a mule. She tamped down hard on the resentment that was building inside. There was no reasoning with him when he got an idea into his head.

"Besides, everyone knows you can't make a marriage work when yer not in the same place. What about babies?"

She swallowed, rapidly losing patience and trying to keep her voice even. "What about them?"

"You pregnant yet? It's high time you were."

Martha shifted uncomfortably in her seat. "Now, Warren, they're not even married. Give them some space."

"With all due respect, sir," Blake interjected. "That's none of your damned business."

Her heart lifted a fraction. At least someone was in her corner. It warmed her that it was him.

Warren turned on him. "Like hell it isn't. It's high time she quit her job and settled down to raise children."

"Who died and made you expert?" Her voice rose and she didn't care. "You're the poster child for an ornery cuss. No wonder you never remarried after mom died." She'd be damned if she let Warren meddle any further.

Blake flashed her a sympathetic look, and turned to her uncle. "You've been married the longest, sir. What do you have to say?"

Eddie wiped his face with his napkin. "Nothing. When you've been married as long as I have, you learn to keep your mouth shut."

She'd have laughed if she wasn't so angry. She cast a glance at Blake. He smiled and winked at her. So he thought this was entertaining?

"Maddie knows her own mind, and that's enough for me."

Gunnar looked at him sharply. "Since when did you get all soft?"

"Not soft. Just practical."

"Seriously, Maddie Jane. Why are you wasting your time doing all that science stuff anyhow?" Axel grunted between bites. "Not like your bosses are gonna let you bring a baby to work." He pinned her with an intent look. "Kids need to be raised outside, learning real things. Not have their nose stuck in a telescope all the time."

White-hot anger and indignation bolted through her. "Are you kidding me?" she cried out, standing, before reining herself in again. She lowered her voice, but couldn't keep the surprise from it. "You are kidding, right?" She looked to each of them.

Oh God. They weren't kidding. Unbelievable. She was related to a bunch of cavemen.

"How about some coffee and pie?" Martha interjected brightly, standing. "Nothing that a little pie won't cure."

"This conversation is over." She swept her gaze haughtily around the table. "Auntie M, I don't know how you manage to keep your sanity around these… these *Neanderthals*." She tossed the napkin she'd been clutching on the chair and turned on her heel, rushing to the door.

She needed to escape. Her anger burned so hot she couldn't see straight. The screen door slammed behind her as she stepped across the expanse of porch and clutched the railing, gasping for deep breaths of air. Bitter disappointment welled up and settled below her breastbone. She'd expected more from them. Especially her cousins. She didn't understand how they could be so backward in their thinking. It was truly stunning.

The screen door opened and footsteps moved toward her. She refused to turn around. Refused to let whoever it was see her cry. Two arms circled her from behind. Blake's unmistakable scent of leather and pine, sweet hay and musk, overwhelmed her.

Bringing relief.

And comfort.

He stayed silent, just holding her. Slowly, her breathing settled to his, and she let herself lean back into him, to rest in his strength.

"Maddie. You know I'll never ask you to give up what you love." His voice was gentle and low in her ear. "You love what you do, don't you?"

"Yes… Deeply." Emotion threatened to overwhelm her.

"And…"

"It's complicated." And becoming more so every day.

"What part of life isn't?" He stayed silent. As if waiting for her to continue.

"I have ideas. Thoughts. Hypotheses I want to explore. With people who will give me the space to think, not just regurgitate formulas I could work out in my sleep."

"What about teaching?"

She laughed bitterly. "Where scientists go to die?"

"Some teaching positions are research based."

"How do you know so much about my field?"

He sighed against her. "Are you happy where you are?"

She shrugged. "I guess. I love my research. I have my

horse."

"That doesn't sound like the answer of a happy person."

So he'd caught the hesitation in her voice. "I didn't have a very happy childhood. It was easier to cope by throwing my life into things that are quantifiable. Predictable."

"But maybe now you're not so sure?"

"Well… I don't know. You scare me Blake." The confession slipped easily from her. He got her. "You make me want things I don't know how to compartmentalize."

He nuzzled her neck, kissing her in the sensitive spot below her ear, sending hot shivers through her body. "Like what?"

Anxiety twisted with hope, and the two expanded in her chest, making it hard to breathe. "Companionship… I guess."

"And hot sex…" His breath tickled in her ear.

"Ha. You're pervy."

"Hmmm." He peppered little kisses along her jaw, weakening her defenses. "Maybe I am. At least where you're concerned. I'm a lot of things where you're concerned, Maddie."

Her insides grew warm and tingly. Like a coal had been placed inside her chest and was cooking her from the inside out. Melting her.

"Ask for what you want, Maddie. Anything. If it's within my power…"

Ridiculous as it was, his offer touched her. Was this the real Blake? Tender, funny, chivalrous? It tore at her. All of this… whateveritwas… would be ending in a few more days. Her father was home, and she needed to get back to Chicago. But she didn't want to go, and that tore at her too.

She felt like she was falling through a wormhole in her heart. The more she fought it, the harder it pulled her down.

Was she brave enough to surrender?

He chuckled again.

She loved his laughter. The way it slid over her like melted butter.

"Stop thinking, Maddie. We'll figure it out. Whatever *it* is. Together."

The creaking of the screen door and the clearing of a throat broke them apart. But Blake kept his arm around her.

Warren stepped outside and narrowed his eyes. "You two get yerselves sorted out?"

She prayed to the Gods he hadn't been there long. She wouldn't put it past him to meddle. It certainly wouldn't be the first time he'd wreaked havoc in her life.

She put on a wide smile for his benefit. "Of course, Dad. There was nothing to sort out."

"Good. Good." He cleared his throat again. "A word with your man if you don't mind."

"What could the two of you possibly have to talk about that doesn't concern me?

"Jes a little man talk. Now run on in and help Martha."

Her radar was up in an instant. He was scheming again. She just knew it. Every instinct in her body told her he was meddling. "Dad."

He turned to her. There was something going on all right. He looked innocent. Too innocent. She glared at him. She mustered her most authoritative, no-nonsense voice. "No meddling. I won't tolerate it. Understand?"

His eyes widened innocently and he shook his head. "Sweetheart, I'm just having a little man to man with your fiancé."

"Don't sweetheart me. I know what you're capable of."

She shot a glance at Blake, who appeared distinctly uncomfortable. "Let me know if he gets out of hand okay?"

He nodded and she turned to go into the house. She had a bad feeling about this.

CHAPTER 24

BLAKE WAITED TO speak until Maddie had shut the screen door behind her. "Walk with me." Warren had stretched his patience beyond the breaking point. He turned on his heel and stepped off the porch, heading down to the corral.

He measured his pace so the old man could keep up without asking for help. They both knew exactly where this conversation was headed. It was time he took the reins in this unholy mess before Maddie got hurt.

He stepped up to the rail and grabbed it, seeking strength from the steel beneath his fingers. A moment later Warren joined him, panting. Damn. He'd gone too fast. Guilt stabbed through the anger. He shouldn't have made him walk so far so soon.

"Need to rest up a bit?"

Warren shook his head. "Nope. Doc wants me to walk. Even if it hurts."

The silence stretched between them. Two palomino brood mares munched lazily on the grass at the center of the pen, their bellies full and round. They'd be foaling soon.

"Say what you want to say, son." Maybe the old man figured out he'd pushed too far at the dinner table.

"You were out of line back there."

Warren stiffened. "Says who?"

"Says me."

"Hmmph."

"Maddie's my responsibility now, and you won't say anything to her that upsets her."

Warren side-eyed him, a sly smile playing at his mouth. "Who says it upset her?"

God, if Warren was anyone but Maddie's father, he'd have laid him flat by now. What Warren needed was a good pounding.

"For a poker player, you sure are dumb when it comes to your daughter."

"I know what's best for her."

"No. You don't."

"Well you sure don't."

The coal of anger flared up, and Blake tamped it down. He would not give in this time. "What century are you living in, Warren? Wake up. Maddie's her own person."

"Is she staying here?"

So he was changing the subject. He could try, but Warren was not getting the upper hand this time.

"We're sorting things out."

A triumphant gleam developed in Warren's eye. Shit. Maybe he shouldn't have been honest. But he was tired of living in a world of half-truths and manufactured misunderstandings. He couldn't do it anymore. Especially where Maddie was concerned.

"So you haven't held up your end of our agreement then."

"You collapsed in my arms before we could make an agreement."

"Well where's the ring on her finger then? How you gonna keep her if she doesn't have a ring?

Blake clenched the railing and took a steadying breath,

turning to look Warren dead in the eye. "I have done *more* than enough to honor any agreement we *might* have had. Dammit, Warren. I'm the reason you're still alive and down here giving me hell." He clamped down his jaw so tight it hurt.

Warren drew himself up with a challenge in his eye. "If she's not stayin' then you haven't done shit, son."

Not even a thank you. Not that he expected it. Not from him.

"If she's not staying *yet*," he gritted out. "It's because I've given her space to sort through her feelings."

"Huh." Warren snorted. "Have you gone soft, son? That's not how you handle women."

Jesus Christ on a pogo stick. He wanted to pound Warren so badly he clenched the rails until his knuckles turned white. If he didn't rope in his anger, Warren would best him.

He turned and focused it on the man in front of him. "And I should take a lesson from your playbook on how to handle women?"

Warren narrowed his eyes and opened his mouth to speak, but Blake lifted his hand to stop him. "That's your problem, Warren. You *don't* know how to handle women. You only know how to push and prod and manipulate. And that stops here. Now."

"Pah." Warren turned and spit, then looked at him slyly. "Don't you think yer the pot calling the kettle black?"

Realization hit Blake like a locomotive. No wonder Maddie railed at him. Didn't trust him. Too often, he'd behaved like her fucking father. God*dammit.*

"When have you ever considered someone's feelings besides your own Warren?"

"When I loved your mother."

"What?" Blake's head reeled back like Warren had slapped him.

"I think Maddie's mother, Janie Danielle knew it, too. Told me she was lettin' me go when she died." Warren's eyes grew bleak. "Your father had everything I wanted. Amelia... land... a son. There was a time when we both loved her. But she made her choice." He turned to Blake, anguish and anger swirling in his eyes. Maddie's eyes. "I hated him."

Blake's stomach dropped like he'd been sucker punched. Warren turned away, staring off toward the creek and the Sinclaire ranch.

"I wanted to make him pay. I thought about seducing your mother, but I didn't want to be like him. Dishonorable."

Blake clenched his jaw in an effort to hold himself in check. Everyone knew Jake Sinclaire had been an SOB. He'd been the recipient of enough pitying glances growing up to figure out at an early age the havoc his father wreaked around town. A sick sensation settled in the pit of his stomach. Warren was laying a trap, bringing up all this old history. And like a fool, he was walking right in.

"Your mother came to me that summer. Asked for help. You were already gone. But she had no money to feed the others."

Blake stiffened. The memory of his mother, crying over the sink when she thought no one was looking rose, unbidden.

"I gave her the money. She gave me the deed. But she knew Jake would beat her six ways to Sunday if he found out. So in one of his drunken rages he came over and challenged me to a game of poker."

The rest was history. Bile rose up the back of his throat. He didn't think much about Jake Sinclaire anymore, but he didn't recall hating him more than at that moment.

Warren's eyes narrowed. "How'd you convince Maddie to marry you?"

Alarm bells started to go off. Shit. Maddie would be beside herself if Warren had overheard their conversation.

"None of your business." He stepped forward, bringing the toes of his boots flush with Warren's and he stood fiercely, waiting for Warren to look him dead on. "And for the record… If you do anything, *anything* to cause her pain." He allowed the threat to hang in the air. "You will answer to me personally… And I guarandamntee you, it won't be pleasant."

Dislike flashed through Warren's eyes. "And why should I answer to you?"

"Because I love her, you sonofabitch. And I want her to be happy."

Hell and damnation.

That hadn't exactly gone as planned. Warren stayed silent, his glare fading from animosity to assessing. "Hmmph."

Blake turned back to the rail, studying the mares. He wasn't sure who had the upper hand. But he knew how to get it back this time.

"Tomorrow my lawyer will be delivering a note to your bank for the full assessed value of the land we lost. I expect the deed to be waiting." He spoke flatly. There would be no negotiating with Warren. Not anymore. "And to cover only the property on the Sinclaire side of the river. The Hansen side can stay with your family. Deed it to Maddie if you like."

He turned to Warren, letting the full force of his anger vent. "And in one week's time, we'll be breaking ground on a hunting lodge. If you do anything to stop it or so much as hint to Maddie about any understanding we may or may not have had, I. Will. Crush. You."

Warren's head snapped back. "Think you can buy me off?" he snarled.

"I am giving you an out. A means of financial independence. To pay your bills and keep your part of the disputed land…and a means to keep your relationship with your daughter intact."

Blake stood there, clenching and unclenching his fist. He'd turned the tables on Warren, but wouldn't put it past him to turn the tables right back. The old man was wily as a fox. And Blake had definitely provoked him.

Warren stood tall, his jaw clenching and unclenching, loathing radiating from eyes that belonged to Maddie. It unnerved him.

"Warren. This isn't an equal sum game. You're not losing anything." He shook his head. "Hell, you're gaining everything."

"Am I?" For a moment, Warren's eyes went bleak.

Jesus, did he have to spell it out for him? "What have you lost, Warren?"

He waited for the answer.

None came.

Blake waited one more beat. "You haven't lost a damned thing. You've gained, and you know it." He narrowed his eyes at Warren. "You once told me a gambler knows when to walk away from the table. Are you taking your winnings or are you going to drag Maddie into this?"

God help Warren if that's what he did. Blake wasn't sure he could hold back if that was his answer. The silence crackled between them. Everything in his body stilled. He didn't think Warren would deck him, but he was ready to react.

"What would my mother tell you?"

"Hhmph."

After what seemed like an eternity, the fight went out of Warren. His shoulders sagged, and suddenly he had the look of a tired, old man. Blake let out the breath he didn't realize he'd been holding.

"We're not done. You and me." Warren speared him with a fierce look. "I still want a grandchild."

"And you'll have a much better chance of that if you stop meddling."

"Who says I'm meddling?"

Blake snorted. "Tell yourself whatever you like. But you know what I mean. Now if you'll excuse me, I've got to get on home and attend to my own livestock."

He reached out and clasped Warren by the shoulder as he passed by. The old cuss would be the death of him. He was a loose cannon who would never be contained.

Blake trudged up the hill, lost in his thoughts. Now that he had the family land back, could he keep Warren under control long enough to convince Maddie to stay?

He didn't want her to go back to Chicago.

Didn't think she wanted to, either.

At least he hoped not.

Hell, if she was willing, he'd even commute. His work took him out of town often enough, laying over in Chicago would be manageable. Being with her had been heaven. He'd glimpsed a future he'd never even allowed himself to imagine, thanks to Jake. As he stepped across the back porch and placed his hand on the screen door, he paused. Maddie's laughter filled the kitchen with a warmth that settled in his gut. Home.

She turned, laughter still in her eyes. "Oh good. You're back. Gonna come in?"

He nodded, not trusting himself to speak.

"How'd your manly conversation go?"

He shrugged. "How do you think it went? It's your dad."

"Say no more." She wrapped her arms around him, standing on tiptoe to place a kiss on his chin. She narrowed her eyes suspiciously. "You okay?"

The urge to tell her he loved her hit him square in the gut. He nodded, beating back the urge to the corners of his psyche. Not here. Not now.

"So I was thinking," she traced her fingers up the buttons of his chest, sending delicious sensations straight to his cock. "Why don't I help you with the remaining chores, and then we can hit the Trading Post?"

His mouth went dry. He cleared his throat, concentrating on her words not her fingers, touched by her offer to help.

"Sure you want to go back after last time?"

She shrugged, a small smile forming.

"Yeah. Things are, um, different now."

They certainly were. Making love had changed everything. Like flipping a switch. Loaded banter had been replaced by an easy intimacy. The touches and glances between them were no longer manufactured, but spontaneous expressions of feeling.

He caressed her cheek with his knuckles, losing himself in the deep blue pools of her eyes. "I have a better idea."

She leaned on tiptoe to whisper in his ear. "Does it involve removing our clothes?"

His cock jerked straight to attention. He smiled slowly and waggled his eyebrows. "Perhaps."

"Then let's get out of here."

The question still burned in him as he kissed her forehead. Was he brave enough to tell Maddie his deepest, darkest secret?

CHAPTER 25

BLAKE THREW HIS weight against the weathered old door. On the second try, the swollen wood gave way to a dark, musty interior. He shined the flashlight around the small space. Except for a fine covering of dust, the room appeared clean and tidy, and Maddie caught glimpses of a large stone fireplace similar to the hearth in the Big House.

She'd been surprised when he'd suggested coming to the homestead instead of hitting the Trading Post. But now that they were here, away from the prying eyes of family and friends, she felt like she could breathe a little easier, be a little more free. Now that they were… whateveritwas… she found herself appreciating more and more the time they spent alone.

"Is there a light in here?"

He stepped into the space, flashing the light back and forth. "There should be an oil lamp… here." He brought it to the center of a little wooden table, and dug his bag for a lighter. He lit the wick and brought down the hurricane, casting the room in an antique glow.

He grinned over at her. "So this is it. This is where the Sinclaire legacy began."

"It's so tiny."

"Pascal, Stands With Eagles, and their two small children lived here until Pascal built the Big House."

She turned, taking in the full room. A bed frame was

centered under a window against one wall, the little table directly across from it under another window. "It's the perfect hideaway."

"It's been used for that before. Whenever we kids had to get away from Jake or sort out a problem, we'd come here. I'm sure the boys snuck a few girlfriends here too."

"Did you?" Her heart thumped loudly in her chest, jealousy pooling in the pit of her stomach. Why did it matter so much what he did long before he knew her? Before they'd fallen in love.

Her knees buckled and she reached for the back of a chair for support as she fell into the realization like a rocket booster plummeting back to earth.

She loved him.

He studied her intently, like he could see through everything to the deepest part of her soul.

A lazy smile curved his mouth. God, she loved that mouth. The feel of his lips on her skin, on her mouth, on her clit. "Only you, Maddie. You're the only one."

Relief flooded her.

He was her only one for so many things. And rapidly, she was coming to depend on him. To offer counsel and support when her father was ornery, to ask questions about the equations she was solving. He sought her advice about the daily operations of the ranch. He valued her opinion. They'd become partners in addition to lovers.

And strangely, surprisingly, she was unafraid. In her mind's eye, she could see their lives moving forward, in the same rhythm they'd developed over the last few weeks. But she didn't live here. Couldn't stay here.

A wave of grief stabbed through her at the thought of this finally coming to an end. That day was fast approaching. Her father's coloring and energy were improving quickly. In the next few days, she'd have to make plans to return to work. A lump lodged itself in her throat like a fish bone, and for a moment, she couldn't breathe.

Grateful for the dim light, she grabbed the container of wipes he'd brought with them and began cleaning off the table with a ferocity that surprised her.

He turned, calling over his shoulder. "I'll get a fire going. Weather's moving in, we're in for a doozy tonight."

She'd learned to trust his instincts about storms. So far, he'd been spot on. While he knelt in front of the fire, she moved to the chairs, wiping and cleaning, trying to focus her jumbled thoughts.

Should she tell him?

She'd never told anyone except a family member she'd loved them. Not even Marcus.

Did he already know?

How would she even bring it up? Was she better off keeping it to herself?

She knew he loved her. He'd said it. Granted, it was in the heat of the moment, and he hadn't said it since, but she'd heard him, plain as day. His declaration had surprised her, opened her, softened her. And as she studied the evidence in the following days, she was confident he did.

It no longer mattered that he'd held back about Kylee. It was obviously water under the bridge for him. And someday, maybe, he'd tell her. Her parents had kept secrets from each other. Even as a little girl, she'd been able to tell. Maybe it was an uncomfortable part of loving someone.

"Stop thinking, Maddie." His arms enveloped her and he removed the wipe from her hand. Turning her around, he cradled her face in his hands, and brought his lips to hers. She sighed into them, savoring his scent, and the way his lips brought immediate hyperawareness to every nerve ending.

He nibbled the corner of her mouth, his tongue flicking out. She opened, receiving him. Sliding her tongue with his in a slow dance that had her core heating like the fire in the hearth.

He lifted his head and a needy little sigh escaped. "Want to talk about it?"

"Mmm mm," she groaned shaking her head. "I want to kiss."

His low laughter warmed her straight to her toes. "Greedy little thing you've become, haven't you?"

She twined her hand around his neck, pulling his mouth to hers. "Yes," she sighed. "I have needs you know. Lots of them."

His hands caressed her hip, flowing over her ass and pulling her close. She rolled her hips into him, reveling in his sudden hiss. So she wasn't the only one hot and bothered.

He pulled away, studying her intently.

Instantly, her guard went up. "What? What is it?"

Did he bring her here to tell her it was over? Time to cool things off since she was leaving soon? Her stomach sank to her toes like a rock.

He drew the back of his finger across her cheek, capturing a wayward strand and twining it around his finger. "You're a marvel, you know? A bundle of contradictions."

Her heart gave a little kick. Where was he going with this?

He tugged on her hand. "Come here. Sit for a second."

He led her to one of the chairs, then knelt between the bags he'd brought, and pulled out two compressed air mats and a pillow. The other bag held two fluffy blankets, two plastic cups, and a bottle of chilled champagne. Light flickered outside the window, followed a few seconds later by rumbling in the distance.

"Blake, what is this?" She couldn't stop the grin from spreading across her face.

He arranged the mats and blankets in front of the fire, then unwrapped the bottle and popped the top, catching the bubbles in one of the glasses. He poured out a little more and handed her a glass. He poured out some for himself then patted the floor.

"Just showing you that cowboys can be romantic on occasion."

She removed her glasses, leaving them on the little table and joined him on the floor, snuggling up to him. He bent his head, giving her a lingering kiss, tongue curling with hers. She could taste the spikey bite of the champagne. She brought her hand to his face, delighting in the sandpaper feel of his end of day stubble.

The thought of that scraping her most sensitive skin sent a jolt of heat to her crux. With every kiss, she fell deeper into this… whateveritwas. With every kiss, she grew more and more unable to crawl out of the hole she'd dug for her heart.

Keeping his mouth on hers, he began to undo the buttons on her shirt. When she moved to help him, his hand stilled her. "Let me, sweet," he muttered into her lips. "Sit back and enjoy."

He brought his lips to her neck, nuzzling and nipping the sensitive spot underneath her ear. Her nipples puckered in her bra and she arched into him, sighing.

After only a week, he'd mapped her body. Memorizing where and how she was most sensitive.

When he'd worked the buttons off, he began caressing her skin in lazy circles. Skimming inside her pants, then working his way across her body and up her ribs until he stopped at the edge of the lacy material of her bra.

Heat oozed through her, making her limbs slow and languid, as his hands left a trail of goosebumps across her torso. She expected his thumb to dive under the material, but instead he traced the swell of her breast, circling her nipple through the lace, hardening it further. A sigh escaped as he flicked this thumb back and forth. Kissing the corner of her mouth, he slowly drew off her shirt and sat back.

"You're glorious, all golden in the firelight. Your hair looks like a halo."

The sincerity in his voice set her pulse thrumming.

"First I'm seductive in silver, now I'm glorious and gold?" She reached behind and unhooked her bra.

"Exactly. A lovely contradiction."

She reached up to remove the strap, but his hand covered hers. "Let me."

The straps whispered down her arms while the lace lingered a moment on her swells, before slipping into her lap. His breath hissed as he brought his fingers up to lightly caress her fullness. The heat from the fire licked at her, sending bumps skittering across her skin.

Light flashed, brightening the room, thunder on its heels. She started. "Storm's here."

Rain opened up on the cabin, drumming on the roof the way her blood drummed in her ears.

He shifted, reaching for the pillow. "Lie back, love." The blankets were cool against her inflamed skin as he helped her settle back. Giving her a slow, sexy smile, he removed his shirt and tossed it next to hers.

He hovered over her, eyes boring into her with intensity. Her skin heated and pulled tight. He traced her with his fingertips, bringing them to rest on the button of her pants. Her breath caught in anticipation.

He slipped a finger inside her waistband, slipping it back and forth before undoing the button and releasing the zipper. Her pussy clenched and heat pooled between her legs. Holding her gaze, he lowered his head, lips caressing just above the lace of her panties. Pinpricks of sensation zoomed straight to her clit.

"Lift your hips, love," he murmured into her skin, still not taking his eyes away from hers.

Each time he said 'love' a tiny thrill swirled through her. Her heart swelled, pressing up inside her. The way he touched her with such care, such tenderness, pierced her. She lifted her hips as an offering. He shimmied off her pants and the scrap of lace, tossing them aside, and brought her hips back down to rest on the pillow.

Lightning and thunder crashed around them. The sound on the roof increased to deafening. But here inside the tiny hideaway, they were ensconced in their own rising storm.

He slipped his hand inside her thigh, caressing down her leg. The movement sent licks of electricity to her clit. She dropped her head back, momentarily lost in the sensation.

"Open for me?" He put pressure on her knee. The words, the simple request, fired her nerve endings in waves, jolting through her like lightning. She dropped her knees, opening her body. She melted under the intensity of his gaze. He hadn't even touched her, yet the pressure built and twisted in her belly.

He slipped between her open knees, caressing her legs in long, firm strokes, each time edging higher, closer to her folds. His eyes raked over her, leaving a trail of goosebumps across her body. She rocked her hips involuntarily.

"Lie still, love."

"I… can't." She bit her lip to keep from moaning.

His low chuckle scraped over her, tightening her nipples, and settling in her aching clit.

He placed a kiss on the inside of her thigh, sucking, then licking the spot with his tongue. At the same time, he brought his thumb to her slit, stroking from entrance to nub, slowly swirling over her clit until it became hard and swollen. Her hips bucked wildly and she cried out, arching.

His lips curled into a smile against her leg. "Shh, love. I'm just getting started." He continued to work his thumb up and down her slit, circling her clit each time he neared, spreading her creamy desire. "So beautiful, so much passion inside you. Let it out, Madison." There was a softness, a reverence, in the way he said her name. Like a prayer.

She gripped the blankets beside her, trying to catch her breath. Her body was no longer her own. And then he was there. His breath tickled her folds, and she gasped, unable to breathe. His hands came up under her knees and entwined with hers.

"I'm right here, love."

She couldn't tell if the buzzing in her ears was the storm outside or the one in her body. Every cell waited in hot anticipation.

He nuzzled the juncture of leg and folds, slowly running his tongue along the outside of her pussy. It took all her concentration to not clench his head between her legs and hold on for dear life. She clutched his hands as her breath came in small gasps.

He slid his tongue up her mound and across, taking his time and avoiding the place she most wanted him to touch. She arched toward him hungrily.

"We have all night long," he murmured into her skin, sending additional ripples of delight coursing through her. "I intend to take my time. No hurrying tonight." She bit back a needy groan. The anticipation was sweet torture.

He released one of her hands, bringing his to her belly, massaging her legs and mound, sweeping her sensitized clit from the top. Heat flushed her like a fever raging through her body. Simultaneously hot and trembling with want.

"I love you, Maddie," he whispered into her skin. She lifted her head, seeking his eyes. "Your fire, your passion." Keeping his eyes on her, he lowered his mouth to her wet folds, sliding his tongue up and bringing it to rest on her clit.

Tears pricked her eyes as she cried out. She reached for him, threading her fingers through his dark waves, caressing his cheek. Emotion broke over her as she rolled under him, unable to tear her eyes from his, locked into his clear gaze like a tractor beam.

She loved this man with every atom in her body.

He slid his tongue over her folds, returning to the deep place inside her to lap more of her, sweeping back up to circle her clit. He moved his head and she arched, grinding into him, her body begging for more. He pressed on her mound, his hand massaging and caressing everywhere at once in long strokes that mirrored the work of his mouth.

There was no more talk. Only little sighs and grunts. She squeezed the hand she held, letting her body move with his head as the tension built and took her higher. As he scraped his teeth lightly over her sensitized nub, she broke, crying out. Her sounds drowned by the cacophony of the storm overhead. And still he moved. Slipping his tongue through her wet folds, maintaining a constant suction, he helped her ride her orgasm to the very end.

As her breathing slowed, he laid his head on her belly, still holding her hand, and caressing her in lazy circles with the other. She wove her fingers through his thick hair, wanting to touch him, be a part of him.

Overhead, the rain still pounded, but the thunder began to recede. Inside, the only sound was the crackle of the fire, and their mingled breaths.

If she could capture this moment and bottle it up, she would. Here, in this place they'd christened with their bodies, the rest of the world stood at bay. She felt more herself than at any other moment. Ever.

He lifted his eyes to hers. Their hazel depths soft and full in the light of the fire.

"I love you." It slipped from her, quiet as a breath. Unbidden. His eyes crinkled at the corners. She said it more firmly. "I love you, Blake."

He shifted up on an elbow, and scooted closer. They untangled their hands, and she brought hers to his face, caressing each curve and crevice, imprinting his features into her memory.

He captured a strand of her hair, winding then unwinding it. Studying the way it curled over his fingers. He exhaled heavily, then brought his eyes back to her. "I have no right to ask this. But I will."

She stilled, her heart beating wildly in her chest.

He looked down at his fingers again, still wrapped in her hair. Her toes and fingers suddenly went numb as the blood rushed inward with a surge of adrenaline. When he looked up again, he looked… afraid. But only for the tiniest of moments.

"Stay?"

The word hung between them. Suspended like a planet in orbit.

"How?"

How could she stay and leave her work? How could she go back to the lab and leave him? Her heart twisted in slow, sinking knots.

He shrugged. His eyes as intense and determined as the receding storm.

"Maddie… I…" He pulled her hand to his heart. "I don't want you to go." His words came out in a breathless rush.

"I don't want to leave," she whispered.

"We can figure this out… Can't we?"

Hope bloomed in her chest. Pushing out fear, swelling and pressing, demanding to be acknowledged.

"This isn't rocket science."

Her smile wavered. "It's harder."

"You're the smartest woman I know. We can find a way. I'm sure of it." His voice grew stronger, more urgent.

"What about my family?"

He gave her hand a little squeeze. "We can handle them. Together."

His conviction touched and terrified her.

Blake brought his hand to her face, caressing her cheek, coming to rest under her chin. He tilted her face up.

"Please… Maddie." His eyes showed the determination of a man who would not be thwarted. "I want to be with you. Don't we deserve to give our love a chance?"

"I…" All the excuses of why this couldn't possibly work, why it wasn't rational or logical or practical, disintegrated in the face of the answer of her heart. She loved him and wanted to be with him.

"Yes." She nodded. "Yes." An ache expanded into her throat and she couldn't say more.

Relief flashed through his eyes. And joy. He crushed his

lips to hers, tumbling them both to the floor. He rolled her on top of him, his hands stroking her back.

"I know it won't be easy, but we can figure it out."

She silenced him with her mouth. Pressing her lips to his and sweeping her tongue inside. He still tasted of her. "Tomorrow." She mumbled against his lips. "Tomorrow. Want… you… now."

He growled in the back of his throat and rolled them over again, pressing his hips to hers. The denim on her still sensitized clit immediately set her need flowing again. She reached for his zipper, thrusting a hand inside to stroke him as he wriggled out of his jeans.

She brought her other hand down to cup his balls. Stroking and pulling, as she gently stroked his rigid shaft. He groaned and thrust further into her hand.

He brought his mouth to her breast, pulling on her hardened nipple, rolling it with his tongue before sucking hard. She arched toward him, giving him more of herself to take into his mouth.

She swept her thumb across the head of his cock, smearing the slick drop of precome across his slit and down the underside where it was most sensitive. He groaned onto her nipple as he thrust into her hand. The vibrations from his mouth sent ripples careening directly to her aching clit, restarting the upward spiral of ecstasy.

"Need you… Inside me… Can't wait." Her breath came in quick pants, she wanted to seal this commitment with her body as well as her heart.

Blake lifted his head. His eyes held a fire she'd never seen. "You're mine, Maddie." In one strong movement, he thrust to the hilt, his balls coming to rest on her slick folds. "Don't forget it."

His voice was thick with passion. She clenched her walls desperately trying to hold on as he pulled out slowly. "Ever." He thrust deeply again, filling her completely.

"Yes," she cried out, half sobbing. "Only you, Blake."

He continued the rhythm of deep thrusting followed by achingly slow pulling back, winding the lust tighter and hotter with each movement. Just when she didn't think she could take another without slipping over the edge, he stilled, holding her in the space between insanity and ecstasy.

He rolled his hips, barely thrusting in and out, and lowered his head to capture one of her tightly budded peaks between his lips. He rolled his tongue around mimicking the rolling of his hips, and she rolled with him, with greater and greater intensity, as the heat inside her burned like a white-hot star.

He pinched her other nipple at the same time he sucked hard, thrusting once again to the hilt. She cried out as her orgasm exploded over her in brilliant sparks and waves, swirling and crashing as he thrust to help her ride it out, taking everything she had, and joining her in his own violent release. She was nothing. She was everything. Every atom in her body vibrated with the universe. She was nowhere and everywhere. A brilliant beam of light and a million tiny points.

A tear squeezed from each eye. And his lips were there, brushing and kissing, murmuring sweet incoherent sounds as she floated back to Earth on a sea of stars.

CHAPTER 26

MADDIE SAT AT the long Formica bar of Dottie's, lazily stirring cream into her coffee. Blake had needed to leave early for an errand to Manhattan and had dropped her off at Hansen Stables on his way out of town. She'd enjoyed a nice breakfast with Martha, but one of the boys had already taken her father into town.

She'd agreed to meet him here for coffee then stay and have lunch with Blake before heading back to the Big House to put in an afternoon of work. She'd made great progress on her research project out here, in spite of the hours she'd needed to spend babysitting her father.

She sighed, unable to keep the contented smile from her face. Being with Blake had… energized her. Her muscles were tired from their long nights of loving, but her mind was another story. It was like admitting she loved him had unlocked some hidden aspect of her creativity. The fresh air didn't hurt either. Even though it was only early April, she'd been outside so much she was starting to notice freckles forming across her nose.

Dottie placed a large sticky bun in front of her.

"Are you trying to fatten me up, Dottie?"

"Just want you to taste a little bit of heaven this morning, sweetie." She waggled her eyebrows. "You look positively languid. Have you been getting enough sleep?"

Dottie's eyes twinkled at her, as a telltale flush crept up her neck.

Dottie patted her cheek. "Aww, sweetie pie. I didn't mean to embarrass you. Just nice to see you two so happy and in love. That's all."

So everyone else could see it, too? There was no reason to hide it.

She looked around the little diner, studying it with fresh eyes. The patrons, scattered about, most in groups of two or three, all wore smiles on their faces. Several had nodded and smiled at her when she walked in. She had to admit, with exception of Kylee Ross, being home this time had actually been… *nice.*

For one perfect moment, she envisioned herself living with Blake on the ranch, periodically driving in for a morning cuppa and the news from Dottie. The buzzing of her phone broke through her reverie. Glancing at the number, she knew she couldn't let it go to voice mail.

"This is Maddie."

"Maddie, Richardson." Of course it was. He was still old-school brusque.

"Yes, hello. Do you have any questions about the research I sent over yesterday?"

"That? Er… no. Of course not. Exemplary as usual." His voice held an edge of condescension.

"Then may I ask what you need? The team and I are skyping at two."

"Er… well… about that." His voice grew brusque. "The fact of the matter is, this long distance communication isn't working."

For you, maybe.

"In what way sir?" She knew exactly what way. He felt the

only way to manage the project was to have the entire team under his thumb.

"It just isn't."

She pushed up her glasses, and forced herself to take a calming breath. "The feedback from the team seems great. And I'm not sure my father's well enough to leave yet. I really think–"

"Ms. Hansen..." She always knew she'd upset him when he reverted to formalities. "The research partners are unconcerned about your father, or anything that stands in the way of successfully completing the project."

He continued, not waiting for her to respond. "You know our organization frowns on long absences."

"But I've been communicating with the team. And turning in my work. I fail to understand–"

"We can't count on you if your loyalties are divided."

"But they're not." Even as she denied it, she knew it was true. They had suddenly become very much divided, and she was having a difficult time processing that reality.

She lowered her voice. The last thing she needed was word leaking out that she was having difficulties with her job. "Look, I recognize that Skype is not your preferred method of communication–"

"It's not my preferred anything."

"Fine, fine. But according to my notes, we're actually ahead of schedule on our research. I fail to understand why there is a problem."

"To put it bluntly, Ms. Hansen, we're uninterested in paying a salary to an absentee researcher."

"But I'm doing my job." She spoke loud enough a few heads turned. Dr. Richardson always seemed to push her buttons. She smacked her forehead. Of course. He was the scientific version of her father. No wonder he irritated the heck out of her.

His voice was clipped. "You are an Associate Scientist whose work is valuable to this community. You are absent. I suggest… *Dr.* Hansen, that if you value your position here, that you will find a way to get yourself on the next plane to Chicago. And in the future, if you have family matters that need to be settled, *you may use Skype.*"

He cut the connection.

If she'd been anywhere but Dottie's Diner, she'd have thrown the phone across the room. Damn his arrogant, condescending ass. Despair sank deep into her bones.

Whatever beauty magazine or celebrity had sold the idea of having it all – of having love and a career, should be selling oceanfront property in Kansas. It was impossible. At least in her field.

Hot tears threatened to spill over, and she pushed up her glasses, focusing her vision on the little bits of creamer floating on the top of her coffee.

She couldn't quit. Her dad needed her help financially. And she didn't want to. She loved her research. But she couldn't quit Blake either. Not after what they'd shared. And she didn't want to.

Where was the balance everyone talked about? Didn't she deserve to have both love and a career she loved? Why should she be forced to give up one for the other?

She picked at the sticky bun, licking a caramel coated pecan off her finger and letting the sugar dissolve over her tongue as she turned the problem over in her mind.

Was this an unsolvable paradox? The way light "knew" to become a point or a wave? Did people just "know"?

She covered her mouth, holding in a sob. The last thing

she wanted to do was draw attention to herself. She would have to go back to Chicago. At least for a few days until she could figure out a solution. Blake would understand. He had to. He'd as much as promised last night. Her aunt, uncle and cousins could handle her father. She didn't feel great about that, but they'd manage for a few days.

She took a sip of the coffee, not tasting it, bitterness sitting heavy in her gut. For one bleak moment, she wished she'd been born different. Less smart, less ambitious… less… her. But that Hansen stubbornness reared its ugly head and slapped her. Hard.

She would never leave her job. She'd worked too hard to get there. She was a fool for thinking she could have love, too. A damned fool.

CHAPTER 27

BLAKE STEPPED OUT of the bank and into the late morning sunshine, and checked his watch. He had just a few minutes before he was supposed to meet Maddie back at the diner for an early lunch.

He'd hated leaving her this morning, but he'd had to make a special trip into Manhattan and needed an early start. They'd stayed up most of the night, making love, talking, making love again. His muscles were pleasantly sore, but he'd do it all over again, knowing she was staying.

They'd checked the river before walking up the hill to where he'd parked the truck the night before. It had burst its banks, but the homestead wasn't in jeopardy.

Yet.

A few more rains and it might be. At least the hunting lodge was planned for higher ground. And with the deed to the Sinclaire land finally back in pocket, he'd have crews breaking ground within a week.

Thanks to the new clients from his last trip to Chicago, he'd be able to run double crews and get the lodge up and running before midsummer. Question was, who would run it? Ben had suggested Brodie, but he wasn't so sure. Although maybe it would be the kick in the pants he'd need to finally step up and become a full partner on the ranch.

"Well, well. What's got you looking like the cat that ate

the canary?"

Instantly his guard went up. "What do you want, Kylee?"

Her eyes narrowed as she stepped toward him holding a cup of coffee. "I want to know what I saw going on at the bank a little bit ago."

"None of your Goddamned business. Now, if you'll excu–"

"I think it's very much my Goddamned business." She glared at him, eyes full of malice, and took a sip of her coffee, refusing to budge. "It looked like you and Warren were getting all chummy at the bank."

He clenched his fist and unclenched it, keeping a lid on his temper. He would not let her get to him. Not today. "What's your point, Kylee?"

"I think you finagled your property back."

His lips flattened. He would not give her the satisfaction of seeing him lose his temper.

"I'll say again. Anything that happened between me and Warren is none of your business."

He stepped aside.

She stepped in front of him. "Not so fast, Blake. That property should go to me and you know it."

Widening his stance, he crossed his arms, glaring down at her. "And what makes you think that?" He clenched his jaw so tight his teeth ground.

She gave him a sly glance. "Jake promised it to me."

"Like hell he did," he bit out. "The only thing he promised you was a spanking. I know. I heard."

Her eyes widened at the disclosure, but she held her ground.

"You know as well as I do who that land should go to." Her features fell and her lip stuck out.

So now it was manipulation. He was done letting her

manipulate him. He'd have been better off letting the shit hit the fan as a young man instead of keeping quiet and protecting his family's honor.

He stepped forward. Throttling the urge to shout, he lowered his voice. "Let's get one thing straight, Kylee. *No one* is going to tell me what to do with Sinclaire land. Not you or anyone else."

She crossed her arms, glaring back at him. "I told you once before I need more money."

"And we've already discussed this. I give you more than enough money for Simon, and you know it. Are you spending it on yourself? How do you think that would appear to the family court judge?" He was so angry he couldn't see straight. She was rotten to the core.

"It's time this town knew the truth about you Sinclaires, Blake." He didn't miss the threat in her voice.

He didn't bother to hide the menace in his. "I'm going to tell you this once. And once only. If you do anything, *anything* at all that hurts my family, you'll be back in family court so fast your head will spin." He crossed his arms, resisting the urge to get in her face. "You know you're already on thin ice with Judge Walker, and I think he'll not take kindly to your more… questionable activities."

She paled and crossed her arms.

"Don't you threaten me, Blake Sinclaire. I've had enough of your family's attitude."

He stepped around her, jamming his Stetson down further on his head. "Goodbye, Kylee."

"I'm not done with you, you hear?" she called after him.

He kept walking. He'd be damned if he gave her one more second of his time today. He had more important matters to attend to.

Her voice carried half the block as he heard her trying to follow after him. "Don't you walk away from me. You'll regret this." He already did. If he'd been smart years ago, he'd have drop kicked her completely out of his life the second he'd had the chance. But he'd chosen honor over prudence. And look what it had earned him for his trouble?

It would all be water under the bridge, just as soon as he spoke to Maddie this afternoon. He could finally explain everything. He touched his hand to his pocket as he pushed open the door of the diner, scanning the room for Maddie.

She sat hunched over the long Formica countertop, her face pinched. Immediately, his heart started pounding.

"Maddie?" He rushed toward her. She turned her face turned to his, stricken.

The door rang behind him again.

"Don't you dare threaten me and walk away, Blake Sinclaire," Kylee cried. The sound in the diner dimmed instantly. "I'm not the only one in town with secrets."

"Kylee, you better not be stirring up trouble," boomed Dottie's voice from back near the coffee pots.

The door rang again. He turned. Warren. Great. A perfect storm, and something seriously bothering Maddie.

Ignoring them all, he stepped to Maddie, full of concern. "Sweetheart. Whatever it is, we can figure it out."

She opened her mouth to speak, but Kylee spoke first, just loud enough to attract attention. "Fancy seeing Warren and Blake all chummy in the diner. What happened to make this happy little reunion?"

Maddie flattened her mouth in dislike. "Why shouldn't they be friendly? Blake saved his life."

"And got a wife and his property back as thanks, it seems."

"Now just a damn minute young lady," Warren huffed. "That's my–"

Kylee sneered. "I know exactly who she is. Little Miss Perfect thinks she's so much better than everyone."

"*Enough.*"

Warren raised his hand, his voice echoing off the diner walls. He waved Blake back. "Let me handle this son." His eyes glinted at Kylee like two laser beams.

"I know all 'bout you, young lady. Don't you drag my daughter into your beef with the Sinclaires. My face may not be so pretty, and I'm old. But I still got fight left. And I know secrets that would turn your legs to jelly." His eyes narrowed. "I even know some about you."

Blake's stomach dropped. No. There was no way anyone knew. No one but him. Unless Jake had let something out in a drunken rage.

Warren chuckled, and reached for a toothpick on the counter. He picked at a tooth, then chomped on the end, staring hard at him. "Jake Sinclaire was a lyin', cheatin' sonofabitch."

"Dad." Maddie spoke sharply, her eyes wide behind her glasses.

"And when he got drunk, he said things."

Blake's hand started to shake, and he swallowed hard, working to keep his face neutral, even as the panic started to bulge up in his chest.

Warren shook his finger at Kylee. "So don't you be pickin' on anyone anymore. You hear? I will not take kindly to that." He took the toothpick out of his mouth and pointed it at her. "And you don't wanna mess with me." He cracked the tiniest of smiles back at him. "Hell, ask Blake."

No one moved in the diner. While no one was looking

directly at them, they stayed silent, straining to hear every word. Hell, this would be all over town before the cows came home.

"I'm not afraid of you old man," she gloated, a triumphant smile slashing her face. "Not after what I saw at the bank."

"And what did you see, Kylee?" Maddie's gaze burned intensely. "What exactly did you see?"

"Warren signing over a deed to property." Her voice held a note of triumph.

Maddie stood, peering over her glasses at Kylee. "I see. And did you see exactly what was on the deed? Or are you just speculating?"

"I know what I saw," Kylee huffed, crossing her arms.

"So it could have been a car, or a horse?" Maddie pounced. "Yes, Kylee, do you know all Hansen horses come with ownership papers? And Blake has purchased a horse from my family in the past." She paused. "You have no evidence, do you? Just a hunch and a mean streak a mile wide."

Warren shuffled, looking at the ground. Blake had never seen the man look so uneasy.

Shit.

This was not what was supposed to be happening today.

Maddie crossed her arms and glared at Kylee. "I suggest you run along. My lunch date was supposed to begin twenty minutes ago." She pushed her glasses up her nose and turned back to the counter, effectively dismissing Kylee.

Warren sagged into a stool next to Maddie. Kylee spun, whipping her head from Warren to Blake. "We are not done. Not by a long shot." She gave him one last glare and stomped out of the diner.

CHAPTER 28

HAD BLAKE AND her father really been so stupid? Anger, betrayal, and bitterness raced through her. How could she have been so blind?

After the door rang, and the noise levels resumed to normal, Blake came and sat on her other side, snaking an arm around her shoulders. "You were great, sweetheart."

She slammed her hands on the counter, and she glared at both men. "Do *not* sweetheart me. Did you really think I'm so obtuse that I wouldn't figure out what was going on?"

"Maddie, you don't–"

"I am not done." She pushed up her glasses, her mind racing. Who to start on first? They were both on her hit list as far as she was concerned. Her heart was slowly squeezing tighter with every breath. She fought the rising panic as questions ricocheted through her head.

She turned to Blake. "So is this why you wanted to marry me out of the blue?" She narrowed her eyes. "It had nothing to do with giving hope to an old man on the brink of death, did it?"

"Maddie Jane–" Her father started to speak.

"And you." She spun around, ready for battle. "Stop talking. You can't stop meddling in my life, can you? Can't stand that I'm the one thing you can't control." All the years of frustration and resentment bubbled up and came spewing out of her like a volcano. She slid off the seat, glaring at him. "Did you fake the heart attack, too? So you could pull the puppet strings again?"

"Maddie." Blake spoke sharply. "I was there when it happened, and–"

She flung up her hand. "I don't care. I want to know one thing, and you better give it to me straight. Was this…" She waved her hands between the two of them. "All an act? Did you mean any of it?"

Despair welled up, forming a lump in her throat so hard she couldn't speak. Tears pricked her eyes, and she blinked rapidly, holding them at bay. "Was it just some game to see if I could feel?" Her voice thickened with emotion. She hardly recognized the way she sounded. "To see if you could bring the cold, calculating scientist to her knees?"

"Of course not." Blake reached for her, eyes full of concern and… and… a flicker of guilt. Her gut twisted.

"Maddie, you know that's not true." Blake leaned to Warren. "Ask Warren if you don't believe me. I love you, sweetheart. Ask me anything."

"I already have." Her gut twisted harder, and she shook her head. "And you won't tell me."

Kylee strutted forward, a triumphant gleam in her eye. "Ask him what else he won't tell you."

Maddie spun around. "Didn't you just leave? This doesn't concern you."

"Oh, I think it does."

Her heart dropped to her toes as a sick hole formed in her belly. A skinny young boy, maybe ten or eleven, with wide hazel eyes and overgrown dirty light brown hair, wove through the chairs. He stopped in front of Blake, his eyes twinkling and his mouth and pockets stuffed with penny candy from the Five & Dime.

"Hi." The boy reached out to hug Blake.

Blake blanched, glaring at Kylee, but opened his arms to the boy, ruffling his hair. "Hey Simon. Why aren't you in school today?"

The boy shrugged, grinning, his mouth so full it was hard to understand. "No school today."

Warren's eyes narrowed at Blake.

Blake cast a wary glance at Maddie over the boy's head. "I can explain."

"You have a lot of explaining to do, Blake." Kylee's voice dripped acid. "Why don't you start by telling Simon who his father is. He's been asking, you know."

"Don't do this, Kylee. Not here."

The boy turned questioning eyes to Kylee, confused. "Mom?"

Blake put his arm around the boy, pulling him close. Maddie's heart tore a bit more.

"Dottie? Can you take Simon back and give him a piece of your best pie?"

He gave the boy another pat, and Dottie hustled him to the back.

Maddie finally found her voice. "Blake? What's going on?"

Warren stood up waving his finger at Blake. "Thought you could keep this from us, did yeh? Well I don't take kindly to doing business with a liar."

"Is he yours, Blake?" Dread pooled in Maddie's stomach. How could the child not be his?

"It's not what it looks like–"

"It looks pretty obvious to me. He's got your eyes. How did anyone not notice?"

"Tell them Blake. Tell them who Simon's father is." Kylee's voice was cold as ice, malice flashing in her eyes.

Blake turned on her. "You've gone too far, Kylee. How dare you bring this up in public? In front of Simon? Is this really how you parent? I should have sued for custody years ago."

Maddie's stomach lurched as if she'd been punched.

"Just try me. I will make your life a living hell."

"You already have, Kylee. How many more lives do you need to ruin before you stop?"

"Aren't you glad this is all out in the open now, Maddie?" Kylee shot over to her. "How does it feel to know that your father sold you out, and your *fiancé* is nothing but a liar?"

The ground tilted underneath Maddie as her vision darkened. She locked her knees and clutched the counter to keep from falling over. She would not give any of them the satisfaction of seeing her crumble.

Kylee smirked. "I warned you Blake, if you messed with our arrangement, it wasn't going to be pretty."

"We have no arrangement," he stated flatly.

"Hmm." She shrugged with a half smile. "Tsk. Tsk. There you go again. Now that your little *fiancée* knows your big dirty secret, I wonder, would Brodie be interested in learning about who fathered Simon?" Her eyes narrowed.

He reached out and grabbed her by the arm. "Leave him alone. You've caused him enough pain."

Kylee pulled her arm away, glaring at him with pure hatred in her eyes. "Don't you threaten me, Blake Sinclaire."

The buzzing in Maddie's ears wouldn't stop.

This.

This was the sensation of her heart ripping out of her body. Even when her mother had died, the pain hadn't been this intense. Hysteria raced through her hot and heavy. It hurt to breathe. This could not be happening. She'd told him she loved him.

A sob escaped, and she slapped her hand across her mouth. "I have to go." She started moving toward the door, bumping into furniture in her effort to escape.

"Maddie, wait. Please. Let me explain."

He reached out a hand to stop her. She shook her head and brushed past him out into the yard.

"Dammit, Maddie, wait."

She stumbled out of the diner, unable to see through the tears. A wave of nausea brought her to her knees and she retched right by his truck. She had to get out of here. Had to get away from them all. As fast as possible.

A *son?* What kind of person knocks up their brother's ex-girlfriend and then lies about it? What kind of person uses their daughter as collateral in a land deal?

Grief rolled through her so intensely she stayed rooted to the ground, rocks digging into her knees.

She retched again, her empty stomach clenching and heaving. She had to move now. Letting them see her like this would only add insult to injury. Taking a shuddering breath, she forced her knees to straighten. Slowly, as if her limbs were filled with lead weights, she rose, leaning against the truck for support.

Boots crunched on the gravel, and a hand brushed her shoulder. She shrugged it off.

"Don't… Don't. Touch me."

"Sweetheart, pl–"

"I am not your sweetheart," she sobbed, turning to stare at him.

His eyes were stormy and wild, his face strained.

Her heart lurched and she turned away, burying her head against the truck. She couldn't look at him. Not anymore. The sight of him pierced her so intensely it stole her breath.

"How could you? How *could* you?" she wailed into her sleeve.

"Maddie, love. I never meant to hurt you. I–"

She lifted her head, catching his reflection in the glass on the truck. "This is not what you do to someone you love. Either of you." She sniffed, wiping her nose on her sleeve, no longer caring about anything.

A hard lump of anger formed in her belly, giving her the courage to continue speaking.

"I'm going," she ground out over the lump in her throat. "Dr. Richardson called. I've been ordered back to the lab. An-and since Dad doesn't need me anymore…" A wave of despair nearly buckled her knees. "I… it's time."

"Maddie. *Please.* Don't go. Just give me until tonight. I can explain." The panic in his voice shattered her.

She slowly shook her head.

"You had all the time, Blake. I gave you everything and you couldn't trust me. How… I-I d-don't know h-how can I trust you after this." She sniffled, brushing her fingers across her face. "I-I'm sorry. I can't do it."

One foot. She just needed to move one foot. If she didn't do it now, didn't rip the Band-Aid off all at once, she wouldn't have the courage to do it. It hurt too much. Choking back a sob, she lurched away, forcing one foot to move in front of the other.

The direction didn't matter, so long as it was away from here.

Away from Blake.

And the mutilated pieces of her heart.

CHAPTER 29

BLAKE PACED THE front porch like a caged lion. It had been hours since the shit had hit the fan in front of God and everyone at the diner. And not a peep from Maddie. Not that he'd expected to hear from her after what happened.

Nausea settled in the pit of his stomach every time the scene replayed in his mind. Until the day he died, he'd never forget the heartbreak on her face, or how the light dimmed out of her eyes. It cut him to the core. He kicked a rock off the porch in frustration.

The visions he'd had of Maddie with his child returned to taunt him. What sick karmic game was the universe playing? Giving him that little spark of hope only to let the wheels of fortune turn against him. His chest squeezed tighter with every heartbeat. He'd been a damned coward, and his chickens had come home to roost.

The Hansens' old blue pickup tore up the road, tires squealing to a stop behind his truck. The doors opened and slammed shut in unison.

"Sinclaire, you're a damned fool." Axel stalked over and stood at the foot of the steps, glaring at him with his arms crossed over his chest.

"So I've been told."

Gunnar joined his brother, his long hair wild around him, giving him the look of a berserker. "For all your bragging about your MBA, you're an idiot."

Bragging? Anger that had been lurking beneath the surface flared up. He didn't brag.

Okay, maybe he did.

A little.

But only a little.

He cleared his throat. Now was not the time to let his anger get the best of him. Especially with Gunnar and Axel. If anything, he needed their help.

"You came from Dottie's."

Axel side-eyed his brother. "News travels fast."

Yeah. Especially bad news. "What'd you hear?"

"That you got yourself in a smack of trouble between Warren and Kylee Ross."

That was an understatement.

Axel squinted up at him. "Didn't take you for the sort who would poach his brother's ex-girlfriend."

"You should have come to us." Gunnar scowled at him.

"Yeah. We know how to handle Uncle Warren."

He narrowed his eyes, scowling. He'd be damned if the Hansen boys were going to stand here and scold him. "And I would have known this how?" His voice dripped with barely restrained anger.

Gunnar studied him carefully. "Maddie called us a while back and asked us to buy out Warren." He paused. "We'd have sold you the Sinclaire portion."

"But you never gave us the chance," Axel chimed in.

Sympathy briefly flashed through Gunnar's eyes. "And we didn't know about Maddie Jane."

Not that the land mattered a bit without her. Right now he never wanted to see the homestead again. It would only make him think about her. How much he loved her. He ran a hand over his chin, shaking his head. "I love her," he croaked hoarsely. "I was going to give her a ring today."

Gunnar's eyes widened in surprise and he glanced over to his brother. Axel nodded, agreeing to a silent question in Gunnar's eyes.

"We'll help you."

"You're an idiot, Sinclaire," Axel added. "But we'll help you."

A wave of despair crashed down on him, hot and heavy, nearly bringing him to his knees. Oh God. If he'd lost her… If he'd ruined his one shot at happiness because he'd been too scared to level with her… He stared out bleakly across the hill.

Brodie's truck came careening up the dirt road, kicking up dust in its wake.

Great.

This was turning into a shit show.

Gunnar turned to study the truck, then met Blake's eyes. "You gonna stand there like an idiot or invite us up?"

He cocked his head toward the porch. "Beer's in the fridge."

Axel rubbed his hands together. "Love me a family showdown."

"Shut up, Axel." He and Gunnar spoke at the same time.

Gunnar popped open a beer, handing the first one to him. Blake clenched the bottle, his heart pounding in his chest. Of all the conversations to have in front of the Hansens, it had to be this one.

Fuck it.

Word was probably all over town anyhow, thanks to Kylee. The story needed to be set straight, fast. And that started with him.

Brodie skidded his truck to a stop behind the Hansens',

blocking them in, and cut the engine before it had even stopped moving. He launched himself out of the cab and stalked toward Blake, his face contorted in fury.

Behind him, one of the Hansens let out a low whistle. Blake opened his hands in a gesture of peace, bracing for the onslaught he deserved.

Brodie didn't stop.

With a guttural roar, he launched himself up the stairs. Brodie had all the momentum, and the punch was delivered with the force of a bison at full charge.

Blake staggered back, beer flying, pain exploding in his nose, teeth rattling from the power of the blow. He struggled to keep his vision from darkening. He'd be lucky if his nose wasn't broken. With a snarl, Brodie came at him again. This time he was ready. At least he thought he was.

The punch landed right in his gut.

Hard.

His breath hissed out and a wave of nausea swept through him, nearly bringing him to his knees. "Wait."

"Fuck you, you fucking lying asshole." Each word was punctuated with a sharp blow.

The desolation in Brodie's voice was powerful. An ache lodged itself in his throat, his heart squeezing. He deserved every blow and then some. It hurt to breathe. Whether from the force of Brodie's blows, or the weight of his own guilt, he couldn't tell.

He raised his hand in supplication. "Brodie."

"Shut. Up." The blow to his jaw sent blinding pain up into his ear. He staggered back and, tripping on Gunnar's boots, fell into the furniture, smacking the back of his head on the heavy wooden spool. Stars shot through his vision.

The fuzzy form of Gunnar stood. "Enough, man. Nobody

needs to die here."

Brodie let out an anguished sob. "He fucking stole everything. My whole life. He stole my whole Goddamned life." He braced himself on the pillar, chest heaving.

Blake sat up, running his tongue over his lip and tasting blood. "I need to explain–"

"Explain what?" He snarled, teeth bared. "How you stole my girlfriend? Then you stole my son?"

This was it. The moment he'd dreaded for the last twelve years. He wiped his hands across his eyes.

"He's not your son."

"Like hell he isn't. I want a paternity test."

"He's Dad's, Brodie." Defeat swept over him as he finally let the admission out. "Simon is fucking Dad's."

Everyone went still as the weight of his words sunk in. For a moment there was only the sound of wind rushing over grass.

"Jesus." Axel muttered.

Gunnar broke the silence. "Who wants another beer?"

"There's scotch in the cabinet next to the refrigerator. Glasses in the cupboard to the left. And bring me a towel."

Gunnar stepped inside, while Axel grabbed a beer and sat back. The hiss of the top opening sliced through silence. Blake sagged back against the leg of the furniture. So this is what utter defeat tasted like. Blood and despair.

Brodie lifted his head, eyes flat. "I don't believe you."

Blake shrugged, the urge to explain gone. Let Kylee do the explaining. She created this mess.

Gunnar stepped back out onto the porch, and tossed him a wet rag. "Clean yourself up. You look like shit."

He was sure he did. The rag stung as he wiped it across his lip then tenderly dabbed his eye, which was quickly swelling.

Gunnar handed him a partially filled glass. "Sinclaire. You're an idiot. You and your inflated sense of honor."

Brodie's eyes narrowed. "Why?"

The word hung heavy between them.

"Why do you think?" He took a gulp of the scotch, savoring the raw burn down his throat.

Brodie's glare burned into him. Condemning him.

"I loved her."

"I know. I'm sorry."

"You never cared about what I wanted."

"Shit, Brodie. You were a kid. With a fucked up girlfriend making fucked up choices."

"She wasn't fucked up."

He rolled his eyes. Did he have to be so stubborn? "For chrissakes, Brodie. She seduced Dad."

Brodie crossed his arms, his mouth thinning. "How do you know?"

Bile rose up in his throat. He took another swig of the scotch, forcing it down. This was the ugly, ugly truth. Truth he'd hoped would stay dead and buried. The truth he was complicit in hiding from his family and the town. Shame, burning hot in his chest, choked him. "Because I saw," he gritted out.

Brodie uttered a strangled cry and lunged at him.

Gunnar and Axel shot up from their seats, and stepped between them.

"Easy fella." Gunnar spoke commandingly. "Let him speak."

Blake waved them away and lurched to his feet, head spinning. He reached to prop himself up against one of the pillars. "No. I deserve it. I deserve every punch he lands."

Gunnar eyed him critically. "You sure? He's already made mincemeat of your face."

He nodded once, a wave of remorse sweeping through him. He swallowed hard, letting the pain soothe him. He deserved this for betraying them all.

"But he still could be mine."

Blake shook his head. "You don't think I thought of that? I ran a paternity test. Stole dad's toothbrush. Besides, you have blue eyes, like mom's. So does Kylee. No way he belongs to you."

The fire died in Brodie's eyes. Guilt and shame weighed heavier on Blake with each heartbeat. His brother had suffered for twelve years. At his hands.

"Tell me what you saw," Brodie gritted through clenched teeth.

Blake stepped to the table and refilled his glass, taking a gulp to fortify himself. He kept his eyes focused on his glass. "I'd come home mid-week from Manhattan to help Emma with a 4-H project. The barn door was open, and I walked in expecting to find her in there working. Kylee and dad were in the throes in one of the stalls. They never even heard me."

It had been so much worse. Even twelve years later, the vision of the two of them was permanently etched in his memory. But some secrets were meant to be carried to the grave. He'd never share that they were both drunk and laughing. It made him sick even now.

Brodie shot him an icy look. "Why didn't you let that sonofabitch take the fall?"

"Did you ever think what that would have done to Mom? You can't ignore a pregnancy in Prairie or a kid who looks like a Sinclaire. It was easier to help Kylee move to Manhattan for a few years." And he'd be damned if he'd sit by quietly and let a Sinclaire baby suffer through no fault of its own. So he'd swallowed his dreams and manned up. For all of them.

"Hmmph."

"For God's sake, Brodie. Pull your head out for half a second. This was about protecting Mom and Emma."

"What about me?" Brodie glared angrily.

"What about you? What would you have done if you'd found out?"

"Killed the motherfucker."

"Making everything worse for everybody."

"So big Blake steps in again and saves the day, without giving a damn how it affected anyone else."

"BULLSHIT."

Now he was pissed. All the anger toward Jake, toward Kylee, and Warren, that he'd kept bottled up for years. All the shame he'd carried… All of it came bubbling up, black and toxic. He stalked across the porch and jabbed his finger into Brodie's chest.

"I sacrificed more than you will *ever* know. Did you ever notice how there was barely any food in the house that summer? Or were you too busy sucking your thumb? Did you ever notice that Emma was being picked on at school, or that Ben was working two jobs?"

His breath came in short bursts. "It was Ma who sold our land to Warren. *Ma*. So she could feed you and keep the ranch afloat." He let that sink in. "Yes. *Warren*." He shot a look at Gunnar and Axel. They shifted uncomfortably. He scrubbed his hand over his face, wincing where his fingers scraped the cuts. "Warren saved our ranch."

He hated making that admission in front of the Hansens. But it was time to bare the ugly truth.

"No." Brodie shook his head in disbelief. "He stole it in a

poker game."

"He and Ma arranged that. She knew it was the only way Dad wouldn't go ballistic."

Brodie's lips hardened to a thin line. "I don't believe you."

He had nothing left. "I don't know what else to say."

"Does Ben know?"

He shook his head.

No, this had been his own private hell. The sleepless nights doing homework so he could work two jobs and keep two families afloat. The fallout with Jake when he refused to acknowledge Simon or even see him. Hell, it wasn't the kid's fault. He'd been screwed by most of the adults in his life.

Brodie's hands clenched and unclenched. He spun on his heel. "I'm outta here."

Blake called after him. "I'll be here."

Brodie gunned the engine, squealing the tires as he backed out and spun the truck around and down the long drive.

Blake kept his eyes on the dust trail kicked up behind the truck. "Do me a favor. Keep an eye on him tonight." Axel and Gunnar stayed silent behind him.

One of them rose and clapped him on the shoulder. Gunnar spoke. "Sure thing. We look out for family."

Blake swallowed hard, gratitude swelling his throat shut. One battle won, at least. He wasn't sure about the war.

CHAPTER 30

THE SPRING WIND caressed Maddie's face as she stood at the fence watching the bison munch on grass. She'd found herself here every day during lunch. Drawn by a powerful melancholy and a crazy urge to stay connected to home. To Blake.

Somehow.

Every day, rain or shine, for the last three weeks, she'd come. It hadn't helped. When she conjured his face, the pain sliced through her like a laser. When she imagined his eyes, she could only see Simon's. Which set off a wave of grief and longing. What would a child of theirs look like? In her twenty-eight years, she'd never considered children. A handful of weeks with Blake, and she was contemplating the whole kit and caboodle.

When would the intense, breathtaking pain stop and the ache set in? She'd give anything for the dull ache. The only thing that came close was a hefty helping of Irish whiskey, which she'd pathetically indulged in her first night home alone, with the help of Jamey. But the hangover the next day had been enough to swear her off booze for quite some time. No, she'd have to take the pain without the help of any toxic medication.

Riding gave her no joy. All she thought about when she groomed Daisy was Iris. And riding with Blake. And other things that had transpired while riding with Blake.

So she walked until her feet hurt, rode until the sharp pain diminished to something close to but not quite a dull ache, and threw herself into her work with a frenzy, working every moment she wasn't sleeping.

There was solace in math. No emotions, and therefore safety. The cold numbers numbed the spiky fragments that remained of her heart.

Blake had called multiple times a day the first week, but they'd slowed to once a day. And she'd stopped taking her phone with her when she went places, eventually giving it to Jamey and reverting to her landline in the lab.

Jamey had reported her father had called, but only twice. He wouldn't grovel. Of course, in his crazy mind, there was nothing wrong with him offering up his daughter like a hog at market.

An obviously pregnant cow wandered close, a wildflower hanging out of her mouth. She pushed her glasses up and peered at her.

"What are you looking at?"

The bison chewed and contemplated her out of one eye. They were magnificent creatures up close. Far more interesting than cattle. More complicated. Moodier. Like Blake.

She crumpled her sandwich wrapper and jammed it into her pocket, turning to make the trek back to her office. Even if she ran to the end of the universe, something would be there to remind her of him.

A car sped by, only adding to her irritation. She'd gotten used to the quiet sounds of the ranch. Of songbirds, wind and hawks. Of crickets and night peepers. Punctuated by the occasional vehicle. She'd found scope for the imagination at home. Space for her to imagine and contemplate. And it showed in her work. In spite of the stress of dealing with her father, some of the best results she'd produced in years had happened down on the ranch. After twelve years of life in the big city, first Boston, then here in Chicago, it surprised her to acknowledge she craved the solitude and space of the prairie.

Back in her office, she was no better. She couldn't focus, and sat staring out the window, turning the same set of numbers over and over in her head. The phone rang.

"Hansen."

"Maddie Jane, when you gonna stop hiding?"

"I'm fine, Axe, thanks for asking." She rolled her eyes. Hansen men were all alike. They just varied by degrees of orneriness. "And I'm not hiding. It's called work."

"It's hiding when your roommate screens your calls."

"Clearly, she's doing an excellent job of it."

They both remained silent for a moment. This obviously wasn't a social call. Axel rarely called. Gunnar was the one she checked in with regularly.

"Is there something you needed?

He sighed into the phone. "You need to talk to your men, Maddie Jane."

"Oh no. I don't think so."

"Look, Warren's pretty frail. Ma won't let him move back to the bunkhouse, and it seems like the piss has been taken right outta him. I think he's real sorry."

She pushed on her glasses as she frowned at the phone. "Dad's happiest when he's meddling. And he doesn't get to do that to me anymore. Ever."

"Maddie Jane, you've never not spoken to him."

True. "He also never tried to use me to make a land deal before."

"Don't you see he misses you? He's just an ole' cuss. So

what if that's what he told Sinclaire? Even if he'd sold me and Gun the property, we'd have sold the Sinclaire side back. And not just to make a nice little profit." She could hear the smile in his voice. "Sinclaire's stand-up."

"How can you say that after what he did?" The tiny little scab forming over the gaping hole in her heart ripped off again, catching her breath.

"Have you listened to him, Maddie Jane?"

"No."

"Maybe you should."

"I saw all I needed to at the diner."

"You don't know the whole story."

"And you do?"

"Yeah… Yeah I do."

"Is that why you called me?"

"Not my story to tell. But this is. I made a mistake a few years back and let someone go 'cause I wouldn't listen. I wish more than anything I hadn't." Regret thickened his voice.

So Axe had his heart broken… join the club.

"I'm not gonna tell you what to do, but just…" He sighed into the phone. "Just don't wait too long, Maddie Jane."

"I'll take that under advisement."

They hung up, and she sat lost in thought, staring out the window.

Over the last few months, her life had been upended and tossed out with a salt shaker. Nothing made sense anymore. She'd lost her trajectory. Everything she thought she wanted, she didn't. And things she'd dismissed before suddenly became important.

She stood, smoothing her skirt, and adjusting her glasses. She could at least take one step. Someday, in the far-off future, if she was brave enough, maybe she'd take another.

She opened her door and marched down the hall, the staccato sound of her heels echoing off the silent walls. She knocked on the second door.

"Dr. Richardson?" She tried the handle, and the door opened. "Do you have a minute?"

The older man peered sternly at her over his spectacles, but waved her in.

CHAPTER 31

MADDIE STEPPED OFF the bus at the Metra station feeling a little bit lighter. She'd originally planned on going back to the apartment and putting in another full evening of work, but as she walked by Frenchie O'Neill's, she slowed.

She'd avoided stopping by the restaurant since she'd been home. The memories were too fresh. Too painful. But Jamey would be there prepping for the evening rush, and the bar would be quiet.

Before she lost her nerve, she pushed open the door, and made her way back through the curtains to the bar. She carefully avoided looking out to the patio. Sure enough, Jamey stood poring over two notebooks at the bar, a glass of whiskey in hand.

Her red curls bounced as her head popped up. "Well, well. Decided to come out of your hidey hole?"

Jamey turned and grabbed the bottle of twelve-year Redbreast. It had been their crisis bottle of choice for years. Pouring her a measure, she slid the glass down the counter.

Maddie narrowed her eyes at her best friend. "Axe called."

Jamey shrugged, a little smile hinting at the corners of her mouth. "I figured it was okay to give him your work number."

"It was." She held out her hand. "I'd like my phone back, please."

"Oh praise the saints. It's about time, Maddie. Don't you think you've put him through the ringer?" She skewered her with a look. "Don't tell me that man doesn't love you. Did Marcus ever call you once, all those years ago?" She raised her eyebrows.

Jamey was right. He hadn't.

"And another thing." Jamey waved the whiskey in her hand. "You know my brother Jarrod. He's not an O'Neill by birth."

That got her attention. Jarrod was the oldest of the O'Neills, and the only one of Jamey's brothers not to go into fire or police protection. Instead, Jarrod had chosen litigation. If she remembered correctly, he'd left Boston for a stint in DC.

Jamey nodded at her questioning glance. "Yep. That cat got let outta the bag right about the time I met you. Jarrod left the family for a bit over it."

"What happened?"

"He was a babe when Ma and Pops met. We'd always assumed they'd done things the old Irish way, but nope. Ma's family had disowned her for havin' a babe out of wedlock, and that's how she met Pops. Pops adopted Jarrod as soon as they married."

Shocked, Maddie took another sip, letting the burn warm her. "Why are you telling me this now?"

"Why do you think, Mads? Pops loved Ma so much her past didn't matter."

"The difference was he knew what he was getting into."

"Maybe, maybe not. My point is you choose to love a person, lumps and all, not the idea of the person. We're not robots, Mads."

Jamey was getting wound up, sloshing the whiskey as she

waved her arms. "Forgive me for saying, but yer behavin' like a spoony feckin' eejit."

And the Irish was out. Always a sign of Jamey's emotional state.

"For chrissakes, the man loves you." She grabbed the phone out of her coat pocket, waving it in her face. "I know. I've listened to the messages."

Maddie reeled back. "What? You invaded my privacy?"

Jamey scowled at her, pouring another round. "You lost that privilege when you made me keeper of your phone. And another thing." She took a gulp. "No one. *No one,* can live up to your expectations of perfection. Numbers might be perfect, people aren't. So quit cryin' whiskey tears that yer man let you down. Newsflash, Mads… they *all* let you down. Men are a bunch of witless fucktards. Big arrogant babies." Her face twisted.

Realization dawned. Were Jamey and Jean Luc having trouble? Maddie hoped not. One of them at least should be happy.

Jamey took a deep breath and pinned her with a gaze so intense she squirmed. "But you choose love in spite of the pain. Because you can't breathe without it."

Understanding slammed into her with the force of a particle smasher. Maddie pushed up her glasses, studying the whiskey swirling in her glass. Jamey was right. Axel was right. She'd only been half-living her life. And the force of Blake's love had blasted away the casing she'd placed around her heart. There was no shutting the door to love ever again. She'd made one step in the right direction this afternoon. Could she take another, bigger step? And then another?

"Stop thinking, Maddie."

Her eyes flew toward the voice with the power to melt her

insides. Blake's eyes raked over her hungrily, setting off a chain reaction in her belly. He removed his Stetson, placing it on the bar. Jamey grabbed a clean glass from behind the counter, poured out another measure of whiskey, and slid the glass down the bar. He reached out and caught it, bringing it to his lips, not taking his eyes off her for a second.

She couldn't speak. Not with her heart squeezing in her throat like it was. So she drank him in greedily, refamiliarizing herself with his planes and crevices. He looked gaunt. Tired around the eyes. Haggard, even. Her heart twisted with the knowledge that she was partially responsible for the pain etched there.

Jamey broke the silence, slamming the bottle of Redbreast on the counter between them. "I'll leave you two. Don't get up until you've sorted yourselves or you've finished the bottle." She left them alone.

CHAPTER 32

THE SOUND OF the bottle hitting the bar echoed through the room. When he'd first come through the curtains, the sight of her sitting alone and dejected had squeezed Blake's chest. Seeing that she was still wearing her blue glasses instead of the black had squeezed it further. At the same time, a little thrill of hope stirred. If he had even half a chance, he'd take it and run.

Her eyes were pools of conflict. At once wary, relieved, and hungry. Her cheeks had hollowed, confirmation of Jamey's report that she hadn't been sleeping. She started to speak, but he shushed her mouth with his finger, shaking his head.

"Me first."

Touching her, after weeks of his body starving for her, sent a jolt of awareness through him. He traced her bottom lip, and was rewarded with her quick intake of breath. Good. Maybe he had a shot after all.

Blake took a deep breath, suddenly at a loss for all the words he'd rehearsed on the plane and every time he'd called. Grasshoppers jumped inside the walls of his stomach. He dropped his hand, reaching to take hers.

He wanted to touch her.

Needed to touch her.

Hold her.

Assure himself that she wasn't a phantom and that this time she wouldn't disappear the way she had in his nightly dreams. He brought her fingers to his lips, pouring all the feeling roiling inside his body into the gesture. She gave his hand a little squeeze.

"Maddie, love. I was so wrong. The whole time I was hammering you to let go, I was afraid to do the same thing. I was afraid that the mess my family made would be too much for you."

"Blake." Her voice was barely above a whisper.

"No." He shook his head, emotion thickening his voice. "Just hear me out… Please?"

Her eyes wide and full of question, she nodded.

"I wasn't lying when I said I love you. I love you more than my own life, and I want to be with you above all else. But you deserve to know everything. Before your dad collapsed, he did try to tell me I had to marry you if I wanted the Sinclaire land back."

She stiffened, but he rushed on. "I don't think he meant it. And the first thing I told him was that I didn't think you'd take kindly to it. And then he collapsed. I should have set the record straight at the hospital, but I'm not sorry I didn't. I think I was already half in love with you. And I paid him more than full price for the land. And only took back what's on our side of the river."

God. He felt tongue tied. Like a teenager asking a girl on a first date.

Her eyes softened and she nodded a fraction. "I talked to Axel earlier today." The corners of her mouth tilted slightly. "He said you were 'stand-up'. That's high praise from him."

So they had helped him. Good to know they'd meant it when they offered. "And you need to know some awful things about my family." He paused, searching her eyes for any clues. Not seeing any, he charged ahead, pushing the fear to the recesses of his mind.

"Jake Sinclaire was an SOB."

"So I've been told," she murmured.

"He was a lying, drinking, cheating sonofabitch." His voice caught. "And he broke my mom. I'd catch her crying sometimes when she thought no one was looking." He took a deep breath. "And… and the reason we lost the property in the first place was because she went to your dad and offered it to him."

She gasped, eyes widening.

He nodded. "Yep. Your ole cuss of a father saved my brothers and sister. Jake had drunk or gambled everything away. There was no food in the house. Mom sent him to your dad for a friendly game that she knew he'd lose."

"Blake." Her hand squeezed his. "I had no idea."

"No one did. One of many dirty secrets our family kept."

He reached for the whiskey and took a sip. She did the same.

"That summer was the worst. I was twenty, working two jobs, and eating at the gas station because I was sending ma everything for food."

"Oh, Blake." She shook her head. "That's too much for anyone that age."

He flashed her a wry grin. "Weren't you almost a PhD by that age?"

For the first time since the disaster at the diner, her eyes crinkled with humor.

"I was. But I wasn't trying to support a family."

The silence between them no longer felt anxious or awkward. But there was still more to tell, and while he felt more hopeful the longer they sat together, hands entwined, his heart still thumped uncontrollably in his chest.

He grabbed his glass and drained it. He studied her intently, gathering his courage.

A kiss.

He needed to kiss her. To caress her mouth with his again.

Then.

Then he could bare his soul once and for all. He tugged on her hand, pulling her closer. And leaning in, brought his other hand to the base of her head, threading his fingers through her hair and disturbing her hairpins.

Her lips were soft as silk beneath his, and a charge of electricity threaded straight to his balls. The urge to crush her to him was profound, but he held it in check, wanting to savor her sweetness, her taste. He would never take this for granted. As long as he lived, he would cherish this brilliant gift in front of him.

She gave a tiny little sigh, and without him asking or pressing, opened under him and flicked her tongue inside his lip.

He melted at the sweetness even as his cock leaped forward. She loved him. He knew it as sure as there were boots on his feet and a ring in his pocket. This was not the kiss of someone saying goodbye. This was the kiss of someone welcoming him home.

He pulled back, resting his forehead on hers, letting his heartbeat come back to normal. "There's no easy way to say this, love. Kylee will never be entirely out of our lives."

She hissed out a breath, stiffening.

"She is Simon's mother, and I can't change that. On paper, I'm Simon's father. And I won't change that."

She gave a little squeak and pulled back. Eyes wide and full of pain.

"Just hear me out. Please. I need you to hear me out."

She pressed her lips together, eyes glistening with unshed tears. It stabbed at him.

"Simon is my half-brother. He belongs to Jake."

"What?" Her jaw dropped, shock and confusion moving across her face.

He nodded slowly.

"I was twenty and trying to protect mom from something I think she already knew."

Maddie reached for her glass, emptying it in one gulp. She grabbed the bottle and poured out another measure, adjusting her glasses.

"Does Brodie know?"

"He does now."

She licked the whiskey off her lips, nodding. In spite of the seriousness of their conversation, the gesture distracted him entirely. Unable to resist, he lowered his head again, his tongue sweeping out to taste the remnants of whiskey. She brought her hands to his face, emitting a little moan, and responded in kind. The whiskey laced kiss warmed his blood, replacing anxiety with hope, fear with love.

"Tell me what happened, Blake."

He scraped his hand across his face, and took a gulp from his glass. "It's ugly. She and Brodie had been on and off. I came home unexpectedly to help Emma with a 4-H project and stumbled across Kylee and my dad. Both drunk and having at it."

She covered her mouth with her hand, eyes huge.

"No one knew I saw them. I couldn't bring myself to tell anyone.

She nodded slowly in understanding. "What did you do?"

"I took off and spent two nights down at the homestead. I was afraid if I saw Jake, I'd beat him and not stop."

She reached for him, entwining her fingers with his. "I'm so sorry. Sorry you saw it, sorry you carried that for so many years. Sorry I… I was so hurt I didn't listen."

He squeezed her and scooted closer, bringing her hand to rest on his lap. "She came to me not long after, pregnant and scared. So I helped her. And after, I didn't feel right just leaving a little baby with her. You know what she's like."

She nodded, eyes fierce.

"How did you manage? Weren't you in school?"

"I was. I didn't sleep much. Didn't eat much. Jake refused to acknowledge the baby, and Kylee threatened to bring Simon to Dottie's if I didn't help her. I couldn't let Mom be humiliated that way. So I tried to fix things on my own."

Maddie pushed her glasses up her nose. "She is hateful, Blake. She doesn't deserve to be a parent."

"The moment I held him, I knew I couldn't turn my back on him. None of this was his fault. But you're right. She's a terrible parent and I regret not taking action sooner. My only excuse was that until very recently I wasn't in a position to be a good parent. And I was afraid. Afraid what people would say. Afraid if I sued for even partial custody, since I'm not his biological father, that I wouldn't get to see him at all. But instead, I've not only hurt you, I've hurt Simon and Brodie too."

"Does he know who his father is?"

"He does now. I wanted him to hear it from me, not anyone else."

It had been tough. Brodie had been so angry at first, but had softened once he met Simon. They'd told him together and Simon's reaction had melted them all. At first he'd been confused, but when he realized he had three big brothers who loved him and wanted to teach him how to ranch, rope, and ride horses, his grin had been wider than a rodeo clown.

"So will you start proceedings now?"

"Already have, for joint custody. The first court date is in four days."

He studied his glass, swirling its contents. His heart started to thump again. Steeling himself, he looked up "Would you stand by me?" He swallowed down the lump in his throat and pressed on. "I meant it when I said I want to be with you. However you want. You don't have to move back. You can fly down on weekends. I can make my travel come through Chicago. I'll do whatever it takes."

She reached out, cupping his cheek with her hand, her eyes soft and shining. "I meant it when I said yes," she murmured.

He didn't realize he'd been holding his breath until it whooshed out as relief cascaded over him. The first inklings of joy ballooned, filling up his chest.

"Does that mean I can give you this?" He dug into his pocket and pulled out the ring that had been burning a hole there for the last twenty-two days.

"I know we've both been guilty of doing everything on our own, and I don't want that anymore. For either of us. I love you, Dr. Madison Jane Hansen. Please say you'll be my partner in life and love? For the rest of our lives?"

He brought her hand to his lips, before slipping the ring on her third finger.

"Yes, yes, yes." She leaned in, wrapping her arms around his neck, and kissed him.

"Do you like it? The ring was my grandmother's, but I

had the diamond replaced with a sapphire to match your eyes."

"It's perfect Blake, stop talking." She pulled on his neck again, bringing his mouth to hers. His hand skimmed her hips, pulling her off the stool to stand between his legs.

They were interrupted by the loud pop of a cork. Jamey had returned to the bar and was pouring champagne into three glasses.

"Redbreast works every time," she grinned. "So Mads. You pull your head out of your arse and say yes to this fine specimen?"

Maddie showed Jamey her left hand. Jamey studied it, then raised her head, eyeing him. "Impressive, cowboy. I suppose I'll have to give you my blessing. Especially since my Irish great-granny matchmaker sense is never wrong."

Maddie snorted and rolled her eyes.

"Well it was right this time. When you gonna do this?"

Blake pulled Maddie close, not wanting to be apart from her for a second. "As soon as we can?"

She nodded her agreement. "There are a few things I need to say first."

"Of course, love." He pressed a kiss to her temple. "Whatever you need."

"First, I'm sorry for running out. I was hurt. And Dr. Richardson had called me back to the lab. He's old school and doesn't understand how collaborative work can be done digitally. I gave him my resignation this afternoon."

Blake frowned, his eyebrows knitting together. "Sweetheart, are you sure? You can't quit your research." He didn't want her quitting for him. Not after he'd seen how happy her research made her.

She nodded, taking a sip of champagne, her eyes clear.

"I'm sure. Very. You're not the only one who's been thinking. After twelve years of concrete jungle, I miss the quiet life. And dad's a cuss, but he's slowing down. I want to come home."

He gathered her in his arms, joy overflowing to the point where tears pricked behind his eyes. He rained kisses over her face until she giggled. "If you're interested, I made a few phone calls. There's a physics position open at K-State. They said they were ready to make a hire soon. I know it's not ideal, and if you want to go somewhere else, I support that. But… I wanted you to know."

Her brows furrowed. "When did you talk to them?"

"Two days ago, before I bought my ticket."

She beamed. She leaned forward and kissed him tenderly. "Hmm. Interesting," she murmured between kisses. "Gary Anderson called two weeks ago inviting me to apply for a new position at their lab." She smiled slyly. "I am brilliant, you know."

"Like a star, Dr. Hansen. Like a star."

CHAPTER 33

Three Weeks Later…

MADDIE PEERED OUT the window of the master bedroom. The day had dawned sunny and perfect without a cloud in the sky.

After a quick breakfast and a ride with Blake, she'd sequestered herself upstairs to buff and puff with Blake's sister, Emma, while Jamey and Dottie set about the food preparations. Jamey popped in and out, mostly to complain about Dottie.

True to her word, Dottie had insisted on planning a wedding party for them, and had reluctantly accepted Jamey's help. That meant Jamey's family, and hers by extension, descended on Prairie, too. The plans had very quickly spun out of control with Dottie and Jamey spending as much time one-upping each other as they did preparing the feast.

Jamey stalked in, slamming the door behind her. "That woman."

Maddie turned from the window. "Let it go, Jamey. She's just a mother hen. She's intimidated by your fabulousness."

"She should be." Jamey tore off her chef's coat and stripped down, walking over to the closet to grab her dress.

"You have to admit, her biscuits are the best."

"Here, Jamey." Blake's sister, Emma, whom Maddie had only met a week ago, handed Jamey a glass of champagne.

"This will help take off the edge."

She, Jamey and Emma had hit it off like three peas in a pod. Emma, only twenty-four, was the Sinclaire baby, and pushed her older brothers around like a boss. Not only was it adorable, it was great entertainment.

"Huh." Jamey snorted. "You've just forgotten what gourmet food tastes like, Mads." She pulled the pale green chiffon dress over her shoulders, fluffing out her wild red curls once she'd straightened the dress. She took the champagne and downed it in two gulps.

"Jamey. Please," Maddie pleaded. "I'm thrilled you and your family are here. Don't let anything else bother you. Please? You make kitchen lint taste delicious."

"Speaking of delicious." Jamey grinned wickedly. "I'd like to taste some of the cowboy hotness walking around here. I cannot get over the amount of testosterone in this town. Makes Chi-town gents look like boys."

That was the Jamey she knew and loved.

Emma giggled. "They're all yours, Jamey. No ranch life for this country girl."

"And at least you have Jean Luc to keep you satisfied."

Disappointment flashed across Jamey's face but was quickly replaced with her brilliant smile.

"Ha. Yes. Cowboys might be nice for a little snack, but they're no gourmet meal. And I won't waste my brilliance on someone who loves slop."

What was up between Jamey and Jean Luc? Maddie made a note to take her aside after the wedding.

A quiet knock sounded on the door. Martha poked her head in. "Are you ready to get dressed?"

Maddie nodded, suddenly wishing it was her mother and not her aunt. Tears pricked her eyes, but she blinked them back. No tears of sadness today. Only tears of joy.

Martha reached for the wedding dress hanging on the outside of the closet door. True to her word, Emmaline had worked magic. The finished effect was stunning. She'd preserved the vintage feel, as well as the hemline, and still managed to make it feel modern. She loved it.

Martha helped her slip it over her shoulders. Jamey fussed with the skirt while Martha set about fastening the 24 buttons up the back. "Tsk tsk. Blake is going to have a hard time with these. Tell him to be patient, or you won't be able to save this for your own child."

She felt the flush creeping up her neck. "Or Hope."

Jamey slapped her thigh, her laughter filling the room. "I knew I loved you, Martha. Usually I'm the only one that makes her blush."

Jamey grabbed the long length of tulle spread out on the bed and pinned it to her hair. "You are a vision. And you deserve every happiness."

Another knock sounded at the door.

Dottie peeked her head in, letting out a gasp as she met Maddie's eyes. "Lordy, Emmaline's good. You look like you stepped out of a fairy tale. Can I come in?"

Jamey muttered under her breath and Maddie elbowed her sharply. "Of course, Dottie. You're always welcome."

Dottie pushed the door open wider, and stepped in, holding a large white box encased in a white glittery ribbon.

"I wasn't sure these would make it in time. Lydia sent you a little something. Made them herself. You don't have to use them if you don't want, though."

Maddie's hands trembled a bit as she undid the box, and the gasps from the other women echoed her own.

Nestled in a bed of tulle was a pair of white leather ankle

boots, a cross between an old fashioned button up boot and a cowboy boot. A tiny H and S embroidered inside a heart in gold and silver adorned the top of the boot. Rhinestone buttons decorated the side.

"They should fit. I had Blake take a peek in your riding boots for the size… Lydia's real sorry she can't get away."

Her heart was literally overflowing. "Dottie. I'd be honored. They're stunning."

She quickly slipped them on. The fit was perfect, and the pointy toes peeked out from under the hem of her dress. She hugged Dottie close. If only she and Jamey wouldn't circle like alley cats, her day would be perfect.

Another knock sounded. This time Simon stuck in his head.

"Are you ready?"

His hair was freshly cut and slicked back, and he stood ramrod straight in his new suit. Clearly he took his ushering job very seriously.

She nodded, her heart fluttering.

She had decided to walk down the staircase behind Simon, Emma and Jamey, and the families agreed that the men – her father, Gunnar, and Axel on one side, Blake, Ben and Brodie on the other – would wait at the foot of the stairs. Then together, she and Blake would step through the doors to the front porch.

There would be a quick and private exchange of vows in the foyer. Neither of them wanted much spectacle. Just a moment to acknowledge in front of their families the promises they'd already made with their hearts. There would be a round of toasts on the porch, and then a late afternoon luncheon and cake. Afterwards, dancing and hayrides until dark. After dark, more dancing, and a bonfire. Simon had insisted on the bonfire.

He held out his arm to her. "You look so pretty. Blake's gonna have a heart attack."

Her heart melted at his admission. The judge had awarded equal joint custody to all the brothers, and Simon would live half time at the Big House. Kylee would still be a thorn in their sides, but the boy had positively blossomed since moving to the ranch.

She bent, kissing his forehead. "Are you ready for your big job, young man?"

He nodded solemnly.

"Remember, you need to help Jamey and Emma down the stairs."

He looked at her nervously.

Jamey grinned and held out her hand, and spoke low, but loud enough for her to hear. "If you do a good job, I'll teach you how to swear in Irish."

His eyes grew mischievous, and he nodded, a grin splitting his face.

They stepped aside to let the older women pass.

Maddie patted her hair one last time, shooting a questioning glance at her best friend and future sister-in-law.

Jamey's eyes pooled with tears. "You're perfect. Go to your man." She winked, blinking rapidly.

She followed them out the door and down the hall, pausing just before the top step, and peeking around the corner.

The men stood in their Stetsons, faces turned up expectantly. They were dressed sharp in black denim and shiny boots, white starched shirts with matching onyx and silver cufflinks – a gift she and Blake had surprised them with this morning.

Her heart swelled watching the emotions play across their

faces. Pride on her cousins' and father's faces, peace on Ben's. And was that hunger on Brodie's face? His eyes were glued to Jamey, tracing her.

She tucked that observation away for later.

And Blake. His eyes shining expectantly, a smile playing at the corners of his mouth. Her breath hitched at the intense joy that surged through her. He was her One. Out of a million billion possibilities. That all the matter in the universe led them here, to this moment.

A grin split her face from ear to ear, and she stepped around the corner, moving forward into the circle of his love.

CHAPTER 34

A LUMP FORMED in Blake's throat as Maddie stepped around the corner, her face beaming and filled with love.

Dammit.

He would not tear up.

He'd never hear the end of it from his brothers. His breath caught in his chest as she descended, her eyes looking nowhere but into his. Maddie glided toward him, still smiling, and stopped.

"You're beautiful," he murmured, not trusting himself to say more.

She raised her eyebrows at him, eyes twinkling. She stood up on tiptoe and whispered into his ear. "Wait until you see what's underneath." Her tongue flicked out and licked the sensitive spot sending a jolt of electricity straight to his groin.

Temptress.

There was no way he could wait the rest of the day to find out.

She stepped back, sliding her fingers down his arm. "Ready?"

He nodded. "More than ready."

His heart started beating faster. After all they'd been through, he was still nervous. Still wanted to please her. "Shut your eyes."

A question arose in her beautiful blues.

"Just do it."

She closed her eyes, and he took the bouquet out of her left hand, and handed it to Jamey. He held open his hand, and Simon handed him a band. Taking Maddie's hand, he brought it to his lips, then slipped silver filigree band above the sapphire and diamond ring he'd given her in Chicago.

Her eyes flew open. Then down to the ring, and back to his face.

She squealed.

"The ring belonged to my grandmother. Is it okay?"

Her smile was the only answer he needed.

His mouth went dry from the emotion. He spoke low, his throat thick with feeling. "Maddie Jane, I promise that I will try in every way to be worthy of your love. I vow to you that I will support you in all things. In health and sickness, sorrow and success. With my body, my time, and my heart. I want nothing more than to go to bed each night wrapped in your arms, and to wake up each morning to your smile. For all the days of my life"

Tears brimmed in her eyes, and she threw her arms around him pulling him down for a kiss. "I love you Blake, for all time." She murmured into his lips.

Jamey cleared her throat. "Somebody hand the girl a tissue before they think she's been left at the altar."

Maddie held out her hand and Jamey passed her a ring. Taking his left hand, she slipped a band over his finger.

"Blake Pascal, I promise to love you, be faithful to you, to share my life, my body, and my whole heart. For the rest of our lives. In sickness or health, sorrow or success. No holding back. Across all space and time and dimension. To the edges of the universe."

Love for Maddie welled up, pressing brightly against his

chest. So intense, he clutched her hands in his, holding on for dear life. Again, he drew her fingers to his lips, reverently kissing each one, before accepting her vow with a kiss of his own.

Brodie clapped him on the shoulder. "I know you want to start the honeymoon now, but the natives are getting restless. It's time to kiss on the porch."

Laughter erupted from the men, while Jamey rolled her eyes. "Is that all you men think about? Kissing?"

"Much more," Brodie muttered baldly as he passed her.

"Oh you're one of *those* are you? All talk and no substance?"

Brodie reached out and pulled Jamey close. "I've got plenty of substance whenever you're ready, honey."

Jamey flushed deep red. And snapped her mouth shut, eyes flashing.

"Enough, Brodie," Blake spoke sharply. "She's our guest, as are her brothers. I don't think you want to mess with them." Brodie wouldn't last three seconds in a dog pile with Jamey's brothers.

Jamey glared at Brodie, and pulling herself up tall, jabbed him in the chest. "Back off you arse weed. You might think you're Mister Hotcakes, but if you can't make soup outta chicken shit, you better not piss off the cook."

Brodie flushed and cast his gaze downwards. Looking back up, he winked and put on his best charmer smile. "Aww shit. I'm sorry, hon."

"Don't you honey me. I will serve your balls for dinner if you cross me." She turned on her heel and swept through the door.

Blake shook with laughter, clapping Brodie on the back. "Better watch out. I think you just met your match."

He pulled Maddie close and stepped through the door to the cheers and catcalls of their friends and family.

Corks popped, and Gunnar and Axel began to pass the champagne.

First, the Hansen toasts came in Norwegian. Next, the Irish toasts offered by Jamey and her family. Finally all eyes turned toward his brothers and sister.

Ben spoke first.

"Blake, you've always been our rock. You've held us together through thick and thin."

"Through the good, the bad, and the ugly," Emma added. Her reference drew a titter from the crowd gathered on the lawn.

Brodie swallowed, clearly wrestling with emotion. "Through laughter and tears, you've sacrificed so we could thrive."

Maddie's breath caught, and he fought the huge lump of emotion that lodged itself in his larynx. She squeezed his hand.

Ben spoke again, his eyes glittering. "All this time we'd never dreamed that you would find your own rock."

"A life partner and soul mate," Emma's voice chimed in.

"A beautiful woman with a heart so big she'd love all of us." Brodie reached out and ruffled Simon's head.

Blake squeezed Maddie's hand. Dammit. He would not let his brothers make him cry. His heart grew fuller with every beat.

Simon pulled out a piece of paper and stood very tall. Looking out at the gathering, he grabbed a glass of water. "Please raise your glass."

Glasses, beer bottles, and soda cans all rose into the air.

Ben stepped forward. "If our many greats granny was here

she'd say the following: Shelter in the storm. Sunshine on your path. Wind at your back. And a heart to warm you by the fire at night." He raised his glass and drained it.

"Jesus, Mary, and Joseph, your granny sounds Irish," Jamey muttered behind them.

Cheers erupted on the lawn and Blake swung Maddie into his arms, kissing her deeply. When they finally broke apart, someone had turned on the music and guests had started to move to the back yard where dinner would be served.

Blake pulled her close, cupping her ass in his hand.

Hmm…

No panties…

He couldn't wait to get her alone.

He kissed her gently, letting his lips linger on her sweet fullness. "Come, wife. Time to mingle, but then I have a surprise for you."

She smiled coyly. "Good. I might have one or two myself."

He leaned into her ear, nibbling just under her lobe. "I hope one is what I felt just now? Or what I didn't feel?" He kissed her neck again, inhaling deeply, letting her fragrance fill him.

"Mmm. Hmmm. Perhaps…"

"Alright, alright, you two. Save it for the bedroom." Brodie approached them with two glasses of champagne. "Right now we've got more important things to do. Like eat."

"And ogle Jamey," Maddie muttered under her breath so only he could hear. He squeezed her hand in agreement.

They made their way around back to the tables laden with barbecue, potato salad, cornbread and Irish soda bread, bison tenderloin sliders from the Sinclaire freezers, fruit salad, Caesar salad, and fancy finger food Blake assumed must be

Jamey's creations.

Jamey and Dottie were everywhere at once, serving, refilling glasses, and directing people to the beer and soda coolers. Someone handed them plates, and the next few hours were spent in a whirlwind of eating, drinking, and laughing.

As the sun dipped low and twilight descended, Gunnar and Axel launched fireworks they had stashed from previous Fourth of July celebrations.

That was his signal. He squeezed Maddie's hand and cocked his head toward the barn. "Come on."

Looking like a guilty teenager with mischief in her eyes, she nodded and followed.

She hitched her dress up around her knees. He stopped, scooped her up and continued over to the corral. He was sick of waiting to be alone with her. Desire got the better of him and he stopped, covering her mouth. He flicked his tongue against her lower lip, and she opened to him with a small whimper, inviting him to go deeper. Deeper he went, sweeping his tongue against hers, letting her down gently so he could palm her ass, pulling her hips against his straining erection.

He tore his mouth away. "Can you wait a bit longer, my love?"

"Are you serious?" She panted. "I've been waiting all day."

"Just a bit longer, I promise. Besides, don't you have surprises for me?"

Her eyes glittered mysteriously in the twilight. "Yes, but I was waiting for the right moment."

"This isn't it?"

She shook her head. "Not yet."

"Well, then. I have something to show you."

Her hand snaked out, grabbing the waist of his denim.

"Oh yes please. Tell me it's time for show and tell."

He gathered up the silky folds of her dress, diving underneath. Bingo. She'd gone commando. His cock twitched against his jeans. His fingers found her slick folds and opened her, diving into her wetness. "Jesus, Maddie. You're always so ready."

She let out a breathy laugh. "It's all your fault."

"God I want my mouth on you now. I don't care who sees."

She laughed again. Low and sultry. "Hold on there, cowboy. It's so much better when we're alone."

"Then let's get the hell out of here."

He pulled her over to the rails where Blaze waited patiently, saddled and ready. Lifting her up, he helped adjust her dress, then mounted behind her. He pulled her close, remembering the last ride they'd shared and where they'd ended up. Spinning Blaze around, they headed around the barn and headed out toward the north pasture.

The noise of the revelers and fireworks faded behind them, and soon they were surrounded by the rising sounds of evening. The first stars glittered in the twilight. Maddie relaxed into him and he sighed contentedly. Only a little further. Just over the next rise. He held his breath, waiting for her reaction.

As they crested, she gasped. "What is this?"

Only a few yards in front of them stood a canvas tent, glowing like a beacon in the fading light. In front of the entrance, a crackling fire danced and flickered. Just outside the ring of light, but still discernible, stood a very large telescope.

Maddie quivered in his arms, covering her mouth in surprise. "Someone was very busy today."

"I had a little help."

He dismounted and turned, pulling her into his arms. He placed a tender kiss on her upturned face. "Come see. I've been waiting for days to show you this."

"When? How?"

"I asked your new boss for a recommendation, then Ben and Brodie drove to Kansas City to pick it up."

She hitched her skirt up and practically skipped over to the telescope, circling it.

He rattled off the stats nervously. "It's a fourteen-inch Celestron with all the trimmings. You'll have to show me how to use it. I've never looked in one."

"I'll show you Andromeda, our nearest galaxy. And the Globular Cluster. It looks like a magic globe." She came back to where he was standing and ran her palms up his chest, leaning into him.

"I want to tour the universe with you, but first I want to take a tour closer to home. Right. Here." He brought his hands up behind her, undoing the pins of her veil. Tossing it aside, he buried his fingers in her hair, tilting her head to expose her neck.

Her lips parted and her tongue flicked out as she dropped her gaze.

Everywhere her body connected with his, tendrils of lust snaked down, binding him to her. He lowered his head, stopping to let his lips brush back and forth across hers, savoring the ripples of passion that flowed between them.

"Maddie?" He lowered his lips to hers, tasting, exploring, savoring. He began to undo the buttons at her back, slowly exposing her to the warm spring air.

"Mmm?"

"You said you had a second surprise?"

Her lashes fluttered and she smiled coyly as she inserted

her fingers into his waistband, fumbling with the button of his denim.

"Well, it might take awhile... About seven and a half more months to be exact."

His hands stilled.

"Are you sure?"

She nodded. "Are you okay?"

Joy burst in his chest, and he threw his head back, laughing. He picked her up swinging her around.

"Yes. Perfectly okay." He lowered her to the ground, keeping her flush against his body, and resumed undoing her buttons. The sooner she was rid of this dress, the better.

"But when did you know for sure?"

"A week ago. But by then we'd already planned for today, and I wanted to tell you when we could savor it together."

He reached the last button, and gently pushed the dress off her shoulders, baring her to the night sky.

Her skin glowed in the firelight. He sank to his knees, trailing kisses down her chest to her belly. He tenderly kissed the slight curve. Keeping his mouth above her soft curls, he quickly doffed his shirt and pulled her hips to him.

"Yes. Savoring is good." Planting one last kiss on her belly, he stood, sweeping her into his arms and stepped into the tent where a mattress covered in soft furs waited for them. "I think we should begin savoring right now."

THE BEGINNING OF HAPPILY EVER AFTER

Did you like this book? Please leave a review! Independent authors rely on reviews and word of mouth. If you enjoyed this book, please spread the word!

Want more?

Receive Notifications for Upcoming Releases
http://tessalayne.com/newsletter

PRAIRIE PASSION – Brodie Sinclaire & Jamey O'Neill (On Sale Feb. 10th 2017)

Out of the Frying Pan
Brodie Sinclaire, the youngest and wildest of the Sinclaire brothers, has just been given an ultimatum. Settle down and run the hunting lodge his brothers have built, or find a new job – on another ranch. His first order of business is to find a cook who will last more than a week. He gets more than he bargained for when the cook he hires turns out to be his sister-in-law's best friend, fiery redhead and Cordon Bleu trained chef, Jamey O'Neill.

And Into the fire
In the span of a week Jamey O'Neill has lost everything. Her boyfriend, her restaurant, and her career – thanks to a devastating health diagnosis. Broke, and desperate to make a fresh start, she agrees to help the Sinclaires get their hunting lodge off the ground. The last thing she needs is a deliciously handsome cowboy getting under her skin and bossing her in the kitchen.

Can They Handle the Heat?
They can't deny their chemistry is explosive, and Brodie sets out to prove himself to the feisty chef. But can they handle the

heat when Brodie is forced to face his past and Jamey wrestles with her future?

Join my newsletter to receive updates on future releases
http://tessalayne.com/newsletter

Join my reader group on Facebook – The Prairie Posse this is where I post my sneak peeks, offer giveaways, and share hot cowboy pics!
facebook.com/groups/1390521967655100

MORE BOOKS IN THE COWBOYS OF THE FLINT HILLS SERIES

PRAIRIE RAPTURE –
Ben Sinclaire & Hope Hansen (coming in 2017)
PRAIRIE STORM –
Axel Hansen & Haley Cooper (coming in 2017)
PRAIRIE OBSESSION –
Travis Kincaid & Elaine Ryder (coming in 2017)
PRAIRIE FIRE –
Parker Hansen & Cassidy Grace (coming in 2018)
PRAIRIE FEVER –
Gunnar Hansen & Suzannah Winslow (coming in 2018)
PRAIRIE ECSTACY –
Colton Kincaid & Lydia Grace (coming in 2018)
PRAIRIE LUST –
Jarrod O'Neill & Lexi Grace (coming in 2018)
PRAIRIE REDEMPTION –
Cody Hansen & Carolina Grace (coming in 2018)

Acknowledgements

Books are not written in a vacuum. This one certainly wasn't. There are many, many kindhearted, supportive, and generous souls who believed in me, and helped breathe life into this story. I am deeply grateful for all of you.

Amanda at Razzle Dazzle Designs – you've made the most amazing cover. You perfectly captured everything I couldn't verbalize but wanted, and I look forward to many more fabulous covers on my books.

To the RDs and my Chatzy ladies – Thank you for welcoming me into your tribe, for your generosity of spirit, your filthy humor, your celebrations of small wins and encouragement when it's tough. Nikki Haverstock – you're the best whipper ever. Zoe York and Sidney Bristol, thank you for all the patient advice, handholding, and leadership. You're a shining example of what it means to be community.

To Cora Seton – I never expected when we reconnected that the course of my life would change. Thank you for your encouragement, feedback, generosity, and wisdom. And most importantly, for your friendship. You are a bright spot in this world!

To Kimberly Troutte – Who I never would have met had it not been for Cora. I have learned so much from you. Thank you for your continued mentorship, encouragement, and your commitment to help me be the best writer I can be. You are the only person who sees my material hot off the press, and I'm immensely grateful for your straight shooting feedback when I've strayed, and your unbridled enthusiasm when I've nailed it. I couldn't be luckier to have you on my team!

To Genevieve Turner and Melissa Blue – Thank you for your expertise and feedback. Your willingness to be truthful has made this book so much stronger. I admire and appreciate you both!

To Virginia – who read the scandalous pages I wrote as a teenager and still liked them. Someday you will get your hockey player named Logan. Or maybe he'll be a baseball player ☺ Thank you for your feedback and encouragement on doing it for real this time!

To my fellow lit nerds Jenny and Kara – Thank you for the wine, the comma splice corrections, the brainstorming, and enthusiasm when I needed a boost. Love you both.

To Rebekah – Thank you for the countless skype sessions, giggles, and words of encouragement along the way.

To my strong, magic daughters – May you learn every day that you are the authors of your destiny and that true love waits for you.

Lastly (and most importantly), to the hero of my life, Mr. Cowboy – You keep all the balls spinning and never fail to encourage me when I need it most. I love you to the end of the universe.

64432799R00189

Made in the USA
Charleston, SC
27 November 2016